FICTION   Gaines, Charles,
GAINES   1942-

Survival games.

DATE			

SURVIVAL
GAMES

Also by Charles Gaines

FICTION
Dangler
Stay Hungry

NONFICTION
A Family Place
Pumping Iron
Pumping Iron II: The Women
Staying Hard
Yours in Perfect Manhood: A Biography of Charles Atlas

Atlantic Monthly Press
New York

SURVIVAL

GAMES

A Novel
Charles Gaines

Published simultaneously in Canada
Printed in the United States of America

FIRST EDITION

Library of Congress Cataloging-in-Publication Data
Gaines, Charles, 1942–
    Survival games : a novel / Charles Gaines. — 1st ed.
        p.   cm.
    ISBN 0–87113–684–8 (alk. paper)
    I. Title.
PS3557.A353S87   1997
813'.54—dc21   97–12379

Design by Laura Hammond Hough

The Atlantic Monthly Press
841 Broadway
New York, NY 10003

10 9 8 7 6 5 4 3 2 1

To Charlotte Gafford

and to Dick Wentz

If a man loses anything and goes back and looks carefully for it,

he will find it.

—*Sitting Bull*

PART
ONE

CHAPTER ONE

It was slaughter weekend, though of course the sheep on Old Ledge Hill did not know that. Twelve of them were in residence there— a big, stately Hampshire ram, six ewes, and the five 6-month-old lambs whose next home would be a freezer in Boston. In early October the ten-acre pasture they occupied was still a rich and sunny one, running up the north-south slope of the hill and lapping a few hundred feet back into the blazing hardwood trees at the top like a soft, emerald tongue. From high up in this pasture an idyllic view opened to the south: a lush New Hampshire valley with sheltering hills rising behind it, a white church steeple and a few neat houses marking the lakeside village of Newbury; and in the foreground, a handsome two-hundred-year-old Colonial farmhouse, painted red with green shutters and white trim, and beyond that an old two-story barn and a trout pond ringed with willows. All in all, it was a view of benign order, proportion and calm, reassuring man and sheep alike that everything was right and safe with the world.

At 5:20 P.M. on Friday, October 7—a hot, Indian-summer afternoon that hung a blue haze over the valley—the Old Ledge

Hill sheep looked up from grazing to watch a Jeep Wagoneer with a canoe on its roof drive up the dirt road to the house, park beside the garage, and disgorge an overweight dog and two couples. The dog, who managed to step on all four people on his way out of the Wagoneer and then ran to the pasture gate to bark at the sheep, was named Brando. He was a three-year-old golden retriever.

"Hush," Clair Joyce told him. She had followed Brando to the gate and was leaning on it grinning as she watched the sheep file down toward them from the top of the pasture at a stiff-legged run, bleating as they came. "They're glad to see us," she said to Bill Joyce, who had come up behind his wife and put his arms around her waist.

"I think they just want some grain," said Bill. "Be quiet, Brando."

The dog looked up at his owners but kept barking and prancing in front of the gate as if looking for a way in. The sheep came on, ignoring him. Clair took the lid off a twenty-gallon plastic trash barrel standing beside the gate and poured a scoop of grain into each of five metal feed buckets just inside the fence. The sheep all tried to shoulder in to the same bucket, riding up over each other's backs and wriggling their way to the grain.

Walking up to the gate, Portia Hurley laughed. "Why don't they just eat out of different buckets?"

"Because they're hungrier than they are smart," said her husband Dray. "I recognize the condition." He reached over the fence and scratched the wooly back of a rooting lamb. "Hello, Lamb Chop. We're getting two of these guys for the freezer this year, right?"

"Can we just please not talk about it until after tomorrow?" said Clair. "And that one's name is Agnes, not Lamb Chop."

"They're all lamb chops to me," said Dray. "I'm sorry but I gotta admit this: Just looking at them makes me hungry."

"Cut it out, Dray," Portia told him. "When does it happen?" she asked Bill.

"The guy is going to pick them up tomorrow around mid-morning. You girls can be gone to the Foliage Festival by then and you won't have to watch him load them." Bill leaned over to kiss the back of Clair's head, but she turned abruptly out of his loose hold around her waist and walked off toward the car.

Still prancing and barking at the sheep, Brando glanced up at Bill to make sure his ferocity was being appreciated.

"Nitwit," Bill told him finally.

"Some bird dog," agreed Dray.

While Bill, Dray, and Portia unloaded the car and put away the food they had brought up from Boston for the long Columbus Day weekend, Clair opened the screened porch and pulled back the drapes in the living room. She and Bill had not visited the farm for almost a month and the old house was musty, so she lit scented candles downstairs and cracked the windows in the bedrooms upstairs. Mrs. Ayers, the wife of a retired neighbor who looked after the house and the sheep for Bill's family, had left cut flowers and stalks of bittersweet in the kitchen sink. Clair arranged these in vases around the house while Bill turned on the patio lights and started a charcoal fire in the grill.

When they had finished all the chores, the four friends poured themselves drinks from a shaker of martinis that Dray had mixed and went onto the screened porch to sit looking out on the pool in the closing dusk.

"To our hosts," said Dray, raising his glass. "It's great to be back at Old Ledge Hill."

Clair said, "And to being together again. We haven't had any relaxed, fun time together in ages."

"And to all our mucho good luck," added Portia. "It's bad luck to forget all our good luck." She stood up and walked over first to Dray, then to Bill, and then to Clair, touching her glass to theirs and giving each one a kiss.

A few minutes later Bill suggested they take a swim.

"We should pack the Jeep while there's still some light," Dray said.

"We have lights on the garage and we've got all night," said Bill.

"What time do you think sunset is?" Dray asked him.

"I don't know. Six-forty, six forty-five."

"Ten bucks says it's no later than six thirty-five."

"Oh, puh-*leeze*," said Portia, and groaned.

"It's what they do," said Clair, smiling.

"Ten bucks," said Dray.

"You got it," said Bill. "But I'm going to get another drink and take a swim before we check the paper."

Dray stood up and stretched. "We can find out what time sunup tomorrow is, too. Legal shooting time is a half hour before sunup, and we ought to be on the lake with the decoys out at least fifteen minutes before that, Billy Boy. That means we're outta here at two or two-thirty in the morning."

Dray, Portia, and Bill had been best friends since their freshman year in college twenty-one years before, and Clair had entered the group only four years later. In that time they had been through much together that was intimate. They had once spent three days stuffed into a two-man tent in Maine's Baxter State Park, waiting out a rain- and windstorm that destroyed the other tent; and they had shared the only hotel room they could find in San José, Costa Rica, for a couple of nights, all four of them with a relentless case of diarrhea. Dray and Portia had even been in the operating room with Bill and Clair when their son, Carl, was delivered by caesarean, and at the rainy funeral for that baby only four months later. They had seen each other bleed, had heard each other throwing up and making love. And whatever lusts or embarrassments or other secret fleshly emotions might once have existed between the two couples were now gone—eroded away by two decades of determined friendship and humor.

"Don't you think Portia's breasts ought to be in a museum?" Dray said. "Honestly."

Naked, as were the two women, he and Bill were lying face-down and side by side on floats in the deep end of the pool, balancing their drinks on the plastic headrests. Portia was walking languidly back and forth in the shallow end, trailing her hands in the water and humming to herself, and Clair sat on the tile edge of the pool, her lovely tanned legs crossed, looking happy. Brando, who had just been banished from the water for the third time by Bill, lay beside her, his chin on his paws.

"What kind of museum would that be?" Bill asked, though he knew his friend was serious. After seventeen years of marriage, Dray still had a limitless reverence for his wife that extended to her every attribute, even those, like her singing voice, that were less obviously praiseworthy than her body. Portia was, in fact, heroically made. Only an inch short of six feet, with hyperbolic, Daisy Mae curves, she had big bones, big hands and feet, big hips, and a truly majestic chest that was still, after thirty-eight years, high and firm. A natural blonde and early bloomer from Tennessee, Portia had been ogled and mistranslated nearly all of her life, and she now wore her body with a practiced, indifferent swagger.

She should play the Queen Mother, thought Bill, watching her, in some film about Amazons.

"Seriously," Dray insisted. "Are they gorgeous, or what?"

"No question about it," Bill agreed, though in fact Portia's big heart, her coltish awkwardness and instant readiness for either fun or sympathy were what he saw whenever he looked at her, in or out of clothes, and her body, including the museum-quality breasts, had long since ceased to stir him.

His own wife's body was another story. Bill could not look for long at any part of Clair—not in the entire time they had known each other, and particularly not in the past few months—without wanting her.

She had been a dancer when she was a child, and she still had a dancer's figure, with long, well-shaped and muscled limbs, wide, thin shoulders, and a slim neck. At thirty-nine, she carried herself like a proud girl, with a high head and a jaunty neatness. Her black hair, a gift from her Italian mother, was thick and long, hanging halfway down her back when she wore it straight. She had hazel eyes, high cheekbones, and a full, expressive mouth that usually carried a cool, prim set to it and gave her face, at first glance, a shy or haughty quality (it was hard to tell which). But on second or third look, a daring hint of voluptuous neediness appeared around that mouth. More than her beauty, it was this vivid undertone of hunger that gave Clair the power she had owned over men since not long into her teens.

Bill paddled the float over to his wife, who buried both of her hands in his hair and tugged. He lifted the arch of one of her feet to his mouth and bit down on it.

"Uh-oh, girlfriend," drawled Portia. "That boy's gettin' kinky. You want us to leave?"

"Forget about it—we got a Jeep to pack, Billy Boy," said Dray. "And five bucks says we're gonna have to replace the cords on some of those decoys. So quit fooling around and let's get at it."

The man sat beneath a big, double-trunked birch tree at the very top of the pasture near the fence, resting his elbows on his knees and looking downhill through a pair of binoculars. He had been there for over an hour without moving. His back was beginning to cramp and he was losing the light fast, but after four and a half months of waiting for her to return, he was not going anywhere as long as he could still see the woman.

He had driven after work to the plateau at the top of Old Ledge Hill as he did almost every day to learn if she was back, and had pulled off the road and was uncasing the binoculars when the Jeep drove up the hill and turned into the driveway. When he saw her get out of the car, he had walked quickly through the woods to the top of the pasture, climbed the fence, sat down under the big birch, and watched her through the binoculars talking to her husband and the other people, then watched her walk back to the car and carry a suitcase and a bag of groceries inside the house. He had kept watching, hoping she would come out again, and had seen the four of them drinking on the screened porch and then head out of the house to the pool, naked and carrying drinks and towels. The pool was surrounded by a fence to the north, but the man was high enough in the pasture so that he could see most of it and the patio surrounding it. He kept the glasses on her as she dove in and swam two lengths with the dog following her, then sat on the side of the pool with her legs in the water and her back to him.

He sat under the birch without moving, slowing his breathing and his heartbeat to keep the glasses steadier in the nearly gone light. In a few minutes more, after her husband paddled over to her on a raft, all four of the people got out of the pool, and he watched her dry herself, starting with her left foot, then wrap her hair in the towel. He watched her hips and back—that straight, thin back that he could not forget shuddering like a dying rabbit in his hands—as she followed the other woman into the lighted house, which felt to him at that moment as though it contained all the wealth of the world, and closed the door.

She did not come back out, and within minutes it was so completely dark that the man could not have seen her if she had, but still he stayed, sitting without moving, watching the old farmhouse through the glasses.

Bill and Dray did have to replace some of the anchor cords on the twelve black duck decoys in the garage. Then they packed the decoys in the back of Dray's Jeep along with waders and rain gear, two 12-gauge shotguns in canvas cases, and boxes of shells.

Bill pulled his hiking boots and an old hunting vest that had belonged to his father out of the garage closet, and threw them into the growing pile of gear in the back of the vehicle. "Are you sure we won't need sleeping bags?" he asked Dray.

"Uncle Stu says the cabin is totally equipped. Bags, cots, Coleman stove and lamps, dishes—the whole nine yards. How about the booze?"

"I put it in. And the cooler with the food in it. Now let's cook some dinner."

"Not until we check the paper, my friend," said Dray.

He took a crumpled *Boston Globe* from the backseat and began thumbing through it. Leaning on the hood of his car, he glared combatively at the paper through glasses perched on the tip of his stubby nose and scratched the bald top of his head, as he did whenever he was about to win a bet.

Bill walked away from the garage onto the lawn and looked up at the sky. The night air was still and much too warm for the season, but the sky was clear, and was predicted to remain clear throughout the long weekend. A full, butter-yellow moon, the hunter's moon of October, had just climbed above the trees behind the trout pond. He looked into the sky and thought of the heat that he and Dray and Brando would have for hunting over the next two days. Then he walked back into the garage. "You know we could just stay here," he said, only half joking. "Go to the Fall Foliage Festival with the girls. Do some canoeing, maybe. Sleep in beds."

"Yeah, right. The bad news is sunset was six-seventeen—you owe me ten bucks, which brings you up to a hundred and twenty, not counting the Cincinnati game you weaseled out of. The good news is sunup is six-fifty. We don't have to leave here until two-fifteen."

Portia and Clair had showered and changed by the time Bill and Dray came back into the house. Portia had on one of her "good mood outfits," a pair of gold, tiger-striped pants, high heels, and a safari hat with a scarf tied around it. Clair had used combs to pile her rich hair at the base of her neck, and was wearing a simple, short, blue linen dress that hung loosely on her by two thin straps and made her look like a little girl. She brought Bill a drink and a plate of smoked salmon with crackers and lemon wedges while he grilled swordfish steaks on the patio.

The grilling fish gave off a fragrant breath of soy and basil marinade. The pool glowed at his feet. The fine old house that he loved and had spent summers and weekends in since he was a child was full of light, and Ella Fitzgerald sang on the CD. His wife stood up on her bare tiptoes, took his face in her hands, and kissed him, pushing a sliver of tongue between his teeth, and Bill felt luxuriantly aware of the sweet, specific wealth of his life at that moment and was very grateful for it.

"I told Dray we should maybe just stay here," he told her.

"What did he say?" Clair laughed. "No, I know what he said."

"He didn't think I was serious."

"Were you?" She kissed him again. Bill took her in his arms, then felt himself going too fast and let her go.

"Do you want me to be?"

"No, I want you and Dray to go enjoy yourselves. You know how he loves this with you. Brando too—he's already gone to sleep on our bed, he's so excited."

"I just don't feel that much like going," said Bill.

"We have all day Monday here. We can leave Dray and Portia at the house to read the Sunday *Times* and hike up to Lake Solitude. You'll feel like it tomorrow. All you need is a good night's sleep."

"I need you is what I need," Bill said, and was afraid for the sake of the nearly done fish to touch her again.

"That, my sweet," she promised, "can be arranged."

After dinner on the porch they walked down to the trout pond and stood watching the full moon reflected in the pond and heard some large animal crashing away from them through the woods.

Portia squealed.

"You're the great white huntress, girl," Dray told her. "Go get it." He turned to Bill, grinning. "Does she look great in that outfit, or what?"

"I am *not* a huntress," said Portia solemnly, sounding a little tight. "And I don't personally know how y'all can stand to kill those little ducks that aren't doing you any harm. Slaughtering lambs and all those things. I think everybody ought to just stop killing everything for a while. Just call a moratorium, or whatever you call it."

"What a load of horseshit," snorted Dray. "You sound like that antigun bunch of Democrat pansy freaks that are trying to put me out of business."

He was standing at the edge of the pond with his hands in his pockets. Behind him, Portia lifted her long right leg, placed her high-heeled pump just below his belt, and pushed. Dray stumbled into the pond up to his knees before he could stop himself, then he turned, bellowing and slipping in the pond mud, and charged Portia, who was backing up, laughing and holding out a stick to fend him off.

"Wouldn't you think they'd grow up *sometime?*" said Clair. Bill had his arms around her from behind, his hands resting on her abdomen. He looked at the moon and didn't answer, feeling stilled by the night, the moon, and the warmth of his wife, who leaned into him now and turned up her face. He bent and kissed her, and Clair made a quiet sound in her throat.

"Hey Clair!" shouted Dray. "Whattya do with an elephant with three balls?" Glasses askew, his face delighted, he was holding Portia over his shoulder like a prize; her gold rear end gleamed at them in the moonlight.

"Y'all, *please* get me away from this little maniac," Portia wailed.

"I don't know, Drayton," said Clair.

"Walk him and pitch to the rhino. My honey and I are going up to bed now. Good-night, kiddies." Dray turned his head and kissed Portia's bare midriff on his shoulder, a world of tenderness in the gesture, then carried her off, stumbling a little under his load, both of them laughing, toward the house. "Bright and early, Billy Boy," he shouted.

Brando lay across their bed on his back with his paws in the air, snoring. While Clair went to the bathroom, Bill opened the French doors to a small deck and stepped outside. In a moment Clair joined him and they stood side by side, looking out over the valley at the lights of Newbury Harbor and the moon-bright lake. Clair slipped her hand under his shirt and made widening circles over his back with her nails, and Bill felt the past few hours of waiting come together in a sudden knot of longing in his stomach. He turned to face Clair and lifted his hands to cup her head. He pulled the combs from her hair and dropped them onto the deck, and she shook her head, spilling hair down her back.

She touched his cheek lightly. "I love you," she said, and stared at him, then said it again, and her lovely, cool face was suddenly overrun with a hot bloom that lit up her cheeks in the half-dark and narrowed her eyes like pain. It was a transformation that left Bill no less breathless now than the first time he had seen it, the day after he met Clair, when she had stepped nonchalantly out of her bathing suit on a beach at Martha's Vineyard and led him by the hand into the sea until it lapped around their chests. She had taken the back of his neck in her left hand and crossed her legs around his waist and, throwing back her head, had guided him into her in the rock of the waves. Then, lifting her head again with a long sigh, she had stared at him through wet, black strands of hair, her face shockingly, almost unrecognizably aflame.

Bill drew his hands down along her throat and slid the straps of the dress off her shoulders. She stood absolutely still and naked in the moonlight, frank and open to the night, and Bill felt, as he did every day now, that he was seeing her body for the first time. He brought his hands up along her rib cage onto her breasts, and passed them lightly over her nipples, touching his reclaimed wife as carefully as if he were cutting a diamond.

"I love you, Billy," she whispered again, and Bill went to his knees then on the deck and pulled her hips toward his face as if they were all of the world he would ever want.

CHAPTER TWO

He came awake a few seconds before the alarm clock was set to ring and turned it off quickly so it wouldn't wake Clair. He lifted a strand of hair from her cheek and tucked it behind her ear, then kissed the top of her head and slid out of bed. He dressed without turning on a light, feeling buoyant and happy and ready for the trip now. Brando was asleep on his dog bed in the corner of the bedroom, and Bill had to tug his collar twice to wake him up. The dog followed him into the bathroom, drank noisily out of the toilet while Bill brushed his teeth, then lay down and went back to sleep.

In the kitchen, Dray already had a thermos filled with coffee. He had poured each of them a glass of orange juice, fried half a pound of venison sausage, made toast, and was cracking six eggs into a pan.

"How can you cook all that crap this early in the morning, let alone eat it?" Bill asked him.

Dray looked up and grinned. His face had not yet settled into the fervent tenacity that characterized it during the day—that made him seem a little tilted forward and on the point of charging something. Now he looked simply tired, and older, Bill thought, than he ought to look. "Couple of sexual athletes like us gotta eat our Wheaties, Billy Boy," he said. "Plus we're marching into some seriously hostile country today, so you'd better load up."

They drove out of the driveway at two-thirty with Brando in his kennel in the back of the Wagoneer. Before they reached the bottom of Old Ledge Hill, Bill had tuned in the country station they always listened to, Dray had lit a trip-christening Swisher Sweet cigar, and they were officially under way.

It was another in a week-long string of still, clear mornings, and so warm that they drove with the front windows down, the car awash with balmy, New England autumn air that smelled sharply of apples and dying leaves. They picked up 104 in Danbury and followed it east through the quiet, dark, hilly countryside over the Pemigewasset River to 93, the four-lane interstate, where they turned due north toward the White Mountains. Dray drove fast over these roads he had known all his life, smoking his cigar and pointing out in the dark the same things he always pointed out: the Lone Pine Tree grouse cover, an apple orchard where he had shot his first deer, the now-closed ski area where he had learned to ski.

Somewhere around New Hampton, during a lull in the conversation, Bill asked him, "So, how's the company doing?"

After a moment, Dray said, "Well, lemme put it this way, my friend, you were probably smart to sell out when you did, even though I thought you were an idiot then and told you so." He smoked his cigar in silence for a moment, driving with his right wrist draped over the wheel. "The fucking lawsuits are eating us up. I practically own goddamn *stock* in that law firm we use. Some asshole'll take off his goggles during a game and somebody'll shoot paint in his eye and he gets in line to sue. Last month some kid shot *himself* in the eye and sued."

"What happened?" Bill asked.

"He lost the eye. Fucking good riddance."

"I meant with the suit."

"Same thing that happens with all of them. They get settled and cost me a fortune in insurance and legal fees. Can't we talk about something cheerier, like whatever war's going on right now?"

"Okay, tell me about where we're hunting."

"Uncle Stu gave me a map. There's this point in the north end of the lake where he says the ducks are thick. We'll set up there and shoot until they quit flying, then we go look for woodcock and grouse along the logging roads he told me about."

"Did he say the birds were thick along the logging roads?"

"You bet," said Dray, his mood improving again. "Would I take you somewhere where the birds weren't thick?"

"Never," said Bill. "So we have thick ducks in the morning and thick woodcock and grouse in the afternoon. Not bad."

"Then we drive up to Stu's camp on the Dead Diamond River to spend the night and do the same thing tomorrow. Drive back tomorrow afternoon. Personally, I'd rather be staying two nights, and we would be if you weren't so pussy-whipped nowadays. No offense."

"It has nothing to do with that, and look who's talking, by the way. It's just that one night in a shack with your snoring is all I can handle."

"My snoring . . .," Dray roared.

Bill grinned, poured himself a cup of coffee out of the thermos, and settled back in his seat. The trip was on track.

They drove past Cannon Mountain, where they skied together two or three times each year, then angled east across the mountainous northern tier of the state, through Twin Mountain and Berlin, and followed the Androscoggin River up to Errol. They arrived at their put-in, on a small river flowing into the lake, at five thirty-five, a few minutes later than Dray had wanted to get there.

"If you hadn't spent so long in the can, we'd be on time," he said, jerking the Wagoneer over onto the shoulder of the road in a spray of gravel.

"What the hell difference does it make? I'm on vacation here."

"*Vacation*," said Dray. "Do you work? I thought you sold your stock in a company that's always getting sued to your best friend for more money than it was worth and then retired." Bill looked at him in the dark. "Just kidding," Dray chuckled, and Bill knew he was. "Let's get in the water."

They took the canoe off the rack and loaded it by flashlight with the paddles and life vests, the dozen decoys, the shotguns and shells, Bill's waterproof camera case, a small cooler of lunch and the thermos. Then they put on their waders and camouflage jackets. While Dray studied a hand-drawn map of the lake, Bill let Brando out of his kennel. The dog jumped up on both of them, then ran around panting and grinning and shaking his fat rear end.

"What makes you think that mutt's not going to be a disaster like last time?" Dray asked, watching Brando pee on both his rear tires.

"I've been working with him some. Don't worry about it," said Bill, though he too was curious how the dog would perform.

Clair had gotten Brando from the pound and given him to Bill two years before when his ancient black Lab finally died in its sleep. Bill had trained and hunted the Lab at a time when hunting was more important to him than it was now, and the dog had been a natural who rarely made a mistake after his first season. When it quickly became evident that Brando had little talent for hunting and was too whimsical and lazy for Bill to train easily, he had discovered that it was actually to his liking now to have a half-assed hunting dog—one who adored Clair and was manically protective of her but only tolerated Bill, who was fine, jolly company around the house and as unpredictable and original in response to commands as the Lab had been dependable. The only other time he and Dray had hunted ducks with Brando, the dog had nearly turned the canoe over leaping from it to swim after a beaver, and Bill hadn't been able to get him back for twenty minutes. Since then, it was true, he had done a little work with the dog, but he had no idea what Brando might do when confronted with an actual duck that needed fetching.

To ensure there would be no repeat of the beaver incident, he tied a leash onto the center thwart of the canoe and snapped it to Brando's collar. The dog sat in the middle of the canoe and began to whine as they pushed off into the black water of the river with Dray in the stern and Bill in the bow. Within seconds they were out of sight of the road, folded into the subtly lightening dark and the sounds and smells of the river, and Bill felt the sharp, clenching, anticipatory excitement of setting out to find something to kill that had always felt wonderfully natural and freeing and ancient to him, and was now the real and only reason he hunted, other than to be with Dray. The small river was lined with tall spruces and balsam fir. Their tops were outlined against the sky, which was already starting to go from black to a deep, cold blue. A gull flew by overhead, followed by a squadron of whistling wood ducks.

"Do you think you can make that worthless fucking pooch quit whining?" whispered Dray. "He's going to spook every duck on the lake."

Bill took a yellow rubber bathtub duck out of his jacket and threw it to Brando. It was the dog's favorite chew toy, brought along for emergencies at Clair's insistence, and it worked—Brando lay down and began to bat at the duck with his paws.

In less than ten minutes they came into the lake to a loon's chilly warble, and paddled north about a hundred feet out from the west shore. From somewhere up ahead Bill could hear the convivial chuckling of black ducks and then, behind the canoe, the unmistakable air-ripping sound of ducks in flight. Dray was leaning hard on the paddle in the stern, and in ten minutes they pulled into a point of thick, stubby spruces. Bill stepped out and pulled the bow of the canoe up onto the rocky shore. He unclipped Brando and the dog jumped clumsily out of the canoe, carrying the rubber duck in his mouth.

They unloaded the canoe on the shore, then carried it up the bank and into the trees. It took them two or three minutes to find Dray's uncle's blind, which was near the end of the point overlooking a shallow bay of the lake. The blind was a rectangular frame of two-by-fours covered on the top and sides with chicken wire into which spruce boughs had been woven. It was just tall enough in the front for two men to stand, and there was a log bench toward the back.

"Some blind," said Bill.

"Helluva lot of work," Dray agreed. "Old Stu likes to take pains. Did you hear all the ducks on the way in? They're thick in here, alright. We're going to whip some ass here, Billy Boy."

"If they don't all get out on us. It's gonna be another bluebird day and they'll move out early."

"We'll get 'em. We'll call the bastards in," said Dray.

Bill carried the guns and shells and the rest of the gear up to the blind. He uncased the two over-and-under shotguns and laid them on the bench at the rear of the blind, then filled the pockets of his camouflage jacket with shells and poured himself a cup of coffee. Out in the marshy bay Dray was wading in hip-deep water, setting out the decoys. Brando swam behind him, holding the yellow duck in his mouth and tangling the decoy lines. Dray looked up disgustedly at Bill, motioned at Brando, and threw his arms open wide. Bill laughed. He was enjoying watching the scene and thinking of how Clair would love it, but he blew the whistle around his neck and Brando turned obediently and came swimming in to shore. A good sign, Bill thought, but he didn't want to take any chances on the dog getting away from him while ducks were flying, so when Brando came trotting up, Bill tied the leash to one of the two-by-four posts supporting the front of the blind and clipped the snap into the D ring on Brando's collar.

When Dray waded in, there were only ten minutes left before legal shooting time. The sky had gone silver-blue now in the east and the stars were paler. They stood at the front of the blind drinking coffee and watching the lake, and Brando sat at Bill's feet, leashed to the blind's corner post. A couple of minutes before legal the entire north end of the lake appeared to explode as hundreds of black ducks jumped into the air at once. Bill and Dray watched as the ducks circled, milling and shifting into formations, then flew off to the west.

"I'm going to call," said Bill.

"They've headed out to feed—every duck on the fucking lake. You'll never turn 'em."

Bill reached inside the front of his coat, pulled out a duck call hanging by a lanyard around his neck, and blew three long, urgent "come back" calls.

Dray chuckled. "A hundred bucks, five-to-one odds you don't turn one."

Bill blew one last melodramatic call, lifting and holding the final note, and a duck near the end of the last formation disappearing over the horizon dipped and turned and flew back toward them.

"Well, I'll be a sonofabitch," said Dray, laughing and scurrying to the back of the blind for his gun.

"Is it legal yet?" asked Bill.

"Close enough. Keep tootin'." Then Dray was back in a crouch, handing Bill his gun. "Not bad for government work, Billy Boy—that deaf motherfucker's gonna come in."

They crouched and watched the duck circle over them, eying the decoys, then make another, lower pass and set, flaring its wings out to catch the air, its orange feet coming up, pitching and canting downward in the air like a leaf falling.

"Now," said Dray, and both of them stood and shot at the same time. Bill watched the duck fold and drop, landing in the curve of the decoys with a splash.

Then the next thing he knew, he and Dray were covered up in chicken wire and spruce boughs. Fighting his head clear, he saw Brando sprinting toward the decoys, the corner post of the collapsed blind, still tied to the leash, bouncing off the rocks behind him.

By nine o'clock they had not seen another duck in three hours, and the day was hot, bright, and windless. They had rebuilt the blind, and now Brando was tied by his leash to a spruce tree, though Bill had not been able even to scold the dog for destroying the blind after Brando swam out through the decoys, towing the two-by-four, and retrieved the duck perfectly, actually sitting to deliver it to Bill's hand.

"I'm gonna take the canoe and see if I can jump something out of that little river," Dray said. "You stay here and maybe I'll push some birds over you."

"You want Brando?" Bill asked him.

Dray looked at him and grinned. "Like I want herpes. I'll be back in an hour or so. You two hold down the fort."

Carrying his gun and puffing on a freshly lit cigar, Dray pulled the canoe out of the trees and slid it down the shore and into the water. He propped the gun, barrel up, against the center thwart, sat in the bow facing the stern, and pushed off.

Watching the canoe recede down the shoreline and then turn into the river, trailing blue cigar smoke and a V-shaped wake over the calm water, Bill felt a sudden, exhilarating freedom descend on him. He grinned and said aloud, "Portia would kick your ass if she saw you smoking that cigar, Hot Shot."

They met in their freshman year at little New England College in Henniker, New Hampshire, and immediately became best friends. They were both good athletes—Dray a lacrosse forward and hockey player, and Bill a Junior National Team goalkeeper in soccer— but otherwise they had little in common.

Bill was the youngest child in a big, histrionic Boston Irish Catholic family, the center of which, for better or worse, was Bill's dapper, hard-drinking, one-armed, lady-loving father, Jack. Dray's father had died of an aneurysm in his sleep when Dray was seven and he had grown up an only child in a silent, bitter home in Andover, New Hampshire, where, with difficulty, his mother kept alive a country store her husband left her with. Dray had worked in the store every summer and school vacation and most week-ends from the time he was ten until he went to college on an ath-letic scholarship, and still managed to become one of the best high school hockey wings in the east. Where Dray was muscular and broad and had a tough, round, bad boy's face, Bill was tall and thin, with hawkish good looks. Where Dray was pugnacious, and rude as a matter of principle to people he didn't like, Bill made an effort to charm almost everyone he met and avoided conflict. And while good grades and athletic success had come easily to Bill, Dray had had to sweat for the same rewards and had won them only because he loved to sweat and was good at it. As an athlete and otherwise, the only game Dray had ever known how to play was charging the other guy's net as often and hard as possible, while Bill was at his best staying in his own goal, assessing and reacting.

The two of them learned early on that their differences made not only for a strong friendship but a good business team, with Bill greasing the skids and Dray pushing things through. In their junior year they wrote and had locally printed a book of college drinking games with illustrative drawings by Portia, whom they had met in a freshman French class and who was by then their inseparable running buddy and Dray's fiancée. Bill marketed the book on weekends by driving to colleges and universities all over the East Coast to set up state and then regional competitions based on the games in the book. Dray went with him, and when Bill had finished winning over a fraternity president or a college-town bar owner, Dray was right there behind him with an order form for books to close the deal. In their senior year they put on a three-day College Drinking Game Olympics at the University of Vermont that was attended by teams from thirty-seven schools; and by the time they graduated, they had sold over twenty thousand books and put $150,000 in the bank.

Before meeting Dray, Bill's outdoors experience had been limited to some sailing and hiking and a little high-yield trout fishing and bird shooting. At the farm in New Hampshire—bought by his parents as a weekend and summer house when Bill was five years old—his father had taught him and his brothers to fly-fish and shoot a shotgun before they could ride bicycles. But on the rare occasions when Jack Joyce skipped a day of work to fish or shoot with his sons, he took them to stocked, private streams in New Hampshire or Vermont where tame trout took the fly on every cast, and to hunting preserves where he would pay to have a hundred pheasants released from cages for their afternoon's sport. Jack Joyce approached his recreations as he did his work, looking for the largest possible return on an investment of time and energy, and then digging into them with a well-dressed, one-armed fury.

Being constantly encouraged to work harder at catching and killing so easy and productive that they required no work at all eventually soured Bill on those activities, and he might never have taken them up again had he not met Dray, who had grown up making his own rods, loading shells, and tying flies, who would fish all day for one old smart brown trout lying beneath a cut bank and crawl three hundred yards over a muddy field for a long shot at a single Canada goose, and who loved hunting and fishing and anything else that could be done intensely in the outdoors with a bloody, joyful, and contagious ferocity.

Less than a week after they met at freshman registration, Dray and Bill were fishing together almost every evening for trout in the Contoocook River and then, a few weeks later, shooting grouse four or five afternoons a week in abandoned apple orchards over Dray's weimaraner. Bill was amazed at how his spirit soared to meet those occasions, how thrilling and absorbing it felt to be bringing growing skill and Dray's level of effort and concentration to bear not on simply collecting game, but on prying it out of nature.

During college and after, Dray introduced him to backcountry skiing, rock climbing, ice fishing, deer hunting, and trapping for muskrat and beaver. Bill learned to enjoy all of those things and became as competent as Dray at most of them, though he never developed Dray's patience at the nuts-and-bolts skills such as fly tying and compass navigation. And for years he had also tried to throw himself into the things they did together with Dray's focus and aggressiveness. Dray believed that the outdoors was a place for doing consecrated battle: a rock cliff was there to be beaten or fallen off of, a set of rapids to be conquered or drowned in, a hunted animal or bird to be outplanned, outflanked, and attacked; and his first principle for dealing with the woods was to enter them prepared with the right skills and with the mind of a predator.

Watching Dray paddle off toward the river, Bill saw his best friend doing what he loved to do and doing it "up to spec" as Dray put it. That made Bill happy, as it had for as long as they had known each other. But he also saw a man who never stopped chipping away at himself. Pushing himself too hard at play in the outdoors, Dray had blown out ligaments in both knees, broken the same ankle twice, and torn a rotator cuff. For years after they met, when Dray was his outdoors mentor, Bill had allowed Dray to push him as well, often into discomfort and exhaustion. Then for a while he had become, mysteriously, another person—someone more like Dray or his father—and had pushed himself too hard in his work and his life as well as the outdoors, and that pushing had ultimately cost him his wife. Now, on his first trip with Dray since reclaiming himself and then Clair, Bill watched the canoe disappear into the mouth of the river and realized with some surprise that he no longer cared a thing about coming into the woods with the mind of a predator, or about doing battle with anything there, or about beating himself up in the pursuit of something to do battle with. The realization felt so liberating and welcome that he almost shouted it out loud. Instead, he shared the news with Brando.

"Relax, old buddy," he told the dog. "You and I are through for good being well-oiled machines."

* * *

He sat on the bench in the blind and looked at the duck he had called back to him, turning it in his hands and smoothing the soft feathers of its breast where the shot had caught it. It was a black duck hen and he wondered what compassion or curiosity could have made her turn out of the flock and return to his calling to get herself killed. Whatever it was, it seemed a female thing to do—some empathetic, instinctive urge acted upon—and he was sorry the duck had not survived that urge.

"Meat," was how his father had always referred to something or someone he had beaten. "Full boat," he would say, grinning and turning over his cards in a poker game with his four sons. "You guys are meat."

In 1945 when he got out of the VA hospital in Boston after losing his left arm up to the elbow, Jack Joyce had borrowed four times his net worth and bought out his uncle's butcher shop in Charlestown. Within ten years he had turned the shop into the largest wholesale meat-packing company in New England. He called the company "Meat, Inc."

His father had killed birds—resting the forearm of the shotgun on his stump and swinging as quickly and smoothly as anyone Bill had ever seen—to put them in the bank. To Dray, killing was about winning and losing. It had been about things other than itself to Bill too at other times, but now, as he held the duck and studied its yellow bill and sleek head and the black eyes that were still somehow alert, it seemed to him that killing was a stone that had caught a particular, irrecoverable light and sparkled like a jewel in his hands for a while and was now just a stone again—the drab gray rock of turning something into meat.

He stood up and hung the duck by its neck in the chicken wire, then unloaded his gun and laid it on the bench. Carrying his camera case with him, he unsnapped Brando from the leash, and the two of them walked down to the end of the point. The day was gloriously warm and vivid. The brilliant red-and-yellow hardwoods and black-green spruces and firs on the shore across from him were mirrored in the still water of the bay, and an osprey circled against the faultless blue sky directly overhead, looking for breakfast.

He took off his heavy camo jacket and waders and then stripped down to his shorts. He set up his camera on the tripod he carried in his camera case and aimed it at a small opening in the woods on the shoreline across the bay. He twisted a 300 mm lens into the body of the Leica and focused it on the opening, then he lay on his back alongside Brando on a big, flat rock just out of the water and waited, feeling happy from having just handled the camera. It was the only tool he had ever wanted to use professionally. He had used it that way when he was younger, when he believed he could do anything; and now, when he again believed, through Clair, that he could do anything, he was using it again.

He lay with his hands behind his head in the warm sun watching and waiting for something to happen on the far shore. He felt sleepy and very happy—happy to be using a camera now instead of a gun, and happy about this long weekend and the second honeymoon to Europe that he and Clair were leaving for in two weeks, and about being a photographer again.

In a few moments he heard a lapping sound rise out of the quiet. He raised his head to see a young moose standing in the small opening in the woods and drinking from the lake. Brando had seen the moose, too. His ears lifted, but he didn't otherwise move or make a sound. Bill got up slowly onto his knees and looked through the lens. When the moose raised its cartoon head and stared in his direction for a full five seconds, water dripping from its snout, he snapped the shutter once and knew he had the picture he wanted. Then he lay back down, put his hand on Brando's head, and went to sleep.

A half hour later he woke and lifted his head again. There were eight black ducks swimming among the decoys, not twenty feet from him. Brando was eying them sleepily. Bill got to his knees again, positioned and focused the camera, and took several shots of the ducks, who seemed not to notice him. They were still swimming and chuckling in the decoys when he lay back down and went to sleep again.

The next time he woke, it was to Dray shouting at him from the canoe.

"What?" he said, sitting up, still as happy as he could ever remember being. "By the way, you owe me five hundred bucks."

"Put it on my tab. I said what happened to your clothes? You look like some fucking woods fairy or something." Dray held up two ducks by their necks. "I got these guys in the river. You see anything?"

"Nothing killable," Bill told him.

CHAPTER
THREE

Clair had not slept well. All night again her dreams had rushed at her like wild animals, and she had waked what seemed like dozens of times to feel for Bill. When, not long into the night, he was no longer there, she had to remind herself carefully each time she found him missing that he was not now still lost to her and irretrievable, but only gone hunting.

Sex had always made Clair sleepy, and her sleep dreamless. But the starved, tireless, yearning sex that she and Bill had been having for the past few months, anytime and anyplace and almost as often as meals, seemed to be stirring her on a level she hadn't even known was there, bringing noises out of her that seemed to come from her childhood or from some past life even, and feelings she had no names for, keeping her edgy during the day and awake at night, and then loosing on her a stampede of dreams.

And the dreams, most of them, were bad. It seemed to Clair ironic, if characteristic of what she knew about the pursuit of happiness, that now that her life was better than it had ever been, her dreams should be nightmares; and that when, only four or five months before, her life had been a waking nightmare, her dreams had been sunlit and sweet.

The morning sickness, anyway, was easing up, and Clair made that number one on her list of gratitudes this morning. She found twenty-two others to recite to herself as she lay in bed, saying each thing she was grateful for out loud and holding it in her mind for a moment as she counseled her clients to do. Her last gratitude, as always, was for the day itself, and as she spoke it she realized instantly what had been causing the needling dread she had felt for days, even weeks: today. Today was the day the man would come to the farm to pick up the lambs for slaughter.

As a professional therapist she was relieved to have dug out and carried into her conscious mind what had been bothering her, but having it there didn't make her feel any happier. She got out of bed, dressed, and went downstairs, where Barry White was professing love loudly and passionately through multiple speakers. Portia was singing along mercilessly in the kitchen and running the blender.

"Is it just me or does that music sound a little sleazy this time of day?" Clair asked her, trying not to sound annoyed.

"It's just you," said Portia. "The man's pure sex, girlfriend. Sex with hair on it. My man Barry under*stands* a woman. I'm making a margarita to go with my *huevos rancheros*. You want one?"

"No, thanks," said Clair, laughing at Portia's breakfast, her momentary irritation evaporating. She sat down at the kitchen table. "Getting started early, huh?"

"Portia's on vacation, honey, and she plans to drink *all* the way through it." Portia turned off the blender and poured herself a frozen margarita. "You sure you don't want to just stay here today? Lie around the pool with a cool one?"

"I don't want to be here when the man comes for the lambs," said Clair. "Besides the fair is fun. Can you be ready to go in about an hour, Porsh? . . . Seriously. I'm not sure what time he's coming."

Portia looked at her, catching something in Clair's voice, and her face went instantly sympathetic. "Sure, baby, whenever you're ready. But first you're going to have some breakfast. You haven't been eating squat lately. You want some fruit?" Portia opened the refrigerator and pulled out berries and a cantaloupe.

"I'm pregnant," said Clair.

Portia studied her for a moment, then put the fruit down on the counter. "You are . . . *pregnant?*"

"Almost two months," Clair said, happy to be finally sharing the news with someone.

"Does Bill know?"

"No. I was going to tell all of you together tomorrow night."

"Sweetheart." Portia walked over and stood behind Clair and began to massage her neck. "This is something you meant to do?"

"Well, I didn't stop it from happening. Bill's wanted to have another baby for years. But after we lost Carl, and then all the troubles we had . . . I didn't know that we should. Now I do. If it's a girl, I'm naming it Portia."

Portia rubbed Clair's neck and shoulders silently for a moment or two. Then she said, "Well, I love you for that, girlfriend," and some small wistfulness in her voice made Clair wince.

"Do you still think about having one?"

"I think about it, honey," said Portia, her voice back to its robust drawl. "But Dray's all the baby this girl can handle. We're going to have to keep you from getting tired and keep your iron up. Portia Hurley's gonna take over your care and feedin', little lady." Portia squeezed Clair's neck suddenly, hard, and let roll a long, musical belch, something she could do at will whenever she was happiest. *"Pregnant!"* she whooped. "What a *hoot.*"

The village of Warner held the festival on the second weekend of October every fall and the whole town was given over to it. There were parades down the main street at midday on Saturday and Sunday, and a band playing in the town bandstand. In the little fairgrounds off the main square there were carnival rides and games, food vendors selling hot dogs and pizzas, candied apples, cider and fried dough, and lumberjack competitions going on all day. Clair loved the small-town gaiety and hospitality of the event, and today she planned to stay immersed in it until late enough to be certain the lambs, and the man picking them up, would be gone when she returned home.

Portia had changed into another good-mood outfit, a sarong-style doe-skinned dress with beaded fringe, bought in Santa Fe, knee-high soft leather moccasin boots, also beaded, and a head-band. A flamboyant necklace of small carved turquoise bird fetishes dipped into her luxuriant tanned cleavage, and her wrists and hands were covered in more turquoise and silver. Watching her long-legged, loose-hipped, in-your-face strut through the crowded small-town festival grounds, Clair felt the delighted pride she always felt in Portia when they were in public, as if her big, outrageous, eye-popping friend were something like a prize llama she had out with her on a rope.

They looked at a few crafts exhibits and watched a man draw a two-minute charcoal of a little girl. The child looked up at Portia with startled eyes and said to a thin, drab woman standing behind her, "Look, Mom. It's Pocahontas." The woman gave Portia a sidelong, bitter glance and whispered something to the child. Portia smiled at the girl, who looked away, embarrassed.

They watched big, shirtless, bearded men compete, two at a time, at chopping down poles with axes, trying to drive pegs into the ground with the falling poles. One of the men stopped in mid-swing to gape at Portia, then said something to her in French with a neat, Gallic grin and went back to chopping fiercely.

"What did he say?" Clair asked her.

"I didn't get that far in French," Portia said, "but I have a pretty good idea. You think they'd evolve some, men, after all this time."

"Ours have," said Clair.

"Because we've trained 'em, honey. As far as I'm concerned, you can *have* these unreconstructed hunks. All that rocket-in-the-pocket, hairy-ape shit is *waaay* overrated as far as I'm concerned."

"You got that right," agreed Clair with such conviction that Portia looked over at her.

The day was warm and bright, the hillsides encircling the town sparkled with dying leaves, and the Warner Fall Foliage Festival was crowded and noisy. The two women listened to the band play a polka or two at the bandstand, then strolled through the fairgrounds, trying out a game or two, buying a few things, and generally enjoying themselves on this matchless fall day until they came to a booth down at the far end of the fairgrounds near the carnival rides.

Clumsy hand-lettering on an old gray piece of plywood nailed above the booth announced NATIVE AMERICAN JEWELRY AND GIFTS. Clair spotted the sign and walked over to the booth. She looked around briefly for Portia without seeing her, then turned her attention to the display. Laid out on the counter on an old red velour cloth were some little birch-bark canoes and crudely carved wooden animals, a few unlined, stiff-looking hides and vests, half a dozen bead necklaces and earrings, and a two-foot alder branch with a handful of black feathers tied with rawhide to one end. All the stuff had a crude, useless look to it. Conscious of someone inside the booth moving toward her, Clair halfheartedly picked up the alder stick and looked up to say something charitable about it, but the words stopped in her throat.

An obese young Indian woman was staring at her from behind the counter with what appeared to be naked hatred. She was wearing a gigantic fringed and beaded leather dress, with feathers tied into her greasy black hair. A knife hung in a skin sheath from a belt around her waist. In the folds of one arm she was holding a foot-long black and brown dog that began to yap when Clair looked up, its needle teeth gleaming from a pink mouth; in the other, she held a naked, brown infant with a runny nose. The woman wore thick glasses. Behind the lenses her small, black eyes seemed to drill into Clair, and her puffy features were locked into some desperate emotion that seemed to Clair horrifyingly out of context.

Suddenly the woman started talking to her, in a low, hoarse attack of words.

"I'm sorry?" Acting, though she didn't want to be, Clair smiled firmly but kindly at the woman—a Katharine Hepburn, here-are-my-borders smile. "I didn't hear what you said."

"I said the Sioux and Comanche chiefs warned General Custer not to attack them. Over and over again they warned him," said the woman, audibly now, and Clair felt a flood of relief: she was talking about General *Custer*; she was just passionate about her people's history, or angry in a perfectly justifiable racial way. . . . "But Custer wouldn't hear them. He ignored the chiefs. Then when the battle of the Little Bighorn was over, the women came onto the ground where Custer and his band of cowards died and mutilated many of the bodies. Do you know what they did to Custer's body?"

"No," said Clair. "I don't. But I imagine you are going to tell me."

"Bet on it," said the woman. "They punctured his eardrums with sewing awls so he could hear better in the next world."

The woman turned around to put the yapping dog and the infant on the floor of the booth. Then she stood up and crossed her arms, staring at Clair with hot, black eyes, her face clenched tight as a fist again, and at that moment Portia walked up. Clair resisted looking at her, enlisting her. She wanted to finish whatever this was on her own terms, without acting anymore and without help, woman to woman with this person. She looked for the true, right emotions.

"I don't know why you're telling me this . . . You seem angry. That was all such a long time ago. I'm sorry for what Custer did, but the best we can all do now is try to be kind to each . . ."

"*Listen* to me, bitch," hissed the woman. "I have a warning for *you*, so clear your ears, because if you don't hear it, I swear to God, I'll cut your tits off and stuff them in your mouth . . ."

"Say *what?*" barked Portia, instantly up on as high an anger as the woman. "What is your *problem*, fatso?"

The woman cut her eyes at Portia and said, "Die, cunt. I pray the spirits of the animals you disgrace with that shit you're wearing will lick your skin off with their tongues."

"Now wait just a *minute* . . . ," said Clair, frantically reaching through her mind for the right diffusing professional words. "Portia, please, can we just leave . . . ," but Portia flicked a long arm out then across the counter and slapped the woman in the face.

The Indian woman heaved her enormous upper body across the counter, flailing at Portia with her fists and screaming.

"You have a *child* back there, please stop it!" Clair shouted at her as Portia calmly grabbed two handfuls of the woman's long hair, put a moccasined foot on the bottom of the booth, and started yanking. Clair saw the woman's face pulled up and sideways, the coppery skin stretched tight, her glasses gone, one black eye bulging and sad looking. *"No!"* she screamed at Portia. *"Stop* it, for God's sake, *both* of you." She reached for Portia, but there was a growing mêlée surrounding them, people shouting and pulling at the two women, and Clair was forced away from the booth into a little opening, where she put her hands to her face and fought the urge to cry.

A little girl came running by, stepping on Clair's foot. She was pulling at a thin woman's hand and shouting, *"Hurry*—there's another, *fat* Pocahontas and she's fighting the pretty one . . ."

Portia drove Clair's car back to the farm after a stop in New London to rent a video. Clair didn't say a word on the fifteen-minute drive along Lake Sunapee, but sat picking at her nails and looking worried while Portia recounted, as she loved to do, her dreams of the night before.

"Look," Portia told her finally at the stop sign in Newbury, "this is ridiculous. For the fifteenth time, it had nothing to do with you. That cop said she had caused trouble out there before."

"I know, I *know*," said Clair irritably. "Listen, I've forgotten all about it. Let's just get home, okay?"

"Yeah," Portia sighed, drumming her fingers on the steering wheel. "I just wish I hadn't hurt her neck. I felt so sorry for the poor ol' fat thing when the cop was taking her off and she was holding that little snotty baby and that dog and all, I swear to God I could've just laid down in the dirt and cried."

It was a little after three when they pulled into the driveway. Clair got out of the car, slammed the door hard, and walked quickly up to the pasture gate. The ram and ewes came running down to meet her. The five lambs were gone.

She turned to Portia, grinning. "Al*right*," she said, making the catcher's sign for "safe" that she had learned from Bill. "*Yes! Now* let's have a drink and start enjoying ourselves."

In their swimsuits they made white wine spritzers and took them out to the pool along with the rest of the bottle of wine in an ice bucket, then lay on lounge chairs in the sun. Around five-thirty Portia went upstairs to take a nap. The hot day was finally starting to cool, so Clair changed out of her swimsuit into a pair of cutoff shorts and a button-down dress shirt Bill had worn the day before that still had his smell on it, and went back out by the pool to pick up with the sexy Lasher in Anne Rice's *The Witching Hour* thinking, finally, now, it was behind her and out of her life and she and Bill were safe and there was nothing but blue sky ahead, and feeling delicious relief like a cramped muscle relaxing for the first time in months.

About fifteen minutes later, just as she was finishing chapter 12, there was a knock at the door in the tall picket fence surrounding the pool. Feeling at last as wonderful as she had every reason to feel, Clair turned down the page of her book and got up to answer it.

Red Sizemore and his cousin Bucky Boudreau had begun this Saturday at 8 A.M. with a couple of Rolling Rock beers and some of Red's homemade jerky for breakfast, taken outside the teepee since Red and his wife were not speaking again. After she drove off with the baby and the dog, gunning the rusted old Hyundai Pony so that it fishtailed down the muddy driveway, they packed Red's Dodge Ram half-ton with the gear they would need up north. The following day was the opening of bow season on deer, and Red and Bucky were going to spend it and the next hunting out of Red's deer camp near the Canadian border. But before they left they had a day's work to do.

First they trailered Red's backhoe to Sutton to dig up and unplug a blocked septic system that belonged to Bucky's goddaughter and her boyfriend. The boyfriend came outside and stood on the back deck of the house trailer, drinking a beer and watching them while they worked. He was a beefy biker with long hair, a goatee, and tattoos running all the way down his pumped-up shoulders and arms. Red and Bucky were digging out the holding tank by hand, their shirts off, up to their knees in sewage. The biker boyfriend stood on the deck, watched them through round, red-tinted sunglasses, and drank his beer slowly.

"I sort of wonder who that guy thinks he is," said Red after a minute or two. "Up there drinking a beer and watching us shovel his shit."

Bucky looked up and saw that Red was changing colors. His face and the freckled skin of his huge torso were starting to go red, and Bucky knew what that meant. "Larry don't mean nothing, Red," he said quickly, and tried to change the subject. "Gonna be hot again today. What do you suppose it was yesterday, eighty?"

"He's grinning at us now. I believe maybe he does mean something," said Red. He lay down his shovel and stood up to his full, imposing height. "Hello, citizen," he said to the boyfriend, the red now well into his voice. "Listen: Either pour that fucking beer out on the deck right now and carry your fat ass inside, or come on down here and party some with me."

Red had a deep, slow, rumbling, low-pitched voice that sounded like the idling of a piece of heavy equipment. Bucky had never, ever, known him to raise that voice, but when he was angry, Red literally went from white to pink to red—his big hands and forearms, his square, freckled face and high bald forehead coloring before Bucky's eyes, like the coming of heat into a stove coil—and that sudden dangerous blush somehow made it into his voice too.

"Come on, Red," Bucky said gently. "Sharon and the babies may be home." He knew the biker had a reputation for being a scrapper, and Bucky didn't want his goddaughter to have to watch her boyfriend get stomped into their own septic system. The last scrapper to oblige Red when his voice was like this was a giant young carpenter in Bradford who, as one of the town selectmen, had written Red asking him to remove some of the old vehicles and scrap metal from his yard on the main street. On a stroll through town the next week with his wife, while Red and Bucky were working in that very yard on a 1959 Norton motorcycle, the carpenter had made the mistake of resenting something Red said to him as he walked by, and Red had broken all fifty-six bones in the man's face, put him in the hospital eating through tubes for a month, and then charged him with criminal trespass.

At forty-five, Bucky's first cousin was still, as Red's wife often said, "chicken hawk and chain lightning," and here he was now in Bucky's goddaughter Sharon's backyard about to strike down her boyfriend, and there was absolutely nothing Bucky could do about it. So he sat down on the lip of the pit and lit a cigarette.

Red and the boyfriend stared at each other silently for two or three minutes, neither of them moving a muscle, while Bucky smoked and waited. Finally, very slowly, the boyfriend tipped his bottle of Miller Lite and poured out what was left onto the deck. Then he stepped inside the back door of the house trailer and closed the door. Bucky laughed with relief, picked up his shovel, and went back to work, delighted with the way things had worked out: His goddaughter's boyfriend was still walking around, and Bucky had yet another Red story for the sports bars in Newbury and New London.

There was no shortage of Red Sizemore stories in any of the taverns or sports bars between Concord and Lebanon, and not all of them had originated with Bucky. Red was hard to miss, for one thing—standing six-foot-six and weighing 260 work-muscled pounds, with a big, creased, florid face that reminded people of John Wayne, gold rings in both ears, and shoulder-length red and silver hair that grew only from the back of his head and was worn in a ponytail. Also, he got around and was known by a lot of people, working in the area at various times as a snowplow driver for the Bradford road crew, an independent backhoe and 'dozer operator, a roofer, carpenter, and woodcutter, as well as doing a little tree cutting, sheepshearing, slaughtering, and cattle trading on the side.

The stories about Red were as various as they were numerous. There were the drinking and fighting stories that Bucky was partial to, and the feats-of-strength and huge-appetite stories that reported him picking up small heifers to load onto trucks and eating two dozen eggs at a sitting. There were the woodsman/hunter stories about his tracking and archery skills, and the size of the deer he killed using bows and arrows he made himself, and all the poaching he was believed to get away with. There were stories about him being some kind of medicine man, about how he could hypnotize animals with his hands and mash out cigarettes on his tongue. And there were lots of stories about Red and women. These were the stories Bucky liked the least.

Bucky was not married himself and never had been, though he was thirty-eight years old and had always wanted to be. He was a short man, little bigger than a ten-year-old boy, with a pit-bull-ugly but cheerful face, and women just didn't seem to like him, even though he believed he understood them and always tried to be nice and respectful toward them. If Bucky *were* married, he knew he would never be unfaithful to his wife, and he didn't like to think that Red was, though he figured there were too many stories around for it not to be true. Joy, Red's wife, was not the best-looking woman in New Hampshire, but she was a wicked good cook and God knew she put up with a lot. Bucky himself would be happy to have her, even if she was an Indian, and if he had her, he knew he would damn sure be faithful to her.

After they finished the septic system they had an early lunch at Bradford Junction and bought six cases of beer. The beer was for their hunting trip up north, but they didn't wait to start on it. They both liked to begin drinking beer in the morning and drink it throughout the day up to supper time, not fast, but at a nice, even pace of about one beer an hour that kept a little buzz going all day. After supper—done for the day working with heavy machinery and saws and other things that could kill you—they went to rye whiskey.

Next, they picked up Bucky's truck and drove it to a house in South Newbury to load up some summer people's lambs for slaughtering. The family, the Joyces, had owned the house for as long as Bucky could remember, but he didn't know any of them. He had heard the parents had moved to Florida and didn't come up anymore. Occasionally he saw one or another of the sons and their good-looking wives down in the harbor, where they always seemed to be laughing, drinking beer, and getting in and out of boats, and their eyes would pass over Bucky whenever they encountered him as if he were a broom standing in a corner. Mr. Ayers had asked Red this year to take over shearing and slaughtering the Joyces' sheep, but Red had never mentioned the family to Bucky and that did not surprise him, since Red had a well-known dislike for all seasonal and weekend flatlanders on and around the lake.

There were no vehicles in the drive or the garage when they got to the house, and Bucky assumed that no one was up for the weekend. The house looked big enough for everyone he knew to

live in, and Bucky wondered with no bitterness or irony why anyone would keep and heat a house large enough for four families
and then stay in it only two or three people at a time and only a
dozen or so times a year. For a lot less money, he guessed, you could
probably rent the entire Mount Sunapee Motel for twelve weekends and the whole month of August and have free cable TV in
every room.

"This used to be the Dwyer place, didn't it?" he asked Red.
He had backed the truck into the driveway and stopped to look at
the handsome old house close-up for the first time.

"Yup. And before that it was the Twists. An apple orchard.
It used to be good for something besides just sitting here."

"Looks like these people have poured the money to 'er."

"They got it to pour, I guess," said Red, sounding angry again.
"You want to back the truck up to the goddamn gate so we can
load these lambs and get on with things?"

"I like architecture is all," Bucky said, backing up.

While Bucky was scooping grain into the feed buckets, Red
looked into one of the road-front windows of the house. Then he
walked over to the pasture gate without saying anything and picked
up the feeding lambs two at a time, one in each hand, by the backs
of their necks, and lifted them into the truck.

They drove the lambs back to Bucky's and put them in a
small catch-pen of sheep wire. When Bucky slaughtered he just
walked around the catch-pen with a .38 Blackhawk, putting the
pistol into the ear of each lamb in turn and shooting toward the
opposite eye, filling the pen up with dead lambs, then taking
them out one at a time to skin. But Red had his own, peculiar
way of doing it, as he did with most things. He carried each lamb
out of the catch-pen to a little field behind Bucky's house where
he put the lamb down, took its head between his hands, and

talked to it for a minute, about anything that came into his mind, it sounded like to Bucky. Every time—Bucky had never seen it fail—Red's voice hypnotized the animal and left it standing rooted in place while he stepped off forty paces, sometimes fifty, and then shot the animal through the heart, using one of his own cedar arrows with wild-turkey fletching and his 60-pound-pull Osage orange longbow.

Red was not only the best shot with a bow Bucky had ever seen or heard about, but also the quickest. The only time out of hundreds, from any angle or distance, he had ever missed a lamb's heart, the lamb had gone down on its back legs and no more than opened its mouth to bleat when Red hit it again, perfectly this time, with the second arrow he always held in his bow hand.

Bucky watched Red kill four of the lambs, placing each in a different spot in the field. When he carried out the fifth and last lamb, Bucky asked if he could shoot it. He had never made this request before but they were going deer hunting the next day for the first time that season, and he had had no time over the summer to practice his bow shooting. Red calmed and rooted the animal and said he supposed so. Bucky went up to the house and came back with his black steel compound, which with its stubby arms and pullies and sighting pins looked like some part off a metal tooling machine next to Red's. He paced off twenty steps from the lamb, lined up, held his breath, and shot the lamb in the butt. The animal started hobbling off, bleating.

"Shoot straight this time," said Red. "I hate to see anything suffer."

By the time Bucky had nocked another arrow, the lamb was forty yards off and trying to run. Nervous now, Bucky missed the lamb entirely with his second shot, but before he could apologize, Red had killed it, at fifty yards with a nearly rear-on shot.

"Good shot," he said, as Red walked off toward the lamb. Red didn't answer. Bucky had the strange thought that it was almost as good to have Red around all the time backing him up as to do everything well himself.

Red didn't answer his fuck-up little cousin because he didn't want to get mad for a fifth time that day. He just thought: I hope you're looking down, Celia. I hope you see.

Even though, or maybe because it turned out to be the day he had been awaiting for months, it had started out worse than most. First thing that morning he had gotten into a fight with Joy because he was going deer hunting and not working another fair with her, and he had to pick up the macaroni and cheese TV dinner she was eating for breakfast—shoveling it down and screaming at him at the same time—and throw it against the wall to shut her up.

Even more than throwing things and screaming, Red hated changing a tire and he had had to do that next when he stomped outside to his pickup and found the right rear flat. Changing a tire seemed to have in it everything in the world he hated, and struggling with the jack on his back in the mud of what passed for his front yard, surrounded by machines and engine parts, listening to the kid squalling in the teepee, the meanness of the life he was leaving crashed down on him in a final spite, as heavy as the truck itself, and Red had cursed up into the shocks of the Ram in the fury of his impatience.

He had let himself get angry for a third time that day at some jerk-off biker with a beer, and then for a fourth when he and Bucky drove up to the Joyces' house to pick up the lambs and it looked like she was gone again. But then he had seen dishes standing in a drying rack and a magazine open on the table and known that she was not gone, and that turned things around. Now with almost everything done that had to be done except the most important thing, and then nothing but new and north ahead of him, Red was in the good mood he should have been in all day and he intended to stay there.

By the time they finished skinning out the lambs, it was almost four-thirty. They dropped off the carcasses with the butcher in Newport as old man Ayers, the Joyces' caretaker, had asked Red to do, then drove back to Red's house in Bucky's truck with the skins, a fifty-pound bag of salt, and Bucky's bow and duffel for the trip. Red kept the skins of most of the lambs he slaughtered, and Joy tanned them into throw rugs and lap robes for the teepee. But Ayers said these people wanted to send the skins off to get them tanned, and asked Red to take them back to the Joyces' farm and salt them down. So he and Bucky transferred the skins and salt and Bucky's gear into Red's truck, already loaded for the hunting trip, and drove back to the Joyces', where he would be going now anyway, with or without the skins.

Her car was in the driveway as he knew it would be, so Red drove down the hill and backed up to the old barn.

"Go ask the people where they want their skins," he told Bucky.

"Why don't you ask? You know 'em."

Red turned and stared at Bucky until he got out of the truck and walked up the hill, bent over at the waist, hands in his pockets.

"Straighten up that back, boy. You like architecture, remember?" Red yelled at him out the window and laughed, feeling so good now that he could look over at the trout pond where he had received the first and only beating of his life when he was twelve years old and not even care about the strange revenge he was finally taking for it now, though looking at the pond didn't make him exactly sorry it was a Joyce she was married to either.

He pulled a beer from the cooler on the seat and cracked it, dropping his empty can back into the cooler. Then he put in a tape of Dame Kiri Te Kanawa singing some of his favorite arias. Red had believed opera was vomit for all those years when Celia played it every night. But when he started thinking about the music his new life would need, he had known immediately it would have to be opera, and he had gone to the library and read about it and then listened to all of it he could get his hands on for the past four months. During those months listening to opera had seemed to set him free, even when he wasn't yet, and now it felt to him like a pleasure he had known all his life. Turning up the volume he noticed that his forearm still had sewage stains on it from this morning, along with dirt and sheep blood from this afternoon, and he wished he had taken a shower before leaving his house. He didn't like being dirty, and it would be a couple of days before he saw a shower again.

He watched Bucky knock on the front door of the house, wait for a minute or two—uncomfortable-looking even at a distance— then walk around the side of the house to a door in the tall fence surrounding the pool that Red had looked down on the night before from the top of the pasture. The door opened and Bucky talked to someone briefly. Then he walked back down the hill, his back straight now, grinning.

He leaned on Red's door. "It was one of them Mrs. Joyces," he said, grinning. "I'd eat a mile of her shit just to see where it come from."

Red turned away from him, shook his head disgustedly, and squinted out the windshield at the house. "Where's her husband?"

"She says he's gone until tomorrow night. She says salt the skins here in the barn and give the bill to Ayers."

"Uh-huh." Red felt his breathing start to quicken with the perfect rightness of it. "You tell her you were with me?"

"Uh . . . why?" Red looked at him. "No."

"Anyone else up there?"

"I didn't see nobody. She's out there by a swimming pool reading a book."

"Salt down the skins and then wait for me in the truck," Red said.

"Where you going?" said Bucky.

"Just do what I said," Red told him so there could be no argument or further questions. "I might be awhile."

He forgot Bucky then, got out of the truck and walked up the hill, seeing in his mind the woman's face.

He was walking past the front of the house on his way to the pool when he saw her through the screen door standing at the refrigerator with her back to him. She was bent over at the waist looking for something in the refrigerator, and Red saw her long, thin legs and the creases at the top of her thighs where her shorts rode up.

He opened the screen door silently and walked up behind her. She was wearing a man's shirt. He reached underneath it and put his.hands on her bare breasts. She stood up with a sharp intake of breath but did not turn around.

Red kept his hands on her breasts and kneaded them. He pulled Clair closer to him, kneading her breasts, and whispered into her hair, "I want you to ask for it again."

CHAPTER FOUR

By the time they paddled back to the car, racked the canoe, and changed clothes, it was after noon, and Bill and Dray were hungry. Rather than eat on the side of the road, they drove for a few miles until Dray found an abandoned field he liked the looks of. He followed an overgrown dirt road to the top of a small rise near the center of the field that afforded them a wide view of the Magalloway River valley.

They let Brando out to run around and sat on the tailgate in the sun, the river lying in bright serpentine coils beneath them, the leaves on this high northern hill gone already to russet and brown.

Dray had made the lunch that morning before they left the farm, and Bill would have known Dray made it if he had been served the lunch at the Ritz Hotel in Boston. They had three sandwiches apiece, each a thick wad of ham slices between two pieces of white bread and that was it—no mustard or lettuce or cheese, let alone an apple or a piece of celery. Dray was always complaining about Portia's "designer food," and the "girly cooking" he believed had taken over all Boston restaurants except for Locke-Ober. He insisted on being in charge of the menus on their sporting trips, and those menus invariably featured lots of pork, eggs, white bread, and beans—the kind of food, Dray said, that men used to eat before women, pansies, and Democrats took over the country.

Though Bill was in no more concurrence with Dray's taste in food than with most of his social and political positions, today he found himself enjoying the absence of a woman's touch in the lunch, the landscape, and the day's activities. He and Clair had not been out of each other's company for more than two or three hours at a time since early June, and though he would not have swapped a moment of that company for anyone else's, he realized now that he had been readier than he knew for a trip with Dray, and he was glad he had not backed out as he had come close to doing the night before.

"A masterful and subtle lunch," he told Dray when they had finished all six sandwiches with some help from Brando.

Dray lit a Swisher Sweet and said, "Hey, you ate it, didn't you? And without any fucking pesto, even."

They drove about an hour north and west to timber company land where a maze of dirt logging roads ran over ridges of pine and hardwoods and through thick spruce and alder bottoms. Referring to another hand-drawn map, Dray drove one of the logging roads until it ended in a **T** with another smaller one that cut east and west through a vast, boggy, tangled sea of alders.

"This is it," said Dray, looking around.

"This is what?" asked Bill.

"What Uncle Stu calls 'Vietnam.' He said we can spend the whole afternoon in this one place if the birds are here." Excited now, Dray got out of the Jeep, let the gate down, and started digging around in the back. "I'm gonna put together a couple of emergency kits in fanny packs. We should both wear one in case we get separated. That's some rough country in there, Billy Boy."

Feeling sleepy and content, Bill continued to sit in the passenger seat, his knees up on the dash. "I thought we were hunting the roads."

"Not here. We're going to walk due north into those alders for a half mile, say, and then grid the cover, and if we don't find anything, we can come out whenever we cut the road."

Bill got out of the Jeep and stretched. Dray handed him a hunter-orange fanny pack. "Compass, waterproof matches, whistle, space blanket, bug dope . . ."

"It's October," said Bill. "There aren't any bugs."

". . . PowerBar, gorp, knife, canteen of water . . ."

"*Water?* That's a swamp we're going into."

"The water in there's probably got *Giardia* bacteria."

Bill laughed. "You're getting even more paranoid than usual, you know that? This isn't the real Vietnam, for Christ's sake— this is bird hunting."

Dray looked at him and shook his head sadly. "You never, *ever*, learn do you? You remember that American pilot a year or so back got shot down in Bosnia that had to eat bugs? You think that kid thought he was going to be shot down? Hell no, but he knew he *could* be and he was prepared."

"That was in a *war*, Drayton," Bill laughed.

"Everything's a war, pal. This is a dog-eat-dog world."

"Then where's Brando's emergency kit?"

"With a master like you, he *needs* one," said Dray. And that was that.

Dray uncased his shotgun, filled his vest with shells, and belted on his fanny pack. Bill lay his pack down in the back while he let Brando out of the kennel and snapped a bell onto his collar. Then he took out his shotgun and some shells, and Dray locked the vehicle. They were a hundred yards into the alders before Bill realized he had left the fanny pack. He didn't even consider going back for it. The woods were dappled with light, cool and marshy smelling. It felt fine to be walking through them, watching Brando's tail for the mad whirling it went into whenever he caught scent of a grouse or a woodcock, and Dray, ahead and to the left of him, pushing through the whippy alders like a bush hog. It could not have felt better or safer, and he wondered how he could have ever tried to use the woods as a testing ground to settle an argument, or as anything but the sweet haven they were.

"Instinct and smarts," he yelled for the fun of it over the crack of the brush. "Remember that."

"Experience and skills," Dray shouted back. "And don't you fucking forget it."

The argument began one summer evening in 1989 while he and Dray were grilling bluefish on the patio of Clair's parents' house on Martha's Vineyard. Bill and Clair always took the house for the month of July, and the Hurleys joined them there for two weeks every year. On their first night together Bill and Dray were drinking gin-and-tonics, grilling fish caught that morning, and talking about deer hunting. Bill had hunted deer from stands for years but had never learned to hunt by stalking as Dray did most of the time. Now Dray was volunteering to spend the autumn teaching Bill to stalk, but wanted him to understand that it would be years before he could expect to kill a deer that way.

Bill offered to bet that he would kill one that coming season.

Dray laughed and said Bill would have no more chance of stalking a deer and killing it that fall than he would stalking and killing Dray.

Bill said he figured he could manage that too, if push came to shove: hypothetically, of course.

Hypothetically as well as otherwise, said Dray, Bill was full of shit: Dray had grown up in the woods—the woods were his natural environment, as the city was Bill's. Sure, over the years and thanks to Dray, Bill had learned a little about the outdoors and even owned a few simple skills, but if the two of them were ever pitted against each other in the woods, Dray said Bill could just sit down on the nearest log and write out his will.

Bill made another gin-and-tonic and allowed that he didn't agree: The jungle of the city business world was a harsher environment than the woods any day, and someone with the instincts and intelligence to thrive in that jungle could apply those same qualities to survive in any environment, and to better effect than some woodsy, nimrod simpleton.

The argument continued over the next two weeks, and by the time they left the island at the end of July, Bill and Dray were permanently fortified behind their positions and, with no way to actually test them out, prepared to argue them abstractly for the rest of their lives.

Dray was living then in Goshen, New Hampshire, where he owned a struggling motel and bar at the base of a ski mountain. There had been very little snow for the past six New England winters and the mountain did no snow making. As a result, Dray's business had been falling off steadily, and Portia's cooking classes and little gourmet shop in New London were no longer making up for the losses.

Bill's fortunes were better. After a year of motorcycling around Europe with Clair and trying to become a professional photographer while Clair wrote plays, he had worked for four years as a photo editor and travel columnist for the *Boston Globe*. Then in 1984, with the last of his money from the drinking games book and a loan co-signed by his father, he had bought a small, underpriced travel business specializing in cruises, and the rest of the big-spending eighties turned it into a large travel company.

In 1989 Bill had a beautiful wife, a three-story town house on Beacon Street, and his own successful business. Despite the loss of a child, he believed he was living something of a charmed life and that he could go on dominating that life indefinitely. Dray, on the other hand, had bunkered himself into a kill-or-be-killed frame of mind. Neither man was much prepared to be out argued on the nature of survival.

In early August Dray mailed Bill a page torn from a farm catalog advertising CO_2 pistols that shot paint pellets and were used by foresters and ranchers for marking trees and stock. Accompanying the page was a typed note from Dray challenging Bill to a one-on-one manhunt on ten acres of New Hampshire woods not familiar to either of them, the loser being the first one shot and marked with paint from these guns, two of which Dray had ordered.

This exercise was carried out on a drizzly afternoon two weeks later. They had outlined with surveyor's tape the boundaries of an eight-to-ten-acre tract of light hardwoods on the eastern flank of Mount Sunapee, and they entered those woods from opposite ends at exactly two o'clock, wearing camouflage coveralls. The results of the contest were inconclusive: Dray found Bill first, shot at him, and missed (the guns, they learned, were erratic at any distance over about forty feet)—and, in rolling out of the way of Bill's return fire, lost his glasses. While he was looking for them on the ground, Bill shot him in the leg with a Day-Glo yellow paint ball and called it a victory for instinct and intelligence. Dray called it beneath contempt.

They both agreed there were a number of things wrong with the test. The field of play needed to be larger, they decided, and there should be more competitors, all of them trying to accomplish a task or goal and survive at the same time, to better mirror the real world. Bill came up with the idea of having four flag stations within the playing field, each with the same number of particular-colored flags as there were players. The goal of this new test—or game, as they were now starting to call it—would be to capture one flag of each color and be the first competitor to make it back to one of two "Home Bases" at either end of the field without being shot.

Once this game was conceived, it had to be played. Bill and Dray made up a list of twenty people and sent out a letter inviting each of them to a weekend of sport, barbecues, dancing, and the playing of the first annual game of Survival!

That game was played on Sunday, October 1, over 110 acres near Dray's house in Goshen. Among the fourteen people who accepted the invitation were a heart surgeon from Colorado, an investment banker and a painter from New York City, a friend of Bill's who was a staff writer for *Time* magazine, a New Hampshire forester, a stockbroker from Boston, and a documentary film director. Dray and Bill never saw each other during the competition. Dray stalked and put out five players before being put out himself without having taken a flag. Bill's plan had been to hide beside the flag station nearest his starting position and shoot everyone who came to take a green flag until he was the only player left. The strategy worked, and he might have won with it except that he missed the fourth player he shot at and was put out when he tried to run. The game was won by the forester, who ghosted through the woods picking up one flag after the other without ever once pulling his pistol from its holster or being shot at by another player.

In December *Time* magazine published an account of the game, written by Bill's friend, and over the next few months, Dray (whose address was given in the article) was buried in letters requesting information on how to get the guns and rules, and how to set up a playing field.

In May Dray drove down to see Bill at his travel company office in Boston. He showed Bill the letters, by then nearly two hundred of them, and said that he had been doing some feasibility studies and believed they could make a business out of the game. They could get an exclusive licensing arrangement with the manufacturers of the guns and paint balls, and sell kits containing a pistol and holster, pellets, CO_2 capsules, safety goggles, a compass, and a set of rules, which they would copyright. He believed they could also come up with some franchising method for spreading the game around the country and creating a national competitive structure. Dray figured their start-up costs would be between twenty and thirty thousand dollars. If Bill would put up the money and handle the publicity, he said, he would do everything else.

In less than a month Bill had arranged for two New England television stations and *Boston* magazine to cover their ongoing games in New Hampshire, and they were in business—with Dray filling orders for kits out of his and Portia's small house during the day and managing a twenty-four-hour convenience store four nights a week. But only two months later it looked as if the new company wouldn't make it. Bill's investment was up to thirty-five thousand dollars, as far as he was willing to go. After a flurry of initial sales, orders had slowed to a trickle and Bill was out of publicity contacts and options. Then two things happened that turned the business around: Dray and Portia decided they would sell everything they had in New Hampshire, move to Boston, and sink or swim working together full-time on the business out of the cheapest apartment they could find; and a publicity magic lantern was dropped into Bill's lap out of nowhere with an unwitting genie in it named Dr. Helmut Schnabel.

Dr. Schnabel was a psychology professor at a small college in the Midwest, and the national chairperson of an organization called Academics Against Violent Entertainment in America. In Boston for a conference, he had seen a channel 4 story on Survival! and immediately put it in ahead of *American Gladiators* as number one on the list of entertainments his organization stridently opposed. Back in Iowa, Dr. Schnabel located Bill and challenged him to a long-distance debate about the game on a Des Moines radio call-in talk show.

From Des Moines, within weeks, Bill and Dr. Schnabel had carried their act to over forty radio and TV talk shows across the country, including *Donahue* and *Nightline*. On each, Dr. Schnabel would rant about how football, hockey, boxing, and now this new abomination were leaching America of its conscience and its "feminine anima," and suggest that Survival! players should be made to serve long sentences of public service working in homes for battered women.

Then it would be Bill's turn. For the first few shows he had answered Schnabel's criticisms of the game by denying them. But the people who called in, 90 percent of whom were on his side, seemed to want more from him. On an important New York daytime TV talk show, Bill broke loose on a hunch and said that, alright, yes, of *course* there was symbolic violence in the game, and by God it was *fun*. It was fun to shoot someone before he shot you. From the beginning of life on the planet, he said, survival had been a violent business, and often it still was. The game presented you with paradigms of survival situations that very well could be encountered in real life and taught you how to come out on top.

"Dr. Schnabel in his ivory tower," he concluded, "seems not to realize this, but it is a competitive, even a violent world out there for many of us much of the time. The game teaches you to take the initiative—to be the hunter, not the hunted."

The program ended with every phone line busy. As Bill was leaving the studio, Dr. Schnabel came up to him, squeezed his bicep, and gave him a quick, weasely grin. "Now you're talking, buddy," he said. "We're going to ride this one right to the top."

And Bill knew that he was right. It felt exhilaratingly new to realize that he was out of his net and running the ball downfield for once and that he could score if he just kept charging and didn't slow down or look back.

That was in December of 1990. By the following March, Dray had moved the business out of his apartment into an office and hired two full-time people, and Portia was able to go back to teaching cooking. By that May Survival! was doing seventy-five thousand dollars' worth of business a month, and Bill and Dray believed it was just getting started.

In July Bill sold his travel business and went to work full-time for the game, doing its publicity and setting up a national franchise network. He began traveling four or five days most weeks, meeting with potential franchise owners, helping to put on games around the country, and debating Dr. Schnabel. He was not often at home even when he was in Boston and neither was Clair, and when they were there together they were like two distracted, irritable strangers forced to sit next to each other on a bus.

Bill and Clair had always loved talking to each other, and from the moment they met had carried on a continuous, impromptu dialogue so absorbing and irresistible to both of them that they talked to each other with their mouths full, all during love-making, even in their sleep. But after the death of their infant boy, Clair had quit talking to Bill or anyone else for a while, and when she began again it was from stages all over New England. She dove back into the acting career that she had abandoned after they were married, and finding that film and paid stage roles were no longer available to her, she took summer stock and repertory parts in Massachusetts, Connecticut, New Hampshire—anywhere a the-atre would allow her to become another person for a few weeks. For a while Bill went to see her plays, then he had had enough of them and didn't go much anymore, and then he was too busy and too absent to go at all. When they were together, Clair didn't talk about her acting and wouldn't talk about Survival! which she considered an absurd waste of Bill's time and talents. Instead of talking, they argued often and read different parts of the paper at meals. They went to bed at different times, both of them falling asleep the moment their bodies were still. They made love some-times not once in a month, and when they did, it felt to Bill like a sad struggle to keep from drowning. Every intimacy they had built up like money in the bank—Clair's rubbing his eyelids as she fell asleep, his inventing secrets whispered to him by their old Labra-dor Luke—was suddenly withdrawn and gone, and they found themselves bankrupt.

For as long as Bill could remember, his father had worked twelve-hour days. When he wasn't working he was bullying or ig-noring his wife and children, closing down bars, flying to London to buy his clothes, sleeping with whomever he could get his one meaty, freckled hand on, and braying jokes or threats at people—and doing all that, somehow, with a good bit of endearing charm. Bill's cool, willowy mother Rose belly-laughed at Jack Joyce's jokes, walked away from his boozy tempers, left suppers for him in the stove at night before she went to bed, and did volunteer work for hospitals, charities, and museums every day as if her life depended on it. Bill had grown up holding this marriage carefully in his mind as the precise antithesis of what he would have for himself, and countless times during his childhood and adolescence he swore to himself that he would be a monk serving lepers in Bangladesh before becoming a man like his father. Then, as suddenly and magically as if a wand had been waved over his life, his father was retired and had moved to John's Island, Florida, where he and Rose slept in the same bed for the first time in thirty years, played golf and croquet inseparably, took tango lessons, and rode from their house to the beach club for lunch every day in a golf cart holding hands; and all Bill could figure out to do about his own emptying and angry marriage was to go from working ten hours a day to twelve.

For three years he flew at this work with his head down. He traveled more than thirty weeks a year. He represented Survival! at gun shows, rooted out new franchises, and continued—whenever either of their enterprises needed a PR boost—to debate Dr. Schnabel, feeling more and more natural in the tough-talking, pontificating role of his debate persona. With only an occasional wistful sense of himself being not himself but familiar nevertheless, he closed down bars and brayed at people. And he took to playing Survival!—which he did with numbing frequency—like a desperado, shooting at anything that moved.

"You know, it's funny," a franchise owner named Earl told him in Louisville or Pittsburgh or Akron over a midnight drink at the bar in Bill's hotel. "I don't know you from jack-shit, but I would've sworn you'd be one of those guys that sits still and waits for the game to come to them. But you're just another Billy the Kid like me."

One Friday night in January of '94 Bill flew back to Boston from a Schnabel tour of the Midwest and drove home from Logan in a snowstorm. He had had three or four drinks on the plane, and the velvety, invisible machinations of his Mercedes caused him to feel expansively tolerant toward the posturing talk-show hustler he had been all week. Unlike Clair, he told himself, he had always been able to live with questions about himself to which he had no answers: he was running just fine, why look under the hood?

Clair was seated at the kitchen table in her nightgown, crying quietly, smoking hash from a water pipe and tearing in half newspaper reviews of her stage performances going back to high school. Neat as always, she had arranged the shreds of paper in a symmetrical heap in the center of the table. It was after midnight and Bill badly wanted to go to bed. He poured himself a glass of skim milk, kissed Clair on the back of the neck, and sat down at the table.

"Bad week, huh?"

"Listen to me," she said, crying noiselessly, stoned, her long, pretty fingers taking each review separately and slowly out of the overstuffed file she had kept since before he knew her, tearing it in two and dropping it into the heap. "Don't interrupt. I was gone, *too*, this week."

"Look, could we do this tomorrow?"

"I went to Los Angeles to see my old boyfriend Harry, because he *asked* me to come see him and because he said he could get me a movie part. And do you know *what*, Bill? *Billy?*" She said his name vengefully. Bill stared at the pieces of newspaper in the center of the table, seeing little parts of Clair in them—a head cut away from the shoulders, her legs, part of her name—feeling, as he had on the death of their son, a vast, black, dimensionless loss yawning between them. "There *was* no part except for Lilly in *Oklahoma!* in the bottom of a Methodist church. And Harry's gotten fat and wears gold chains and drives a black Corvette that he hates to get wet and has this fucking helmet kind of hair." Bill put his hand up to touch her cheek and Clair slapped it away. "Kind of armor. Like you, except on his head, not his heart and his dick."

"You're acting, Clair, and I don't care about the guy anyway. Can we go to bed?"

Clair stood up suddenly, unsteadily, and swept the torn newspaper and the water pipe off the table. A long, thin piece of paper clung to her nightgown. She picked it off and held it up to her upper lip like a mustache and stared at Bill, crying, then wadded the piece of paper and threw it to the floor. She stood in front of Bill sobbing, her arms hanging thin and defeated-looking at her sides. "Do you care about *this*, you absolute asshole? Harry wanted me to give him head in his car the way I used to. Do you care about that?"

"Did you?"

"No. And I'm not acting, goddamnit. I'm through with acting, just like you want me to be." She stood looking at him, sobbing now like a child. "Oh God, I miss you, Billy. Where did you go?"

Bill stood up then and took her in his arms and held her and rubbed her back for a moment across the gulf. Then he went to bed.

That night frightened them both, and they clutched for each other in their sleep until Bill went out of town again. Clair quit acting as she said she would and began seeing a Reality Therapist. She tried to get Bill to go with her and he did go once or twice, but during that period he and Dray were negotiating to buy a plastics company in Ohio so that they could manufacture their own pistols and he had a hard time concentrating on what the earnest young woman had to say. It didn't seem to bother Clair when he stopped going: Reality Therapy by then had taken the place of acting in her life and she was on her way to becoming a therapist herself. Then one day she seemed to just give up trying to get his attention, and she was more even-tempered after that.

In March of '94 Bill and Dray signed a big contract with IBM, which wanted to use the game for executive "team-play" training. In June they signed another, bigger contract with the U.S. Army and hired a perky blond ex–aerobics instructor named Candy Mills as a publicity assistant to Bill. And in July, at a gun show in Las Vegas, Bill took Candy back to his room at the Sands with its hot tub and a mirror over the round waterbed and began there an athletic but enervating two-month affair.

He ended it that September when Clair called his hotel room in Atlanta at one in the morning to tell him his grandmother had died. Bill had been in the bar. Candy had answered the phone and gotten confused about what to say.

When Bill got back to Boston late the next day, Clair had already packed her clothes and moved to her parents' house on the Vineyard. Bill didn't think much about his feelings or behavior even then, although he knew they were about to change again, and irrevocably this time. He fed Brando, made himself an omelette, drank most of a bottle of red wine, watched a baseball game, and took a sleeping pill.

The next morning he went in to see Dray at the office.

"Do you remember how all this started?" Bill asked.

"Over a lot of gin-and-tonics," Dray said, studying him.

"How much is my stock worth?"

"Maybe six hundred, seven hundred thousand. Maybe five. Whatever somebody would pay you for it."

"Will you buy me out?"

"Not without trying to talk you out of it. This is not the time to sell, Billy Boy."

"Would you, though?"

Dray stared at Bill for a full minute before he answered. "Rather than someone else doing it."

"Think about it. Whatever figure you say is fine." Bill got up. "I'll be at home."

For the first two or three weeks after the collapse of his life, he wandered around the ruins like an earthquake victim, looking under rubble and finding absolutely nothing of his own. The feeling produced in him by realizing he had been living someone else's version of his life was beyond sorrow and guilt: He felt simply, irrecoverably lost, and powerless to get found.

Dray came by to see him regularly, bringing pizzas or fried chicken and once an entire four-course meal cooked by Portia, and would sit in the kitchen with a glass of Scotch watching Bill pick at the food, neither of them talking. Then one Saturday morning Dray came by with no food and said, "Get your clothes on. We're driving down to Hartford. The guy who owns the franchise there is putting on a fifth-anniversary Survival! game this afternoon. A lot of the people who were in the first one are going to be there, and he says you have to play in it. I say so, too. Don't even try arguing with me."

Bill went. He talked to people, ate a plateful of ribs, and enjoyed himself at the barbecue before the game. When the game started he walked to the flag station closest to his starting point and sat down with his back against a big pine, fifteen yards away from the twelve blue flags that were hung on a clothesline between two trees. There were eleven other players in this game, including the forester who had won the original one. Bill shot him first when he slid noiselessly out of the woods to take one of the flags. During the next hour he shot eight more players as they ran or walked or crawled out of the trees to take a flag, and not one of them saw him, though Bill was sitting in the open. Then he stood up, took a blue flag from the clothesline, collected the other three flags from around the field at a stroll, and walked out of the woods to one of the two Home Bases, having found and reclaimed one small but valuable piece of himself.

In early November he began walking for an hour or two each day with Brando on a leash and taking pictures of whatever interested him. Between Thanksgiving and Christmas, he started jogging twice a day in the Public Gardens, and through January and February his photographic walks took up more and more of the rest of his day. In March he made a darkroom on the third floor of his house and taught himself color processing, and toward the end of that month he did a freelance job for the *Boston Globe*, then another for *Boston* magazine. Later that spring, through a contact on the *Globe*, he picked up a two-day shoot from *Architectural Digest* and an assignment from the *New York Times*, and he took on an agent.

In May Clair moved back from the Vineyard to a rented guest house in Chestnut Hill so that she could resume her practice. She still wouldn't talk to him on the phone, so he sat down and wrote her a long letter. He began with a cheerful, newsy report of what he had been doing. Then he told her that he had looked through some of her books on various types of therapies, on shamanism and meditation and yoga. He had read the passages she had underlined in those books and learned through them of an awful suffering she had borne that he had been ignorant of. He said it was like learning she had had breast cancer while he was out of town, and it was for his stubborn blindness to that suffering that he had blamed and hated himself most over the past few months. He told her that, unforgivably, he couldn't even remember exactly when she had become a therapist herself, but he was proud of her for doing it and believed she must be a very good one.

He told Clair that he had no idea how to explain the strange, long sabbatical he had taken from himself and no excuses for it, but that he was now remaking a careful, attentive life that she could occupy the center of for the rest of time, and that if she decided to come back to him, he would love her with his new heart to within an inch of her life. If she would not come back, he would still love her and wish her well and hope that they could be friends because he could not imagine any life without her in it somewhere.

A little less than a month later, Bill's father died of a heart attack while sitting on a dock with Rose in Vero Beach watching manatees. After his brother Sean called to give him this news, Bill went for a run. As he ran he cried for the first time since the death of his son, with a tearing mixture of sorrow and joy for the manner and place of his ardent father's death, and when he finished he felt looser and lighter than he had in years.

He stood between his mother and his wife at the funeral. It was the first time he had seen Clair since October. She was willowy and haunted-looking, and there was a gauntly erotic look about her, a predatory need in her eyes that frightened him and also made him want to haul her to the ground and make love to her right there in the cemetery.

After the service she told him that she was going up to the farm for the weekend and had arranged to have the sheep sheared while she was there. When he asked her if she had gotten his letter she said only, "Yes. Thank you for writing it."

That following week Clair called and invited him to dinner. The hungry neediness seemed to be gone out of her face and they had a fun, easy evening; Bill left early after kissing her on the cheek. They had two more dates that week and every night the following week, and though he thought he might go crazy on those dates with wanting her and with knowing that she wanted him, too, he ended each evening early with a kiss on her cheek.

On Saturday, June 24, at ten o'clock in the morning, he had just come in from a run, showered, and was dressing when the doorbell rang. He was still pulling on his shirt when he opened the door and found Clair standing there between two suitcases. "Hello," she said. "You can just take that shirt right off, if you don't mind."

It wasn't until that moment that Bill felt himself begin to breathe again for the first time in almost nine months. And beneath the joy and gratitude that overwhelmed him as he took Clair into his arms was the recognition that he had somehow survived the most important game he would ever play, and that smarts had had absolutely nothing to do with it.

They spent three hours slogging through "Vietnam" without finding a single woodcock. What kept them there that long, and kept Brando dashing back and forth with his tongue lolling and his tail whirling, was more of the whitewash droppings of woodcock on the ground than they had ever seen anywhere. They kept thinking that with all that fresh sign, there had to be birds somewhere in the enormous cover, but the woodcock had apparently just left the place on their migration south, and they had left it to the last bird.

When they came out of the woods Bill and Dray were scratched, drenched with sweat, and exhausted, and Brando had been reduced to a slow waddle. But as they trudged up the dirt road toward the car, the dog's tail started spinning again and he plunged into a hawthorn thicket just off the road.

"Come out of there, Brando!" Bill shouted, worn out with the dog's unproductive excitements. "No bird, no *bird* . . . "

But a bird appeared—a grouse, clattering out of the thicket and rocketing straight down the road. Bill, who had unloaded, could only watch it fly, but Dray snapped his gun closed and fired, and the bird tumbled in the air and fell dead in the center of the road. Brando pounced on it and trotted back to them, his eyes glittering with excitement above the big cock grouse in his mouth. Bill knelt and took the grouse. Then he rubbed Brando's muddy ears. "That's a fine dog," he said, and felt the day click shut perfectly for him.

They drank a couple of beers on the drive to Dray's uncle's cabin, riding with the windows of the Jeep open, enjoying feeling the day cool and the good tiredness from walking, and the quick buzz the beer gave because they were tired.

Their plan was to have a drink or two of Scotch once they reached the cabin, then Dray would fry up the pork chops and potatoes and onions he had brought for dinner. They would go to sleep early and could wake later the next morning with only a half-hour drive to the river for duck shooting. It was a plan they had each looked forward to and talked about all day, so when they finally located the cabin, in a little clearing beside a nearly dry riverbed, and went inside to find it trashed and looted, it felt like a personal disaster.

"A bear, you think?" said Bill.

"Bears don't steal things." Dray spat on the floor, which was littered with broken crockery and glass. "There was supposed to be a Coleman stove in here, sleeping bags, lanterns . . . They even took the fucking woodstove." He kicked a dangling piece of stove pipe. It creaked and fell to the floor.

"Who do you think did it?" asked Bill.

"Some thieving, backwoods locals, I guess. I'd like to fucking *know* who they were—I'd fill some woodchuck asses up with number-four shot."

"You'd shoot 'em, huh?"

Dray turned around and glared at him fiercely. "You're fucking-A I'd shoot 'em. What would you do?"

"You shoot people in the game, not in real life."

"Believe it, pal," Dray said, still glaring. "I'd shoot the bastards in a New York minute."

"Okay, fine. So what do we do now, killer?" Bill had his own answer to that question and was even happier with it than he had been with their original plan.

"Tough it out. We've still got food and a roof over our heads. We build a fire outside to cook on, sleep on the floor . . ."

"There's nothing left to cook with."

"We cook the chops on a fucking *stick*, goddamnit."

"The windows and doors are all busted out, Dray."

"So *what*? You said yourself, there's no bugs. It's warm. We'll survive. You got any better ideas, chump?"

"As a matter of fact, I do," said Bill.

CHAPTER
FIVE

The little man had just stood there staring at her with a gap-toothed grin. He had a round, homely face, and his stringy arms were streaked with what looked like blood, but there was something well-meaning about his eyes and Clair was not alarmed.

"Can I help you?" she had asked him finally.

"Is Mr. Joyce here?" the man said.

"No, he's not. He won't be back until tomorrow night. Can I help you?" she had asked again.

"I have your skins," said the man, still grinning.

Clair had stared at him, a little nervously now. "You what?"

"Your *sheep . . . skins*," the man said slowly and distinctly, as though talking to a child. "Richard Ayers said you wanted them."

"Oh," said Clair. She had moved closer to the door to look behind the man into the driveway. "Thank you," she said briskly. "Please salt them down in the barn down the hill. And can you send the bill to Mr. Ayers?"

"No problem," said the man. He had stood there, grinning lopsidedly, his eyes watching her politely.

"Fine, then," said Clair. "Thank you." He still hadn't moved, but she closed the door to the fence and locked it.

She had thought to go back to her book by the pool, but the conversation left her anxious. There had been no sign of Red Sizemore. He had taken the lambs and was gone, she told herself, and simply sent this little man back with the skins. She had forgotten about the skins, and was sorry now she had told Mr. Ayers she wanted them. She didn't like the thought of the bloody skins in her barn, nor did she want anything around to remind her of Red, particularly in the barn. She would get Mr. Ayers to come and get the skins tomorrow, she thought, and he could ship them off to be tanned.

Clair had carried the wine bottle and ice bucket back into the kitchen then and decided to get started on supper by making a salad. She had noticed the open kitchen door and the unlocked screen door and thought she would sit at the counter to make the salad and enjoy the late yellow light on the apple trees across the road. She opened the refrigerator and pulled out a cucumber and some scallions and put them on the counter, then leaned over to open the lettuce drawer.

When the hands touched her, cupping and holding her breasts with a sudden, hard heat, Clair's body jerked upright as if stabbed, but her mind wasn't shocked or even surprised. She drew her breath and held it, and felt him kneading her breasts, his hands hot and hard, and first thought, how dumb: telling the little man that Bill was gone, the unlocked screen door—*God,* how dumb; and then, only, that Bill would know now unless she did everything perfectly.

He pulled her to him and she felt the back of her head come against his chest, and he was rubbing her nipples now with his palms. Clair felt them go hard and her body flush warm over its shock and anger, and then he was leaning over her and she could smell him, and he was whispering into her hair for her to ask for it again.

She thought for a second of screaming, of fighting, running. Then she saw him in her mind, and fighting and running were not options. Face it, she told herself. Calmly. Bring your strength.

She reached under her shirt and pulled his hands off her, and he let her do that. Then she turned around, facing little higher than his stomach: the dirty, open shirt, the reddish mat of hair on his chest, the smell of him, strong now, the smears of blood on his shirt. Not able to look at his face, willing her voice to be calm and strong, she said: "Not ever. I have nothing, ever, to ask you for again. And I hate you for those phone calls. I want you to leave my house and never come here again."

It was what she had wanted to say and it sounded strong to her, and with that small confidence she raised her head and looked into his face to show him her strength. But his face, looking down at her, was sealed and unhearing, as she had seen it before, and for the first time she felt fear for herself, like a bright thin sliver of light appearing in her mind, the crack of light from a door opening, with panic behind it. She tried to seize her thoughts and hold them tight to work out what to do, but they slid out from under as she stared at him, and all she could see was his face the first time she had seen it.

It was May and she had come up to the farm for the weekend, during the most miserable period of her separation from Bill. It was a bright, stirring spring Saturday before the black flies, and Mr. Ayers had been up earlier to say a man was coming to shear the sheep in the barn. Clair had seen the truck drive up and park by the barn around noon. She ate a tuna salad and smoked a joint, her second of the day, and sat down to read, but the restlessness of her misery that wasn't going away had her up pacing in ten minutes. So she filled a thermos with ice water for the man shearing the sheep and took it down to him.

He had spread old blue blankets on the dirt floor of the barn and was kneeling there astride one of the ewes with wool shearings all around him. He didn't hear her over the electric shears when she walked in carrying the thermos, and the sight of him had jolted her and taken her breath: his great, hard, freckled, shirtless torso, his greasy black jeans and big silver belt buckle and heavy steel-toed work boots, his long, coarse red and silver ponytail; and, when she finally said something and he turned to look at her over his shoulder, his face—which was hard as his body and big-featured and cold-eyed and lined and red and used and humorous. The sight of him had stopped her breath, and maybe it had been the marijuana, but she felt as if she were looking at a bull, an old red bull, and then a grizzled Minotaur, its strong wide black thighs astride the sheep, holding a rear leg aloft and drawing the wool away from it with the shears in soft white peels, revealing the pink skin underneath.

"I thought you might like some water," she said when he looked up at her.

He stared at her for a long moment, still holding the ewe's leg, his eyes traveling over her. Then he motioned for her to put the thermos on the table on which he had laid his tools and went back to his shearing. Clair could hear the other sheep, milling and bleating in one of the stalls behind her. The barn was warm, shot with sunlight falling through the open double doors. It smelled of disinfectant and sweat. A fly or two buzzed around her head.

"My grandfather taught me to shear," said the man. "He said it was the most personal thing you could do to an animal that was legal . . ." He went on talking quietly about his grandfather, as though to himself, and Clair had never heard such a voice—it seemed to her to have something of the hoarse rumble of the sea in it, something of far-off thunder.

She carefully placed the thermos on the table and saw that her hand was trembling. Then she walked quickly out of the barn and back up to the house with the sight and sound of the man burning in her head. She made a cup of coffee and smoked another joint while she paced on the porch to the restlessness of her misery and now something else too. Then, ridiculously she decided to try to take a nap. She was walking up the stairs to do that when she turned and walked back downstairs, through the kitchen, outside into the warm, lilac-fragrant air and back down to the barn and into it, and then stood there with her hands on her hips looking at the man now as if he were a perfect workhorse for sale, to put to her plow, and she had the money on her. And he, still on his knees over another nearly naked ewe, looked back at her with his own familiarity.

After a moment he went back to his work and Clair stood there in the fly-buzzing, vinegary-smelling, sun-shot barn, feeling her misery subside mercifully under the marijuana and her excitement, and waited.

"Do you want something?" he asked after awhile without looking up, drawing the shears down the last of the wool on the ewe's stomach.

"Yes."

"Ask for it."

Clair said, "I want you to hold me. I just need someone to hold me."

He stood and lifted the shorn ewe with one hand by the back of its neck and swung it up and into the stall and she saw for the first time the real height and width of him. He picked up the thermos from the table and drank from it, and Clair looked at his narrow hips and Minotaur thighs in the black jeans and felt herself starting to breathe quickly. She prayed this would be alright. He put the thermos down and walked to her and pulled her into him, wrapping his arms lightly around her back. He held her that way, lightly, for a moment, and she put her arms around his waist tentatively and lightly, too. Then her hands went to his back and Clair was gone, beyond help, and she wanted nothing light anymore.

"What else do you want?" he said.

"Nothing," she lied, her breath coming so quickly now, she could barely speak.

"What do you want?" he said. "Ask for it."

And she threw back her head then and looked at him, his face closed off now and unhearing, and her own feeling as hot and damp and urgent as she was beneath, so that she paid no attention to the warning in his face and asked for exactly what she wanted with the first blind pleasure and release that she had had in months.

"That's not what you want," he told her. He put his hands on the back of her head and separated her hair and brought the two halves of it over her shoulder in his hands and stroked them, pulling his hands over her breasts. He said, "You don't want me to leave. We need to grease your hair, C. J." And Clair felt the door open wider on the bright panic in her mind. She tried to keep her eyes on his face. She forced herself to look into it, trying to make him see her. "I know what you want," he said. "You should have told me on the phone. I would have come to get you. I was calling to tell you I know how to give you exactly what you want."

"No," she said.

"Your husband was here with some other people and now they're gone and you're here alone. For what?" He drew the back of his hand down her stomach slowly, turned it over, and drew his fingers back up between her legs.

"*No,*" Clair shouted, backing up. "He is here. He's hunting and he could be back any minute, and I did not come here for that. That's over forever, and I want you to leave . . ."

"Ask," he said, following her.

"Leave now," she said to him, backing toward the screen door, "and I won't tell my husband."

He snorted and said, "No, you won't tell him anything, and you didn't before. You don't want him to know, and if he knew, he might do something to get himself hurt, and you don't want that either. This is you and me."

Clair's back was to the screen door, her mind blind now with fear and telling her nothing. She was about to open the screen and run, hopeless, toward Mr. Ayers's house when Portia walked into the kitchen and stood there, just inside the entrance with her hand to her mouth, her eyes big and alarmed.

"What . . . ?" Portia began, looking back and forth from Clair to the man.

"This man is leaving now," said Clair quickly. She glanced at him and prayed he would do it. "Thank you for bringing the skins. Good-bye."

He looked at her, seemed to consider for a moment, and grinned. He turned and looked at Portia, grinning, and Clair thought, maybe . . . maybe . . . then he turned back to Clair. He put his hands on either side of her head and stared into her eyes as if he owned her, as if she were something he carried in his pocket. He stared at her, holding her head, and for no good reason at all Clair felt herself going calm.

"That's right," he said. "We're all leaving now."

It was almost nine o'clock when Bill and Dray pulled into the driveway of the farm. They were in a heated discussion about the continuing value of Roger Clemens to the Red Sox when they arrived, and both of them were out of the Jeep and walking up to the kitchen door with Brando charging ahead of them before they noticed that the house was dark, and then that Clair's old Volvo that she kept at the farm was gone. The kitchen door was standing open. The screen door was unlocked.

"That's strange," said Bill.

"What? They probably went out for dinner."

"The door being open. Clair never leaves it open when she goes out."

"Hey, they're women," said Dray. He turned on the kitchen light. "You want to unload the Wagoneer?"

"Let's leave it till tomorrow," said Bill. I'll get the charcoal going, then we can clean the birds. Why don't you make us a drink?" As he walked through the kitchen, Bill noticed that some food and an ice bucket with a wine bottle in it had been left out on the counter, and that too, in Clair's always meticulously kept kitchen, struck him as unusual. They had decided not to stop for dinner but to cook the three ducks and the grouse when they got home. Bill had wanted to call the house to tell Clair they were coming back, but Dray hadn't wanted to stop. Bill had asked Dray if he had heard yet of cellular phones, and Dray had said he couldn't afford the use it would get from Portia, and besides the girls were probably out on dates anyway. On the patio, pouring the charcoal into the grill and lighting it, Bill decided to think only about getting the duck breasts rare but crisp on the outside while not overcooking the grouse—and maybe Clair would get back in time to eat some of it.

Dray walked out and handed him a Scotch-and-soda in a tall glass with ice. Though Bill had enjoyed the day, he was very glad to be home now, waiting for Clair, and not sitting around a fire outside a looted cabin eating pork chops off a stick. He had enjoyed being with Dray and Brando and the hunting, even though he had fired only one shot; and he had been happy to learn that he could still make the trips with Dray and find a way to take pleasure in them on his own new terms. Those terms, he had discovered today, meant refusing ever again to have anything to prove in the woods, and refusing to pretend to be anyone but himself there. It meant lying on a rock in his underwear, if that was what he felt like doing, and then coming home when he wanted to for a tall Scotch-and-soda with ice.

"Why don't you just let me throw the birds in a pot and boil 'em?" said Dray. "It'd be quicker."

"The trip's over," Bill told him. "I'm in charge of the food now."

When they finished eating, it was ten-thirty with still no sign of the women, and Bill couldn't come up with anything else to keep his mind off Clair's not being there.

"They should be back by now," he said to Dray as they put the dishes in the dishwasher.

"Maybe they went to a movie."

"They rented a video. It's in the den."

"So maybe they watched that this afternoon and *then* went out for dinner and a movie—how the hell would I know? Besides, it's nice having the place to ourselves. Christ, I'd *pay* somebody to get the old lady out of the house for a whole night once in awhile, wouldn't you, Billy Boy?"

Bill knew this was residual hunting-trip talk—he had never known anyone, man or woman, more devoted to and dependent on a spouse than Dray—but it was not a subject he could joke about now. "Brando's out of dog food," he said. "I'm going down to the barn to get a new bag."

"What's the video?"

"*Junior.*"

"It's funny. You seen it? It's funny. I'm gonna put it on, and you need to watch some of it, my friend, and lighten up." Dray put his hand awkwardly on Bill's shoulder then, squeezed it, and looked him in the eyes, his relentless face tired but younger-looking than it had been in the morning. "I'm glad everything's worked out so well for you and Clair. I've been meaning to tell you that. She's happy. You're happy. And I'm proud of both of you."

It was the sort of comment that Dray would rather chew nails than make, and it made Bill realize that Dray was as nervous as he was.

"Thanks," he said.

Dray squeezed Bill's shoulder again and stuck out his tongue. "What's that?"

"Your tongue."

"Lesbian with a hard-on. Ten bucks says they're here inside a half hour."

Bill took Brando with him on his walk down to the barn. The night was bright enough not to need a flashlight, calm, and too warm again. When they got within about fifty feet of the barn, Brando charged it, barking, then stood in front of the closed barn doors barking nonstop, the hair standing up on his back. Bill walked up behind him and saw a dark, glistening stain that had spread from under the left barn door onto the concrete apron. He knew immediately it was blood, and with his mind gone suddenly blank he stood there staring at the stain. Brando was still barking, but cowering now behind Bill's legs. He knew he had to slide open the doors, but it took him a full fifteen seconds of standing there, conscious only of his pulse beating loudly in his head, before he could make himself do it.

Lying on the barn floor just inside the left door was a bloody heap of skins—lamb skins, he saw when he forced himself to walk over to them—and for a second they had no meaning to him other than as some gruesome sign or portent. Then it came to him what they were doing there, and Bill sat down on a pile of grain bags and said to himself, "Thank God."

Brando had now retreated out into the road and was crouched there whining. "It's okay," Bill told both of them, feeling relief run through him like adrenaline. "It's just the lambs. It's nothing but lambskins."

He picked up a bag of dog food, hoisted it over his shoulder, and closed the barn doors, still feeling high on relief. It wasn't until he was halfway up the hill that he started to think about the skins being there and realized that Red Sizemore must have brought them, as Bill had asked Mr. Ayers to have him do, and that realization started a new discomfort in him.

He had never spoken a word to Red Sizemore, though he had known who he was ever since his oldest brother, Brendan, pointed him out and spoke his name one summer day about thirty years before in Sunapee Harbor, and told Bill that their father had given that boy a whipping a few summers before for poaching trout in their pond. Bill hadn't known whether to believe Brendan or not—he had never heard about the whipping, and that night when asked about it his father would neither acknowledge nor deny it—but he stared at this Red Sizemore anyway and continued to stare after Brendan tied their father's beautiful 1956

Garwood mahogany speedboat to the dock and walked up the hill to the general store.

Red was about fifteen or sixteen years old then but already big as a big man and wearing a drooping red mustache. He was sitting on an old Harley-Davidson in the harbor parking lot, smoking and talking to an older man, also on a motorcycle, who had a monkey on his shoulder. Bill had the strange thought that the two of them and the monkey were maybe planning a robbery. He stood in the bow of the Garwood envying Red his mustache and the old yellow Harley he was on, and wondering if the tough-looking boy-man really had been beaten by his father, and if so, if he had cried. Bill wished that Red Sizemore would look at him so he could see his face, and after awhile he did, turning his head in the middle of a laugh away from the man with the monkey, his eyes cruising down the parking lot as if it were a floor he danced on every night and stopping on the ten-year-old boy standing in the beautiful vintage boat. Red's eyes landed on him hard, and Bill could see that they were full of pride and humor and the ownership of things he knew nothing about, but after a moment of Bill staring back at him they softened with something that looked like his own curiosity, and Red lifted a forefinger, held it near his cheek for a second, then popped it away again in what felt to Bill like a little salute to what each of them had that the other could not have. Bill had lifted his hand in his own small salute, then hopped off the boat and walked up the hill for the ice cream cone he and Brendan had come for.

Since then he had seen Red Sizemore maybe a dozen times, coming out of the Bradford post office or in the Pub in Newbury Harbor, and they would nod to each other if their eyes met, and Bill always felt that the nod carried with it an acknowledgement of some small intimacy still between them of curiosity and sympathy. Then about two months ago when he and Clair were up alone for their first weekend at the farm since getting back to-gether, Bill had seen Sizemore on the street in Bradford, and this time when they glanced at each other there was something new and unmistakably insulting in the huge, ponytailed man's expression. Bill had held his eyes as he walked past him, refusing a polite impulse to smile; and then Sizemore did—a slow, patronizing smile, a cards-holding smile—and nodded.

Something about the encounter bothered him now more than it had at the time. He had written it off then as just a look, after all; at worst, just a form of the game playing Bill knew some of the locals liked to engage in with seasonal residents. But now, as he walked up the hill in the dark, the exchange seemed more loaded than that—more personal in some way, with a gloating in the man's attitude that ended for good the old, amicable standoff between what they each had and knew.

Red Sizemore had been in his barn that afternoon, and Clair was, unaccountably, not at home. He knew rationally that the two facts had nothing to do with each other. But that didn't stop his discomfort from growing—by the time he reached the house—into full-blown fear.

CHAPTER
SIX

When the big blond woman walked into the kitchen it changed everything, and for a moment neither Red's mind nor his body could tell him what to do. Her being there meant that Clair was not waiting in the house alone for him as he had believed she was from the moment Bucky told him the husband was gone. It also meant he could not stay there at the house for a few hours in her bed to tell her his plans as he wanted to do. He wasn't sure what else it meant, and for just a moment after she walked in he thought his mind might be about to tell him simply to leave. But more decisions were made for Red by his body than his mind, throwing him into action that often surprised him and leaving his mind to catch up when it could.

He took Clair's head in his hands and pressed on her jaw and at the back of her skull the way he did with the sheep.

Then he turned to the blond woman who said, "If you hurt her, I swear to God I'll kill you," but looked frightened when she said it. He walked over to the woman and put his hands on her head too and pressed. She tried to pull his hands away but couldn't, so she stood there looking at him, her eyes frightened but not cowed, and finally she calmed down, too.

"Let's go, ladies," he told them then. He took them each by a wrist, and, squeezing with just enough force to let them know for certain in their muscles and bones that nothing was possible but what he wanted them to do, he kicked open the screen door and led them out of the house.

He drove them down to the barn in C. J.'s Volvo, pulled up beside the truck, and honked the horn. Bucky came out of the barn, grinning politely when he saw the two women in the car, and walked up to Red's window.

Red said, "Ladies, this is my cousin Bucky Boudreau. Bucky, this here is C. J." He nodded at Clair sitting next to him, then turned to look at Portia in the backseat, "And I don't believe I know your name."

There was a silence. Bucky ducked his head to look in at the two women. As he looked between them, his head bobbing politely in greeting, no one said a word and Bucky's grin eventually faded. He stood up straight, wiped his hands on his trousers nervously, and said, "What's up, Red?"

"Just do what I say and don't get squirrely on me, Bucky. Close them barn doors. Then I want you and the lady in the back there to take this car and follow me and C. J."

"Where we going, Red?" Bucky asked, his voice bright with nervousness.

"*Nowhere*," said Portia. "We're going nowhere with you." She made a sudden jerk forward in the backseat as though she had just come awake. "You two maniacs are leaving here *now* if you don't want the cops up your asses, and my friend and I are going back up to the house." She grabbed the rear door handle and yanked at it cursing, but Red had locked it from the driver's seat. Portia fumbled with the lock, pushed it up; then Red reached over the seat, took a wad of her yellow hair in his right hand, and whipped her head around hard to face him.

Hurting her but not too much, he smiled and said, "I don't think you under*stand*. You're going to have a nice time with my cousin here while C. J. and I get caught up. Nothing's going to happen to you. Bucky's a gentleman. In fact," Red laughed, "you've probably never been safer. But something's seriously likely to happen to Mrs. Joyce here if you cause any trouble." He let go of Portia's hair slowly and patted her head twice.

Bucky leaned his head in the window, fully squirrely now, Red could see, and said, "Red, can I talk to you for a minute?"

"Please let us go," said Clair. "Please." She faced Red, and it disappointed him to see how frightened her face was. "I know you're not a bad man, and you don't want to get your cousin in trouble . . ."

"*Red . . .* ," said Bucky.

Red realized that he wasn't getting his point across entirely, and that they had been sitting in the barn driveway for too long. He felt his face getting hot, though he didn't want to get mad. "That's enough talk." He said it softly, but everyone shut up.

He got out of the car and guided Bucky into the driver's seat, running his hand fortifyingly over the little man's back and shoulders. Bucky chewed on his lower lip and pushed the button that motored the seat closer to the pedals. Then Red walked around the car and opened the passenger door. After a slight hesitation Clair stepped out. "Do you want to get up front?" he asked Portia. She was looking out the window, along the road toward the house, and didn't answer. Red slammed the door so hard, the car rocked. He took Clair's hand, led her to his truck, and helped her in.

"Where we going, Red?" Bucky asked him again in a small, resigned voice.

"Up the road." He got in the truck, opened the cooler, and offered Clair a beer.

"No, thank you," she whispered, sitting prissily, her hands in her lap, staring straight ahead. Red opened a beer for himself and drained it in four swallows. Then he opened another, catching up, put it between his legs, and started the truck. He pushed the tape back into the deck and Kiri Te Kanawa was on the high notes that he liked in "Vissi d'arte" from *Tosca.* Calming down, he looked over at her again, and, despite the way she was holding herself and the bitchy, terrified expression on her face, it was almost exactly as he had imagined it. She might have been his wife sitting there, riding with him out to the lake for a barbecue and some bow shooting at Dale's house. He put the truck in gear, pulled out of the barn drive slowly, and turned down the hill.

"My name for you is C. J.," he said. "That's how I see you."

At first, that day, he had thought of her as just another piece of strange, no matter who she was married to. When she walked into the barn and he looked up at her and saw immediately what she wanted, he had thought she was a little skinny for his taste and a little wrought-up, which he didn't like in a woman, but why not? Because she was wrought-up he wanted to be sure she knew what she was doing, so he made her tell him exactly what she wanted from him, and when she finally did that, throwing her head back to look at him, Red felt like he had been hit with a cattle prod. He realized he had never seen before that moment, not even in the tits-and-ass magazines, what real lust looked like on a woman's face—uncoquettish, frank as pain, ruthless. It made him think for a second that he was looking into his own face.

Red dropped his jeans and hers. He took her panties and blouse off and she jumped up onto him, crossing her legs around his back and rode his dick like cantering a horse, her butt slapping his thighs, her hands clutching his hair, her head thrown back, moaning and cursing like a Claremont bar waitress. When she came he had his hands on her long thin lower back, and he felt it shudder and shudder in his hands like some animal dying. Then he laid her down on a pile of wool and fucked her his way, supporting his weight on his elbows and driving into her so she'd know he had been there, his mouth sucking one small, perfect tit and then the other, and her grunting under him like she was digging hard earth, working at it as hard as he, sweating, wanting it driven into her and taking everything he gave, rolling her head in the wool and grunting and raking his back with her nails. Then she came again under him with such force and abandon that it made him begin to come, too, and he had rolled her over on top of him in the wool, feeling the shudders of her coming against his own and equal to them, and had seen at that moment in the rafters of the barn the first clear vision of his new life.

It was the lust in her face when she asked him for what she wanted that he couldn't forget and that tormented him after she was gone. It had seemed a lust for all of him at once— not just his dick but *him*, his life, his thoughts, his future—and it had seemed to have behind it the same determined ruthlessness with which he himself wanted things and took them. In Red's experience, once you wanted something you didn't slow up or stop until you owned it, all of it, and he didn't know what to make of her slowing to a walk after he had fucked her in the barn—standing up with his come glistening on her smooth, tanned thighs, getting dressed and looking at him now with a kind of cool caution.

They went up to the house together, and finally he was inside that house and sitting there like he owned it while she made coffee and asked him about himself and his life and was as nice as she could be but also cool and careful. He wanted to go to her bedroom—the same one, he imagined, where old man Joyce had slept—but she said no, that wasn't possible, and Red was so stunned by her that he didn't take what he wanted but just left the house after the coffee when she asked him to leave. She told him that he could not come back to the house, but that she would meet him at the Mount Sunapee Motel the next day at noon for an hour or two before she drove back to Boston. Red waited in the motel parking lot until twelve-thirty, then drove to the house to find it locked and shuttered and her gone. Then he walked around and around a big maple tree in the front yard, hitting the thick, ridged bark with both fists until they were numb and bloody because he had something important to tell her, and he had not taken over her bedroom the day before and fucked her there all afternoon and then told her, as his body had clearly told him to do.

At forty-five years old, Red had realized within the past year that who you are is what you have, and that he was the proprietor of a life full of junk. He had been born with the will and the strength to take whatever he wanted, and ever since Celia died he had done just that—striding through his life as if it were one of the huge antique flea markets that he occasionally went to with Joy, going from booth to booth and taking everything that caught his eye, filling up his truck over and over with what now turned out to be nothing but old, broken scythes and pitchforks and cracked serving platters and paintings of tigers on velvet and place mats that said WELCOME TO SEATTLE.

He knew now that he had walked right past all the valuable things. For all those years when he thought good music was Ozzy Osbourne he had walked past everything of any value—though he could have taken those things just as easily as all the junk—because he hadn't *known* what to want. Not knowing, he had filled up his life with junk, and now he was sick of all of it. He was sick of the know-nothing, Copenhagen-chewing carpenters and plumbers and mechanics and masons and roofers who he drank with at night and worked with during the day; and the scaggy, boozy women he took to bed, with their lank hair and thick legs and missing teeth, their pale New Hampshire skin and all the cheap rings on their fingers and little tattoos on their shoulders and ankles and butts; and of the four wives he had had, each dumber and lazier and less able to dream than the one before. He was sick of digging out septic systems and foundations, and laying roofing shingles and painting houses and bulldozing roads and all the other junk work he did to earn a living. He was sick of living in a teepee with a jealous 240-pound aboriginal woman, a squalling infant, and a hundred tons of metal in the yard. And he was sick to death of being the only shark in a little piss-pot goldfish pond and of living up to the reputation that being that had earned him.

A few months before, Red had waked up feeling his age and known that if he was going to start over, knowing what to want this time, he had better get at it. Over the past few months he had identified a few components of that new junkless, independent life and had spent fifteen or twenty nights in the public library in Concord learning about opera and chinked-log-home construction and Shaker furniture and beekeeping, but he had no idea of how all those things fit together until he rolled a climaxing flatlander woman over on top of him and saw up in the barn ceiling his future as clearly as if he were watching it on television. Then, as he began to climax himself, Red felt as if he had just walked away from a plane crash.

Her lusting face tormented his mind day and night for the next three months, and he called her seven or eight times over the summer, telling her that he knew what she wanted and would give it to her, getting all of that out each time before she hung up. Whenever her husband answered the phone, Red hung up. Then in August, when he was still sure she would come, he had seen the husband in Bradford walking out of the IGA, and Red had looked at him—telling him with his eyes that he would take her, that he already had her; telling this man whom he had nothing against and had always kind of liked what he wished he could have told the man's father: that he had walked back into that full, perfect life of his and taken more than a few trout this time, and what the fuck was he going to do about it now? Then Red nodded his condolences.

The next time the husband answered the phone, Red held the receiver until he said "Hello" three or four times, then whispered very slowly, "I . . . fucked . . . your . . . wife." He had wanted to tell the man that, and once he had he didn't care about ever seeing him or talking to him again, and he finally called it even with the one-armed old man too.

Red quit making the calls by the end of August, and by mid-September he had given up on Clair voluntarily stepping into his future, but he went on planning that future anyway. Then she was there at the farm and the husband was gone, and Red believed she had planned to come back to him all along and knew that the time had arrived to set the sails on the proud black ship with the skull-and-crossbones flag that his next life would be. But when the blond woman appeared in the kitchen it changed everything, and for a moment he had not known what to do. Then his body had him take both women to the barn, and there it became clear to him exactly what to do.

* * *

Neither of them spoke for nearly an hour. Red drove north at under fifty miles per hour, nursing his beer, and Clair sat with her hands in her lap, her face very pale, staring straight ahead out the windshield. She cried once, holding the heels of her palms over her eyes and sobbing for about a minute, then she stopped and went back to the way she had been. Red didn't say anything to make her realize there was no reason to cry because he wanted to save all of what he had to tell her until they were at the deer camp and he could look her in the face.

Finally, she just began talking, her voice as calm and personal as if they were old friends who had been talking all along:

"When I met you my husband and I were separated and I thought we wouldn't get back together, even though I wanted us to, and I was very unhappy about that. I used to be an actress and had a little bit of a career and that was over, too . . ." She paused and looked at him across the truck cab for the first time. Red drank his beer and didn't look back but was conscious of her eyes staying on him when she went on talking. "I felt like I was drowning, do you know what I mean? I couldn't get my breath, I couldn't think, I was just in this suffocating misery that . . . Listen, Red, in my profession we try to get people to see the truth and then tell it. Well, the truth is, I used you, and I'm terribly sorry for that. I had never been so miserable in my life as I was that weekend. I needed someone to hold on to . . . And you were there and I was attracted to you and I let things get out of hand. I am *very very sorry* for that, Red, and I am sorry for not being fair to you. But I'm sure you are a good man and an understanding man. My husband and I are back together now. We love each other, Red. I love him, and I don't want to be with anyone but him, and my life is happy now. It's exactly what I want. I don't want anything else. Do you hear me?"

Red didn't indicate that he did or did not. She did not speak again for a minute, and when she did, her voice was not as calm but now like a scared child's, and she sounded like she might cry again, and Red felt himself getting mad, though he didn't want to.

"Please let my friend and me go home, Red," she said. "Just stop here, *please,* and let us drive my car home and you can go on about your business and no one has to know *anything* about any of this . . ."

Red had just turned onto Route 104 at Danbury. It was almost seven o'clock, and when he turned east a line of hills behind them took what was left of the day's light, and he switched on his headlights. Buzzing at them like wasps just then down a long straightaway section of the road were two Ninja 750 motorcycles, ugly little crotch rockets, their riders lying out nearly flat along the fuel tanks, coming fast and abreast in the narrow opposite lane. Red waited until the motorcycles were fifty yards away, then yanked the truck over the dividing line into the other lane. Clair screamed as one of the bikes shot off the road to their left and spun out on the shoulder into a ditch and the other veered around the truck to their right and was run off of that side of the road by Clair's Volvo behind them, with Bucky sitting on the horn. She kept on screaming for another quarter of a mile down the road.

"Part of my personal road safety program," Red told her when she finally shut up and huddled up against the door, "is to try to improve the reflexes of the idiots that ride those organ-donor bikes."

C. J. didn't say anything else.

About a half hour later Red pulled into a shopping center in Plymouth and parked in front of an Osco discount drugstore. Bucky parked beside him.

"I thought I'd buy you and your friend a few things," he told Clair. "Hairbrush, toothbrush, whatever you need."

"Will you tell me where you're taking us?" Clair whispered.

Red turned in the seat and put his hand on her shoulder. He picked a strand of hair off her face and tucked it behind her ear. "I'm taking you up to a place in the woods where we can talk. I'm not going to hurt you or your friend and I'm not going to make you do anything you don't want to do. Your friend can leave tomorrow. That's why I had Bucky bring your car. And you can go with her if you want to, but you won't. Now I want you to wait here in the truck for a minute while I talk to Bucky, then we're going in that store and I'll buy you whatever you want."

Red got out of the truck, walked around the Volvo, and leaned down to Bucky's window. He smiled at Portia in the back-seat and said, "How're we getting along?"

"Fine," said Bucky. "Where we going, Red?"

"You killed those men on the motorcycles," Portia hissed at him. "I'm going to tell the police exactly how . . ."

"They *wasn't* wearing helmets, Red," Bucky said.

"Hey, LIVE FREE AND DIE—isn't that our state motto? We're going to the camp, Buck, same as before." Then he looked at Portia. "Lady, where you're going you won't be telling anyone a fucking thing. Now listen to me: You be a good girl, you'll be back in South Newbury by tomorrow noon driving this car. But you do one fucking thing I don't like, and you got yourself to blame for what-ever happens to C. J. Now she and I are going in that drugstore there for . . ."

"Looks like she's already going, Red," said Bucky. Red turned around and saw Clair running through parked cars toward the drugstore.

"You get out of that car, I'll break her neck," Red told Portia, then sprinted after Clair.

"Don't hurt her—she's *pregnant*," Portia shrieked at him.

He caught her just before she reached the door, grabbing her by the upper arm and squeezing it.

She looked up at him furiously and tried to pull herself free. "*Fuck* you, mister," she shouted. "You let me and my friend go right *here*, goddamnit, right *now*, or I start screaming and I won't stop for *days*."

Coming out of the store just then were two teenaged boys in baggy shorts and turned-around baseball caps, carrying skateboards. Clair clutched at one boy's T-shirt with her free hand and said, "Hey guys? This man is *kidnapping* me . . ."

Red snapped her against his body and said to her slowly, "Anything you buy here, or anywhere else, your friend in the car is going to pay for. She'll pay Bucky and she'll pay *big*, you understand me? Fuck off, kiddies," he said to the teenagers. "Family fight."

The boys dropped their boards and skated off without even looking at Clair.

She watched them go. Still squeezing her upper arm, Red could feel her wilt and give up then, and he knew he wouldn't have any more trouble with her.

He led her through the store by the hand and bought a bag full of whatever came into his mind for her and an identical one for Portia. As they were headed for the checkout counter Clair suddenly seemed to cheer up and added a yellow chiffon scarf to the items in their cart. Out in the lot, Red gave Portia her bag, and then, since it was cooling off, he went to the back of the truck, pulled Bucky's camouflage hunting overalls out of his duffel, and handed them to Clair. She put them on, and when they got into the truck she tied the yellow scarf around her neck, put on some of the iridescent purple lipstick he had bought for her, and brushed her hair while he watched. Then she tossed her head and smiled at him, and asked him for a beer.

Red stopped again two and a half hours later when Clair needed to pee. They were on Route 145 between Colebrook and Pittsburg in the remote northern tip of the state, with Canada to the west and north of them and nothing but woods in any direction. They had not seen another car in twenty minutes, and Red just pulled off on the side of the road and the two women walked into the woods while he and Bucky pissed by the car.

"Mine's hungry," said Bucky. "I told her I'd cook some venison chili when we got to the camp. Turn's out she has a cooking store and she makes venison chili, too, but she uses poblano chilies and I don't, and I put beer when I have it in mine and she don't . . ."

"Fine," said Red. "You make up some venison chili when we get there and bring me and C. J. some over to the bunkhouse. Otherwise, stay in the cookshack."

"Are we kidnapping, Red?" Bucky asked him. "Mine says we are. I told her I didn't think we were, that we wouldn't do that. Isn't that right?"

"That's right," said Red, not wanting to talk anymore about his plans. "Don't worry about it."

"Nobody's going to get hurt."

"Nope."

"And we're not going to get in trouble."

Keeping Bucky out of trouble had been a major part of his life, as he had promised his aunt Celia it would be before she died. Now that was nearly over, too. "Nope," he said again. "That big one looks like she can get down. She'll probably be all over you like white on rice tonight."

"She's married," Bucky said.

Red laughed and said, "These kind of women don't care anymore about that than the other kind." But Bucky didn't want to talk anymore about it.

Twenty miles north of Pittsburg, where towns and habitation ran out, they turned onto a rutted and decayed dirt road that led to the hunting camp, and one hour and fifteen miles later, they were there, closer to the Canadian border than to the nearest person or phone or paved road. It was twelve-thirty in the morning.

While Bucky got the diesel generator going and carried everything into the cookshack, Red lit a fire in the sweat lodge and heated a pot of water on the propane stove. Clair and Portia stood close to each other in the cookshack. They were quiet, but they no longer looked, Red thought, like sheep in a slaughter pen.

When the water was ready, he left Bucky and Portia to cook and led Clair over to the smaller, windowless bunkhouse. Inside, he turned on a bare overhead bulb, poured the warm water into a plastic mop bucket, lit a kerosene lantern, and then turned off the bulb. He led Clair over to one of the four cots in the room and told her to sit on it.

"What are you going to do?" she asked.

Red brought the mop bucket over and got on his knees in front of her. He carefully took off her sneakers and socks and rolled up the overall pant legs to her knees. He kissed each kneecap, then lifted her feet into the bucket. With a bar of soap he had brought from the other building he began washing her left foot, sliding the soap slowly over the top and around the toes, then bringing it up gently into her arch.

"Talk to you," he said.

Bucky had known from the moment he saw the expressions on the faces of the two women in the Volvo back at the Joyces' barn that some kind of fat was in the fire, but one look at Red had told him there was not a thing in this world he could do about it other than whatever Red told him to do.

At first he had thought his first cousin might have finally just gone crazy, something he frequently seemed on the verge of doing, particularly in the last few months. Just *stealing* two women? Two rich, flatlander, *married* women—just stealing them and their car and heading north without explaining anything to anybody? Bucky had seen Red do some weird things, especially where women were involved, but this took the door prize. He was so accustomed to going along with the unarguable autonomy of Red's will that it took the big woman to point out to him that what Red was doing—and having him do—this time might be more than a little against the law.

"We're talking *kidnapping* and grand theft auto, so *far*, my friend, and we're not ten miles from the house. What are you, a moron? You're committing serious *crimes* here," she had answered when Bucky tried to console her by saying that Red didn't really mean any harm.

"No ma'am," he told her firmly. "Like I say, I don't know what we *are* doing exactly, but we wouldn't be kidnapping nobody. And Red and I don't even like Volvos. You can't get parts." But it worried him.

Smart as Red was, Bucky believed that way too often he thought with his dick, and this appeared to be a perfect example. But if he had just wanted to breed the Joyce woman, why hadn't he done it in the house? And why did he call her some initials like they were friends, and why was he taking the big one with them? Bucky thought about these things for a while after they left the Joyces' barn and then decided, screw it, he'd find out sooner or later what was going on, and whatever it was, he was confident Red would get them out of it.

The big woman didn't say another word to him, even though he talked quite a bit to her, until Red ran the motorcycles off the road, which was another thing Bucky wasn't crazy about.

"Now you can add vehicular homicide, or whatever they call it, to the list, mister," she commented icily when Bucky got the Volvo back in control after nearly hitting one of the bikes head-on. He could still see it and its rider in the rearview mirror, lying bent up together and smashed in the ditch on the shoulder of the road. "You're never going to see *anything outside of prison* for the rest of your life."

"Oh I wouldn't worry about them boys, ma'am," he told her gently, though he was certainly worried himself. "They grow 'em tough up here around Danbury."

At some point after the stop in Plymouth when the Joyce woman tried to run off, and after Bucky learned they were going to the deer camp and calmed down a little because that was a place where no one could find you even if you *were* doing something wrong, the big woman began to talk. Bucky had been rattling away about how he had started cooking for himself at seventeen when his mother died and had gotten pretty good at it and even read a few cookbooks and learned how to bake his own bread, since the bread you bought in the stores was like eating food off the floor, and how his favorite bread now was sourdough . . .

"You make your own starter?" Portia asked, her voice startling him so much, he jumped.

"Why, yes I do," he said, grinning into the rearview mirror at her. They talked about starters and then other kinds of breads and tarts and muffins, then moved into soups and stews.

"I make a wicked good venison chili," Bucky told her.

"Oh yeah? So do I," said the woman, who by now had told him her name was Portia, "with poblanos and fennel. Jesus, this is making me hungry." She barked a short laugh. "Can you believe this shit? I'm being kidnapped and I'm *hungry*."

"I'll make you some venison chili when we get to camp," Bucky said. "I don't have no poblanos and I never heard of fennel, but I've got beans and beer and deer. And I told you before, you're not being kidnapped."

On the long, slow drive up the dirt road to the camp, they talked about mousses, deglazing, making stocks and vegetable purees, and the woman loosened up. She had a deep, raunchy laugh that Bucky liked, and she seemed to say anything that popped into her head, which he liked, too, after he got used to it. "Like baby shit it tastes!" she had said once, on the subject of the green stuff in a lobster. "It looks and tastes *exactly like baby shit,* and people sit around and *oooh* and *aaah* over it."

A little later she asked him, "So what's the story on this Red character?" Bucky asked her what story. "The boy *definitely* doesn't seem to know how to take no for an answer," said Portia. "Are you really cousins, or is that just some woodsy figure of speech around here?"

Bucky told her they were cousins. He told her that both of Red's parents had been killed by a train when Red was eleven, and Bucky's mother, Celia, Red's mother's sister, had taken him in to raise along with Bucky by herself, since her third husband had just taken his eighteen-wheeler and beat feet for California, and she never got a fourth before she died of stomach cancer thirteen years later. By then, Bucky said, Red had moved out, but he was still more like a big brother than a cousin, and he still looked after Bucky and kept him out of trouble.

"What kind of trouble?" asked Portia. "He seems like the one to get in trouble."

"He is, mostly," Bucky said. "I only get in trouble because of him or when I lose my temper, which is practically never, unlike

Red. I can kind of blank out when I do, though, and then usually some shit hits the fan . . . It's like a medical problem."

"Oh," said Portia. A moment later she added quietly, "You poor little thing." And it sounded to Bucky like she was talking about a sick child or a dog run over in the road.

After they finally got to the camp, and Red and the Joyce woman went over to the bunkhouse, Bucky started on a venison chili; after watching him for a while, Portia said, "Screw it. What else have I got to do?" and started helping. She pushed up her shirtsleeves and chopped onions, green peppers, and tomatoes and rolled the chunks of venison tenderloin in flour and drained the cans of beans, working to make a meal right along with him the way he had dreamed of some woman doing since he was seventeen years old, though he had never, in even his horniest dreams, pictured one as stacked or beautiful or tanned or sweet-smelling or round-hipped as this woman was. Or as tall.

"How tall are you, if I might ask?" he said as politely as he knew how while the deer was browning.

"Five eleven and one-quarter," said Portia. "Stocking-foot."

Bucky stirred the meat and felt some strange little twist in his heart at the image of her stocking-footed. "I'm short," he admitted.

"My husband's short. All the biggest studs I have ever known have been just about tit-high to me."

Bucky wanted to turn around and check, but he kept stirring the meat and felt another little twist in his heart. "I'm glad you got friendlier," he said. "You and your friend are safe here for tonight, and Red says you can go home first thing tomorrow, so we might as well try to be friendly."

When the chili was ready he took a couple of bowls of it and one of his fresh baguettes to Red in the bunkhouse. Red was on his knees, doing something to the Joyce woman's feet in a bucket. "Bring me a bottle of whiskey," he told Bucky without turning around. Bucky put the chili and bread down on a table by the door and went and got the whiskey and put it there, too, then closed the door and wondered if things were going to get even weirder that night or just level off and start seeming normal.

After he and Portia ate and cleaned up, Bucky opened his own bottle of rye, poured a drink for himself and one for her, and asked her if she wanted to watch a movie.

"You have a movie theatre around here?" she said, seeming to mean it.

Tapes, he told her. They had a TV and a VCR, he said, pointing them out over in a corner of the shack under an eight-point buck's head, and tapes. What would she like to watch? Portia said she didn't care.

There was an old, ratty green couch in the center of the cookshack in front of the woodstove and she flopped down on it, facing the TV, kicked off her shoes, and propped her head on the arm with her blond hair spilling over it and her drink resting on her stomach. Bucky stood by the sink staring at her for a moment, wondering if marriage was full of moments like this one, and for the first time in his life feeling, if vaguely—like a soft push in the back of his head—everything he was without.

He walked over to the TV, kneeled down and started going through the tapes. He would show her *How To Rattle Up Your Buck* first, he decided, since they were in a deer camp, then a tape that he and Red had made of the two of them ice fishing on Lake Sunapee the winter before last.

"You like *Aladdin?*" he asked her.

"Why not?" Portia sighed, and Bucky added it to his selections.

CHAPTER
SEVEN

When he was eight years old a dalmatian he had been given for Christmas a couple of years before ran away, and Bill had hardly eaten or slept or spoken to anyone for four days until a man in Dorchester found the dog and brought it home. For a month or two after getting the dog back, he hadn't let it out of his sight except to go to school, even sneaking it out of the backyard into bed with him at night and carrying his meals outside to eat in the dog's pen. Having had the dalmatian and lost it, and then miraculously gotten it back, he couldn't stand to think of losing it again, so he had glued his life to the dog's until his father finally noticed what was going on and gave the dalmatian away for good to teach him not to care about loss. But the lesson hadn't worked.

In the months following Clair's return, Bill had known an almost flawless happiness. It was as if he and Clair were living two lives simultaneously: the best of their old one, when they were in their twenties and couldn't get enough of each other's body or mind, and a thrilling new one that seemed to Bill to stretch out before them like a road paved solid gold with the inexpressible preciousness of having each other and living together each day, with the sense that they could accomplish anything they wanted so long as they did it together, and with a new faith in each other, stronger at its welded places, that felt unbreakable to both of them. But gradually over those months, he had learned that that happiness had a price: Every time Clair was late getting home, every time she was supposed to call and didn't, the dalmatian fear would begin to simmer in him, and he would glimpse, stirring it, an ugly little gremlin of dread that had moved in to the very center of his being.

He fed Brando in the kitchen, then he walked into the den and sat down on the sofa. Dray was in the wing chair watching *Junior*.

"They're not back," Bill said. "I think we ought to go look for them."

"I'm watching my man DeVito."

"Listen to me, Dray. There was food left out on the counter and the door was open, two things Clair never does when she leaves. It's eleven o'clock. They would be back by now from anywhere they could've reasonably gone . . ."

"Reasonably? Since when are women reasonable? Maybe they went to Boston because they can spend more money down there. Will you relax? If they're not home by one o'clock, I'll get worried, too. Except I'll be asleep by then."

Bill went back into the kitchen and called Richard Ayers. He apologized for waking the old man up and asked him if he happened to know where Clair and Portia were. He did not. Then Bill called the New Hampshire Highway Patrol office in Lebanon and learned that the only traffic accident in their area of the state that day was a double motorcycle fatality near Danbury. He called the three area restaurants that he and Clair frequented, and they were all closed. And finally, Bill called Red Sizemore's number in Bradford. It was busy. He paced around the kitchen, and ten minutes later the number was still busy. He tried it three more times over the next thirty minutes and it remained, infuriatingly, busy.

He walked back into the den and told Dray he was going to drive to Bradford to ask the man who had slaughtered the sheep if he had any idea where Clair and Portia were.

"Why him?" said Dray. "I thought the girls weren't going to be here when he picked up the sheep."

"He brought the skins back sometime today and left them in the barn. He might've seen them. I just want to talk to him and his line is busy."

"Go for it," said Dray.

Bill stared at him watching the TV. "You're full of shit, you know that? You're as worried about them as I am, you just won't admit it. What kind of bullshit is that? I'll see you later."

"Wait a minute, goddamnnit," Dray shouted after a moment, and followed Bill into the kitchen. "Alright, alright, we'll both go."

As they were leaving, Brando got up off his dog bed and ran to the door, wagging his tail and grinning, and Bill decided to take the dog with them. He locked the kitchen door and left a note closed in the screen telling Clair where they were in case she and Portia got back while they were gone.

Bill drove the Jeep. The big hunter's moon was high over Bald Sunapee mountain and it gave Lake Todd, when they drove past it, a hard, sinister shine. At the stoplight in Bradford Bill turned left onto Main Street and passed the IGA where he had seen Red Sizemore a couple of months earlier. "This guy is kind of a hard case," he told Dray. "He may not like getting waked up if he's asleep."

"I don't blame him one damn bit," Dray said, and yawned.

Near the end of the street Bill pulled up in front of a weedy corner lot that was crammed full of rusted automobile bodies, motorcycles, engine blocks, snowplows, the front half of a school bus, a dump truck, a backhoe, and a bulldozer. Big boulders also lay around the lot, evidently unearthed in the excavation of a finished, concrete block basement that occupied the center of the lot and was all there was of a house. Standing to one side of the basement was a teepee. Bill had heard that there once had been a house on the lot and that it had been destroyed, right after Red got married the last time, in a fire that many locals believed was caused by "debtor's lightning," but no one had been able to prove that, and Red had collected on the insurance. He had heard that Red and his wife lived in the basement in the winter and the teepee the rest of the year, and that the wife was an Indian, and a lot of other things about this man that he had no desire to hear.

He turned off the engine and the headlights and stared into the lot, realizing for the first time that he had always been a little afraid of Red Sizemore.

"Nice spot," said Dray. "How would you like to come into the office of your real estate company one morning and the boss says, 'Bill, I got this corner property over in Bradford I want you to handle. It's not for everybody, maybe . . .'"

"Wait here," Bill said, and got out of the car. "I'll just find out if he knows anything."

After picking his way over the lot to the teepee, he stopped ten feet away from the flap that served as a front door and said, "Hello . . . excuse me."

He was answered by furious, high-pitched barking, and in a moment the flap was thrown back, and a fat Indian woman stepped out into the moonlight and glared at Bill with cold black eyes behind thick glasses. She was dressed in a huge white cotton nightgown and her long black hair was braided into pigtails. She was holding a needle-toothed, bat-eared, yapping little dog with eyes as fierce and black as her own.

"Is Red Sizemore here?" Bill asked, smiling politely at the woman.

"Red *Sizemore*," she said elaborately, "is *not* here. Red *Sizemore* is up at his friggin' deer camp in the north woods with his trusty little cousin, Tonto." She narrowed her eyes and looked Bill up and down. "Well aren't you a pretty thing?" she said, and then to the dog, "Shut up, Chief Joseph—you wake that baby up, you're stew meat."

"I'm sorry to bother you so late at home," Bill said, "I tried calling but the line was busy . . ."

"I take it off the hook at night," said the woman. She smiled suddenly, and Bill saw for the first time that she was young. "So my fans won't bother me."

"Right," said Bill, smiling back at her. "Good idea. Look, my name is Bill Joyce. I live up on Old Ledge Hill. Red slaughtered some lambs for me this morning, and then he brought the skins back and put them in my barn. I've been gone all day, and when I got home my wife and her friend weren't there and they still aren't. I'm starting to get a little worried and I thought maybe Red might have seen them. You know, that he might . . . have some idea . . ." While Bill was talking the woman's face had become tight, and she was staring at him now with an unmistakable, chilling hatred. ". . . where they went," he finished.

"I am Abenaki," she said. "I am descendent of Massasoit the Wampanoag sachem, and of Squanto the corn grower. We taught you people to grow corn and you cut off our hands. I am descendent of Pontiac the Ottawa, murdered by you in Saint Louis, and Tecumseh, driven into Canada by you, whose brother Tenskwatawa, the Prophet, has given me the gift of vision, and of the great Sauks, Black Hawk and Keokuk . . ."

"Look, Mrs. Sizemore . . . ," Bill said.

"I also attended Vassar College on a full fucking scholarship, dickhead. I want you to know *exactly* who told you this: *Keep your goddamned whore wife away from my husband.*"

Bill stared at the woman and felt the gremlin stir.

"What," he asked her after a moment, "are you talking about?"

"I tried to warn her myself, but her cunt friend nearly got her throat cut getting in my face, so I will tell you what I tried to tell her: Red is finished with her, and if she brings her skinny twat around him again or gets him to call her in Boston again, I'll fill it up with lye and sew it shut with barbed wire."

Bill was too stunned to have any idea what to say to this, other than what he prayed was the truth: "You've made a mistake, lady. My wife doesn't even know your husband."

The woman studied him for a moment, her expression cooling from rage to contempt. "Is there anything on *earth* as pathetic as a white man," she said. "Is your number in Boston five-five-five five-eight-seven-two?"

Bill couldn't answer her. Suddenly, horribly, he knew who had made the series of what Clair had claimed were crank calls that had plagued them all summer, and also who owned the voice that had whispered Bill's worst nightmare to him over the phone in August.

"*Eight times* she made him call her this summer. She fucked him first when he went up to shear your sheep. The calls started right after that, plus I saw it in a vision. Maybe they fucked once or twice after that."

"All right, that's enough," said Bill. "You can just keep your dirty mouth *shut* from now on about my wife. Where is this deer camp? I want to know exactly where it is." Behind him he heard a car door slam and then Dray walking through the lot.

The woman regarded him, her small black eyes thoughtful and contemptuous behind her glasses. "You want a face-off with Red about your wife?" she asked quietly, staring at him. Dray walked up then and stopped beside Bill. "You and your little buddy here gonna go draw down on *Red*? Mister, Red is chicken hawk and chain lightning. He's natural disaster. If he wanted your wife, he'd take her like a hawk takes a field mouse, and you wouldn't have a damn bit of say in it. But it's *her* who wants *him*. You keep her away from him is all you need to do."

"Who the hell is she talking about?" asked Dray. "Clair?"

"I want you to tell me where his camp is," Bill said to the woman. "I'm not leaving here until you tell me where it is."

The woman stared at him, her expression softening a little. "He doesn't have your wife, hon. When he's hunting is the one time Red never thinks about pussy. And he's not interested in her anymore anyway. We're going to Canada next month like my totem Tecumseh to trap and hunt and raise our son Black Feather in the woods."

"I want to know where the camp is," said Bill again.

"Okay, fine," she said after a moment. "Your ears need cleaning too, buster, and I don't give a shit who sticks the awls in them." She swept the teepee flap open and disappeared inside.

"What in the *fuck* is she talking about?" asked Dray. "Is she talking about Clair?"

"I'll tell you about it in the car," Bill said, and then was silent.

In a moment the woman stepped back out of the teepee holding a rolled-up topographical map in one hand and a bottle of vodka in the other. She handed Bill the map. "North of Pittsburg," she said. "It's marked on there. You boys want a drink of firewater for the road?"

"No, thank you," said Bill. "I appreciate the map."

The woman tipped up the vodka bottle and took a couple of swallows from it. "You won't when it gets you there," she said. "Joy gave it to you, tell him. My name is Joy. My real name is Swift Otter."

Bill drove slowly back toward South Newbury on 103 and told Dray everything the Indian woman had said and about the phone calls that summer. Dray was silent for a minute or two, then he said, "Do you think it's true?"

"I don't know. Not the way she's got it, but there may be some truth in it. Clair was in a lot of pain. I think he has her, Dray. Has them both. I swear to God I do."

"Why?" said Dray after a pause. "Why would he?"

"I don't know why. And maybe he doesn't. But I'm going to find out."

"Okay, listen. Two things," said Dray. "First of all we've both been up for nearly twenty-four hours straight and Pittsburg is a helluva haul. We could go in the morning. And second, if you think he has them, why don't we call the police?"

They had reached the turnoff to Old Ledge Hill. Bill pulled over on the shoulder of the road and said, "I'm going now. And I don't want to call the police, because I could be wrong. Are you coming or not?"

There was another reason he didn't want to involve the police, but Bill couldn't bring himself to think about, let alone mention to Dray, the possibility that Clair might be with Red Sizemore because she wanted to be.

"Okay," said Dray. "Let's do it."

PART TWO

CHAPTER EIGHT

She had learned by the time he ran the motorcycles off the road that neither panic nor reason nor screaming would save her; and when she tried to run away in the shopping-center parking lot and he caught her, and mashed flat her anger with the hopeless strength of his hand and the threat against Portia, Clair gave up.

She walked with him through the drugstore, letting him lead her by the hand and seeing nothing she could do to help herself, and then they walked past a rack of cheap, bright chiffon scarves. She looked at the rack and saw the scarves, and it was like stage lights going on in her head. He bought one of the scarves for her, and she tied it around her neck in the truck, after putting on a pair of overalls he gave her. She smeared on some outrageous lipstick, brushed her hair, and suddenly she was in costume: with the help of God, she could *act*, was what she could do.

A couple of hours later he pulled over on the side of the road, and she and Portia walked into the woods and were alone for the first time since the nightmare began. Portia wanted to run right then, but Clair knew he was waiting for that and would catch them before they got twenty yards into the woods. She had seen his quick, murderous temper with the motorcycles and knew that they had to avoid invoking that temper.

"He says he'll let us both go tomorrow if I don't want to stay. I think we have to just go along, Porsh. Just go along and not upset him and pray to God he means it."

Portia unzipped her jeans and squatted in the undergrowth next to Clair, shaking her blond head. "Girlfriend, girlfriend," she sighed. "Jesus Christ, are you as scared as I am? What is the *story* with this guy?"

"I'm so, so sorry I got you into this, Porsh. I could slit my throat, I'm so sorry."

"Well we're here, and I guess you're right—about all we can do is go along to get along. The one I'm with is actually kind of pitiful and harmless. Yours is scarier'n *shit*. Baby, how in the *world* could you have . . ."

"Oh God, not now," said Clair, standing up. "I'll tell you about it when we get home tomorrow. I love you, Porsh."

Portia stood and took Clair into her arms and hugged her and stroked her hair. "I love you, too, sweetheart. You and Junior keep your chins up. And don't worry about me—all my guy wants to do is talk about cooking."

After another eternity of driving through lightless, houseless, peopleless woods, they came to two little shacks at the end of a rutted, twisting dirt road, and Clair knew the moment she stepped out of the truck into a remoteness as palpable and hostile as cold that she and Portia were unfindable here—beyond help from anyone.

Act, she told herself.

After the men turned on a generator and then lights and moved some things from the truck into the larger shack, Red took her to the smaller one and told her to sit on one of the cots in the lantern-lit room. Then he took off her shoes and socks, rolled up her pant legs, and began to wash her feet in a bucket, and the strangeness of that jacked up her fear again. She sat on the cot and told herself: Act loose and nice and interested in him; be kind and calm and pray he will do what he says he will do in the morning. She told herself just to get through the night, just get to the day, and pray that he wouldn't hurt anyone.

Washing her left foot, he brought the soap up under her arch and pulled down gently against her toes with his thumb. It felt exquisitely good, and the pleasure reared brusque and wild into Clair's consciousness and mixed there so strangely with her fear and desperation that she moaned, asking herself how in the name of God she had gotten herself into this situation.

"Does that feel good?" he asked her.

"Yes," she heard her stage voice say. "You are very good at it." And right there, she realized, was part of the answer to her question.

Men and acting.

Men and acting had been twined together in her mind for as long as Clair could remember. Or longer. She knew she had to have started performing for her father before she could remember it, because her earliest memories were of already-practiced performances in front of the armchair in his den—of dancing and tumbling for him, flirting with everything she had for whatever attention she could pry out of that quiet, handsome, ironic scholar who was forty-six years old when Clair was born. And she had kept it up—dancing for him in her first recital, heartbroken if he missed even one school play.

Somewhere in her preteens her father became other men, never boys, and she was as dramatic and flirtatious and needy with them as she continued to be with him: Mr. Hopper, who directed her in two seventh-grade plays, and Mr. Maglio. And at boarding school there was Mr. Curtiss, the head of the drama department, who taught her to act, starred her in every school play from her sophomore year onward, and slept with her five times in the winter and spring of her senior year, introducing Clair to what seemed at the time nothing much more than a natural extension of acting.

Then, while she was at Brown, a friend from the Yale Drama School sent an agent over to Providence to watch Clair in *Little Women*. The agent was scouting for a small part in a Woody Allen movie, and Clair got the part. She played it wonderfully, and for two months in the summer before her senior year, Woody Allen was her father.

After she graduated she moved to her parents' summer house on Martha's Vineyard and, temporarily without a man in her life, began writing plays. She did some television and was up for a series the following summer when she met Bill, who had come along to the Vineyard on Dray and Portia's honeymoon. Bill stayed with Clair for two weeks after Dray and Portia left and then asked her to travel around Europe with him for a while. She called her agent, Wolfie Stang, and told him she was going, and Wolfie said, "This is as weird a way to fuck up as putting horseradish on peanut butter. I'll be here when you get back, doll, but will the jobs?"

They weren't, and neither was Wolfie.

For a few years, just before and just after Bill sold his travel company and went to work for Survival!, Clair had believed that she might go crazy from loss: from the death of their baby boy who drowned in vomit in his crib before he was six months old; from wondering what she might have accomplished had she gone to New York that summer instead of riding around Europe on a motorcycle; and from the metamorphosis of the gentle, attentive man she had married into a boorish, work-addicted caricature of his father and brothers.

To flee the loss she acted, snatching up every victimized, man-obsessed role she could find, from Blanche in *A Streetcar Named Desire* to Ophelia, in any theatre in New England that would have her. And she looked for a break, another Woody Allen part out of nowhere, that would give her a life. Then she thought to call Harry.

She had acted with Harry at Brown, and he had been her first real love. His father was a car dealer in New Haven. He drove a French blue Starfire. He was well dressed, on the swim team, tall and good-looking with a swimmer's lean, big-backed body. She met him when he played Tom to her Laura in *The Glass Menagerie*, and they were in six plays together after that before they graduated.

They went to hear Barbra Streisand in concert in his Starfire and down to New York to dance at Roseland, and when his father died at the end of their senior year Clair felt sorry for him and suggested they get married and move to the West Coast and find jobs working in a theatre. But Harry was a practical person with a new degree in urban planning, and he told Clair long-distance from New Haven that he saw no future in acting for either of them and that they could talk about marriage after he had his graduate degree and a job. Clair said, "Good luck, Harry. I'll probably love you for the rest of my life, but don't ever call me again."

And he hadn't. She had called him, getting his number from his mother in New Haven, who told her Harry was quite successful in real estate in Los Angeles, and single. He laughed when he heard her voice and sounded nice. He told her that she had been a big influence on him, that he had dropped out of graduate school, had a hippie phase, played music, and worn his hair long. He had been married once, he said, for a year.

Clair told him she was happily married to a wonderful man. She had kept up with her acting but got a little stale from time to time doing repertory, and if he ever heard of a nice little movie part or something quick in a play, she might think about coming out to read for it. Two weeks later Harry called back and said that he had found a sure-thing part for her, small but plum, in *Pet Sematary II*. The director, he said, was a friend of his.

Clair flew out while Bill was somewhere in the Midwest, without telling him she was going. Harry picked her up at LAX in a black Corvette. When the passenger door swung open, Clair leaned over to put her bag in the little backseat and saw him through a reeking fog of hair spray and cologne and wanted to sit down right there on the curb and cry. But she didn't; she got in the car and smiled when he kissed her on the cheek.

He drove fast down the Santa Monica Freeway toward town. It was starting to thunder, and he told her that the Corvette had never been in the rain. His voice was the same, but that was all. His hair had been brown. Now it was a sprayed-stiff, dyed-black *helmet*. And he had a whole other person inside his skin with him, having more or less doubled the weight of his swimmer's body. He had on white, ironed shorts, white anklet socks, black shades, and gold chains.

His wife had turned out to be a drug dealer, he told her, but he was over that now. He talked about suing a tenant who "did him" out of $350. Then he told her that he had really been very much on his own journey since knowing her, and that she had set him on it. Art, he said, was the only important thing. After his hippie phase he had learned to play the guitar and then played it in a blues band all over the world. Even in Morocco. And Clair thought: *That's* where he gets his style—black blues guys have hair like that.

"This car has never been in the rain," he told her again, miserably, when it started to rain. "It's maybe going to be alright. I can fix it in the morning."

He took her to her hotel and waited in her room while she showered and changed. Clair stood under the hot water beating down on her and thought: This guy has been ruined by me—the sharp-car-driving, backstroking stud has been wimped out and ruined over an idea he got from me. No fucking wonder I'm in a mess.

He took her to an Iranian restaurant, and it was pouring buckets by then on his black Corvette. She bought a bottle of wine and planned to drink it all. He told her he made forty-five thousand dollars a year on his real estate, so he would be a perfect stay-at-home husband for someone. Then he let her pick up the check, and said he wanted to take her to some blues clubs. She said she was too tired and asked then for the first time about the movie role.

"I guess they cast it already," he said, building a little pile of breadcrumbs with his knife. "Sheila called me this morning after it was too late to reach you. But I have these friends who are doing *Oklahoma! . . .*"

In the parking garage of her hotel he asked her if he could come up, and Clair kissed him quickly and said she would rather he not, that she really was very tired. She would call him the next morning.

"No you won't," he said sadly. "You've gone beyond me now, I guess." He took off his shades for the first time all night and looked at her, and she saw that his eyes were red and ruined, and she was swamped then by a great wave of pity for him and for herself and believed she had never felt as lonely before in her life. "You pretty much screwed up my life, really," he told her.

Clair longed for one pretty thing to happen, one thing not dreary and sad that would take them back for a moment to when they were both young and undefeated artists in his Starfire.

"It's okay, but I want one favor from you," he said in a surly voice that she remembered. "I think you owe it to me. The way you used to do it in the car."

She saw her ingenue self—the beautiful young Clair, as in love with him as he wanted her to be, in love enough to save him, unzipping his shorts, dropping her head regally into his lap . . . Then she stepped out of the Corvette, slammed the door, and ran into the hotel.

She checked out that night and waited at the airport for the first plane that would get her back to Boston. And she returned there feeling more victimized than ever and in a pillaging frame of mind. From a book about tigers that she bought in the airport and read on the plane, she learned that in the nineteenth century along the Malabar Coast of India, Hindu women had enticed cobras to enter their vaginas as a way of worshipping Shiva, the God of Maleness. Between Bloody Marys, she shivered and wanted to snatch up one of those cobras and wring its neck, but she knew what the Hindu women were getting at.

And over her third Bloody Mary she determined to just take the next thing she really wanted—exactly as a man would take it—to make up for some of what she had given away as a woman.

A few months later, after trying out every self-help program she could find, she began seeing a Reality Therapist and came to believe through her work with that woman that it was not the situations that life presented her with that mattered so much as how she behaved in them. That slant on administering her life felt like acting to Clair, and it became so central to her functioning that she began eighteen months of study and supervised practicums and was certified as a therapist herself. Then with a new career that

felt a little like her lost one and a well-learned approach to dealing with pain, she believed that the worst was behind her and that
she was ready for anything up ahead. She still loved Bill; she would
do as his mother had done: pretend that her needs were being met
and wait until they were again.

That worked for almost a year until the night in September
when she called Bill in Atlanta to tell him his grandmother had
died and got a baby-voiced woman who said she would tell Bill to
call home as soon as he got back to the room, or, if she was asleep,
she would tell him in the morning. Then Clair learned that she
hadn't even known what pain was.

That following spring, desperate and miserable with living
by herself, wanting and needing Bill and wanting and needing to
believe the things he had said in the letter he wrote her but not
seeing how she could ever have him back, she had gone up to the
farm for a weekend and taken there some giant, grizzled, red-haired
sheepshearer—her payoff to herself from the night with Harry in
LA. She had taken him seeing Bill's face instead of his hard, dangerous one when she wrapped her legs around him and fucked him
as she had Bill their first time in the sea at Martha's Vineyard, and
Bill's face when the man was on top of her, pounding into her.
And it was not only Bill she had fucked along with the sheepshearer, but her not having Bill and maybe never having him again,
her gone child and acting career, her going beauty, the death of
her father-in-law. Clair gang-fucked all those miseries in her life,
along with Bill and the sheepshearer, and then threw herself
against them in her orgasms like the surf on rocks.

The next day, with a clearer head and less pain, and determined
now to find a way back to her husband, she returned to Boston, stepping out of the day before and putting it out of her mind as if it were
a one-minute cameo, and putting the man out of her mind, too, until
three or four weeks later when he began to call her.

She was happy again—maybe happier than she had ever been, with Bill back not only to her but to himself, with her practice and getting pregnant, a second honeymoon to Europe coming up, even acting again with the Charles Playhouse. The calls were the only blemish on that otherwise perfect and deserved happiness, terrifying her not only with the man's lingering presence in her life but with the possibility that Bill might find out about him.

Then the calls stopped and that was that, she told herself. She was terrified for a few days about the possibility of seeing the man that weekend at the farm when he came to get the sheep, but when that didn't happen, Clair had settled into her lawn chair by the pool with her book and a completely free and happy mind.

Then the next thing she knew he was in the house, and his hands were on her head, squeezing out her strong, unsubmissive self and pinning her to the spot like her own fate. And a few desperate hours later all Clair knew to do to influence that fate was to make the man her father and act to him.

"Why are you washing my feet?" she asked him, trying to keep her voice unfrightened.

"My ex-wife is Abenaki. They believe you should clean the feet and purify the body with sweating before you move to a new place." He was stroking the arch of her right foot now with the soap and Clair closed her eyes, not knowing what to do with how good it felt. "You're pregnant," he said.

She opened her eyes, jolted again with fear. "How did you . . ."

"Your friend. Is it mine?"

"No," she said quickly. "It's not." Act, she told herself. "Do you have any children? We lost a baby nearly twelve years ago, so obviously this means a tremendous amount to us . . ."

"Kids aren't in the program where we're going. And I don't want to see you big. I'll take care of it. Now listen to me, C. J., because I'm going to tell you how it's going to be . . ."

He started talking in the harsh, one-toned, growling whisper he spoke in sometimes. He talked as he dried her feet on an old towel and then washed his own big, pale feet and dried them, leaving her and himself barefooted, telling her first how the rest of the night would go. They would eat the chili and the bread now, he said, and he wanted her to eat it all because she would need the energy for the morning. Then they would purify themselves in the sweat lodge and he would tell her in there about the life he was taking her to. He would do her hair as he wanted it, then they would sleep for a few hours here on the floor on bearskins he had tanned, and a little after dawn he would take her with him into the woods so that she could watch him stalk and kill a deer with a bow and an arrow he had made.

He quit talking then and brought a bowl of chili and half the bread to Clair where she sat on the cot, then poured a water glass half full of whiskey and gave it to her. He poured another glass almost full for himself and sat with it and his chili and bread across from her on another cot and began to eat.

Clair knew that she needed to find the right lines here, but she had no idea what they could be or where to look for them. The effort of trying to figure out who and how she should be, and to find some dramatic logic to a situation that seemed to be getting more and more bizarre, had exhausted her and given her a headache. It occurred to her that maybe the man was a psychopath and there was no logic to be found, but that thought was too frightening to hold and so she dropped it. She took a small swallow of the raw whiskey and then another, wanting enough to calm herself and lose the headache but no more.

"Eat," he told her.

Clair broke off a piece of the bread and ate it along with a spoonful of chili. "You told me I could leave tomorrow with my friend if I wanted to."

"We will be back here by nine or ten o'clock with a deer. That's when you can make up your mind."

"You told me I wouldn't have to do anything I didn't want to do." Clair heard herself starting to whine and that made her angry.

"You won't," he said.

"Well, I don't want to go into the woods with you in the morning," she said, her head pounding, her voice rising and going shrill in spite of herself. "I don't want to go to a sweat lodge or sleep on bearskins with you."

He looked up at her, his face and neck darkening suddenly in the lantern light, and whispered, "Eat. And shut the fuck up."

The sweat lodge was a small dome-shaped hut out back of the bunkhouse made of animal skins stretched over saplings. The man led Clair to it barefooted and had her remove the rest of her clothes outside while he took his off, too. Then he held the flap open, and Clair bent and stepped inside and he followed her. There was a fire pit in the center of the hut, in which a fire of logs had gone to coals. He put stones on the coals and then told Clair to sit on the dirt floor.

He sat across the pit from her, his legs crossed, the light from the coals flickering across his torso, his face in shadows. Out of those shadows for the next hour he told Clair exactly how and where they were going to live. He leaned over once in awhile to pour water on the stones from a can, and his face when it came into the light was more vulnerable than she had seen it before. The pressing heat and the whiskey she had drunk made her sleepy, and his voice made her think of the sound of the incoming tide among the rocks at Gay Head. She held that image in her mind, sitting cross-legged as he was, with her body as open to him across the fire pit as his was to hers, and she listened to him.

It was a harsh, remote, independent life he described, a life for two tough people reliant only on each other and a few hand-made things: cabin, canoe—things made with skill, as he put it—and time. It was a life of loon calls and cold nights by a fire, chopping wood and trapping and growing vegetables and salting fish on the shore of a lake in Canada with the nearest neighbor fourteen miles away. It was a life severed of all connections—a complete, initiated life, and perfect, Clair thought, in its needing nothing outside itself—and she had no doubts as she listened to him describe it that this man could make such a life for himself and her, and then sustain and defend it.

It was also an inescapable life, and Clair realized for the first time when he had finished talking that if he did not let her go later that day as he had promised, she would probably never see Bill or her own life again.

Outside the hut he toweled her off and then himself. He wrapped the towel around her and picked her up and carried her back into the shack, saying nothing now, and Clair felt, in her drowsiness, as if she were being carried in the teeth of a storm wind.

He let her dress, and while she did, he brought into the shack from the truck a bow, a fringed quiver of arrows, and a duffel bag.

He laid out on one of the cots a wide, beaded belt with two sheathed knives on it and dressed himself out of the bag in moccasins, a shirt, and trousers, all made of fringed, honey-colored deerskins.

"Did your wife make those clothes? They're beautiful," she said, watching him.

"I made them."

He sat behind her on the cot and worked what he told her was bear fat into her hair, stroking and kneading it into her hair and scalp and massaging her neck, then braiding rawhide thongs into the long glossy black fall of her hair, and his hands were rough but at the same time soothing, and they thrilled something in Clair and put into her mind a picture of herself kneeling by the fire in the cabin in Canada while he did this to her each evening.

He rubbed the fat into his own hair as she watched, and she tied it off for him with thongs as he told her to do. And that too raised an unfamiliar thrill in her and she felt her hands lingering on his coarse red and silver hair.

He built a fire in the woodstove, though it was not cold, and spread in front of it three bearskins, one on top of the other, that were as black and shiny as lake water in the lantern light.

He took her hand and led her to the skins, and Clair lay down on them.

He turned off the lantern and lay next to her, and she could smell the buckskins he was wearing and the bearskins she was lying on and her own skin and his, and she felt strangely but utterly safe.

He raised himself over her and Clair could barely make out his features in the light from the stove but she could see that there was something new in them now—almost a child's longing, she thought.

He unbuttoned the top straps of her overalls, bent and kissed her throat, her chest. Clair felt his breathing on her chest and was painfully, wonderfully sleepy. She thought it must be after three o'clock. Bill, she thought . . . Bill would not even be getting back to the farm, would not even know she was gone, for another fifteen or sixteen hours. And she felt a million miles away from Bill—broken silently away from him, somehow without regret or fear, and floating off like a chunk of silver ice into a blue, northern lake.

He slid his hand into Bill's shirt and rested it quietly, hot, on her breast. Clair closed her eyes and was conscious of herself being taken, drawn away irresistibly as if by an undertow, and of giving herself up to it. She moved her hands up to his back and rested them there, and felt them wanting to explore all the wide, humped, tapered strength there.

"We're going to go slow," he said, whispering against her chest. "Just tell me what you want right now."

And she did that.

Around five-thirty in the morning, when *Aladdin* was over, Bucky got up to make some cookies for Portia and realized he was drunker than he felt in his mind. He and Portia had put away almost half of the half-gallon bottle of rye in the past four hours while watching five hunt/fish tapes and then *Aladdin*. Bucky had not gotten out of his chair during that time except to change the tapes, and now that he was up trying to make cookies, he realized his body was good and drunk and that his mind must be, too, even though it didn't feel it. He supposed his mind didn't feel it because it had been too busy over the past four hours trying to hold up his share of the conversation and trying to make Portia like him.

Bucky wanted her to like him because he had decided he liked her more than any woman he had ever met other than his mother. He liked her sense of humor and her laugh. He liked the way she said whatever popped into her head, and the way she hadn't seemed to be afraid of Red, and a lot of other things—including her pretty, been-there, done-that, but-still-ready-for-anything face and her body, both of which he liked a lot.

At one point, while she was watching him ice-fish on the tape and asking questions about it, seeming interested, Bucky even thought maybe he was in love with her. And for the rest of that tape, which he had watched maybe thirty times already, he tried to picture what her life was like when she was back home in Boston. After awhile he saw a mansion in his mind out of a James Bond movie he had watched recently on TV and Portia lying in a lounge chair out on a blue-tile patio beside a pool overlooking the sea. She had on a bikini, and her huge knockers were just barely contained by the top, and she was reading a magazine with a pair of Ray-Bans dropped down low on her nose. A glass door in the mansion behind her opened and a butler walked out to the patio carrying a silver tray with two tall, frosty bottles of Rolling Rock on it. And Bucky looked for himself in the picture, thinking he had to be there if it was Rolling Rock on the tray, but he could not find himself.

Though lust was an old friend of Bucky's, he knew very little about love. But he believed he knew you had to know somebody longer than a few hours before you loved them, and he supposed by the time the ice-fishing tape ended that that was why he couldn't find himself in Portia's life back home and that it probably wasn't really love he had been feeling for her while she was watching him drill holes in the ice. But it was something he had never felt before, and he was proud of it, whatever it was.

"What's that thing called again?" she asked from the couch. He had just run the cookies in the oven: chocolate chip. He poured himself another drink, then walked unsteadily over to the couch and poured two fingers of the rye into the glass resting on Portia's stomach.

"What thing?"

"The little gizmo the turkey guy was using to call. The one made out of a prophylactic?"

"Snuff can," said Bucky.

"I want to tell Dray. He'll love the idea of using a rubber to sweet-talk a male turkey—what an absolute *hoot*. At least I think it is," she added after a second. "Did you pour me some *more* of this shit? You little devil!"

It was the second time she had mentioned her husband since the car, and Bucky didn't like it. When the cookies were ready, he put them on a paper plate and sat down at the table and started eating them. "Cookies are ready," he said after he had eaten two.

"Aren't you going to bring me a couple?" she asked. He looked over at the couch and saw her long, tanned arm stretched out languidly along the back of the couch, the long, thin fingers with the long, bright red nails holding her drink.

"I'm not that fucking butler of yours," he said. "Get up and get 'em yourself."

In a moment she stood up and walked over to the table. She took a handful of cookies off the plate and sat down opposite him, looking sleepy. "Portia didn't mean to press your button, Little Buddy, and I don't have a butler," she said, and yawned. "Well we've *finally* almost got us a new day here. What time do you think your King Kong cousin is going to let me and my friend drive out of this paradise on earth?"

A number of things about what she had just said irritated Bucky all at the same time, as well as her tone of voice, but the thing that bothered him the most was her calling Red King Kong. King Kong, he knew, was a monkey.

"His name is Red, and he does what he wants to do when he wants to do it," he said stiffly. "And once he's made up his mind to do something the Devil himself can't stop him. That's what my mom used to say. She said that's what made Red different from other people. So you wish you were home right now, or what?"

Portia looked at him and smiled, and Bucky could see for the first time that she was drunk. "What the hell do you *think?*" she said. "You're not such a bad little guy and this has been real, movies out here in the woods and all, but I want to be there when my husband gets home." She chased her second cookie with a swallow of rye, then she put the glass down on the table, twisting it with her long tapered fingers, looking at it dreamily and smiling again. "I've been in love with that ole loud thing since I was eighteen years old and he still winds Portia Hurley's clock. We're everything to each other, Buddy, I mean Bucky—kids, dog, parakeet, the shootin' match." She threw out her arms dramatically and knocked the plate of cookies onto the floor.

Bucky stared at the cookies; then he slowly poured himself another drink and saw his anger for the first time. It was always like he just looked up and there was this tiny black cloud way off in a clear sky. It was still small, and he wanted not to talk for a while and try to let it disappear. He said, "I got some more tapes if you want to see 'em. It'll make the time pass before you go home."

"Sure," Portia said, standing up. "Whatever. Whaddya got, *Snow White? The Lion King?*"

"Nope," said Bucky cheerfully. "These are different." He walked over to the television and rooted underneath it among the tapes. "Frienda Red's and me named Pat Hayward brought these up. They're wicked different, if you know what I mean." He found one of the tapes and pushed it into the VCR and couldn't help grinning. Squatting in front of the TV, he looked at himself in its glass face and grinned at the anger growing in him, knowing now it was too big and too close to stop.

"What's it called?" asked Portia. She was back on the couch. Bucky looked at her and saw her in the lounge chair by the pool in her bikini with the butler bringing her and her husband the Rolling Rocks.

"*Cock Tail Party,*" he said, and went and sat down.

The film opened with a guy answering his doorbell. All he's got on is a black bow tie, and he's got a schlong about two feet long. At the door are two other guys with bow ties and big schlongs— and three girls, naked, too, except for red bow ties around their necks. The girls have tits the size of watermelons and are blowing party whistles with their twats when the guy opens his door.

Portia said, "Now waaait a *minute*, Little Buddy. I got no business watching this thing with you." But she made no move to get up, and in fact settled back into the couch and even laughed once when one of the girls used the schlong of one of the guys to stir her drink. And neither did Bucky move to get up, but poured himself another shot of rye.

When *Cock Tail Party* was over he put on *Pussy Thorpe's Canine Christmas in Jamaica.* This one was kinkier, involving a German shepherd in a Santa Claus hat, and after two minutes Portia said loudly, "Okay, that's it. I'm not watching any more of this sicko shit," and threw a pillow at the TV. "Is this the kinda shit gets you off, Little Buddy?"

"Don't call me 'Little Buddy' again. I'm not no dog and I don't eat off the floor," Bucky told her, watching the tape but not see-ing it anymore, just seeing what always looked to him like the inside of his own skull.

"Okeydoke, *fine*. Big ten-four," said Portia, standing up. "It's six forty-five and it's almost light outside, thank *God*. Portia Hurley's gonna go pee, Mr. Whatever-your-name-is. Then I'm gonna check on Clair and get the travel schedule from Godzilla . . ."

She was almost to the door when Bucky caught her by the arm, spun her around, and tore open her shirt.

"Jesus Christ," she said, looking down, and Bucky heard surprise in her voice, along with anger and shock, and was happy to hear it.

Portia turned and ran for the door. He stepped in front of her and picked up a big Phillips-head he had used to adjust the generator. "You ever been screwed with a screwdriver?" he asked her, grinning.

Portia made a little moan in her throat and said, "Get *away* from *me*." Then she hit him in the mouth with her fist and tried to claw her way past him to the door. Bucky dropped the screwdriver and put his hands on her breasts. *"No!"* she shouted, and hit him again.

That time it hurt and Bucky hit her back, cracking her on the cheek and nose as if she were a man, and she stumbled, crying out, and ran for the kitchen. Bucky followed, kicking her until she was down on the floor, covering her face with her arms and moaning, "Oh Jesus, please God . . ." He dragged her by one leg across the room, lifted her around the waist, and heaved her onto the couch. She landed on her back, looking up, crying and spitting at him, and Bucky could see that he had broken her nose.

He took off his shirt. She spat bloodily onto his chest, and then what little light of consciousness was left in Bucky's head went out, eaten by the black cloud. He leaned over the couch and hit Portia again in the face as hard as he could and felt her jawbone break. He grabbed her jeans and panties at either hip and jerked them down, and she was sobbing now, with blood running from her mouth, and trying to kick him. Bucky dropped his pants and shorts, and she came up behind the arm of the couch, her fists swinging wildly at him and screaming, and Bucky leaned down and picked up the half-gallon whiskey bottle by its neck and hit her with it in the head, and she dropped like she had been shot onto the arm of the couch. He lifted her under the shoulders and pushed her back onto the couch, and when the back of her head hit the other arm, her eyes opened and she stared at him, but there was blood coming out of her ears now, and he could see there was no need to hit her again.

He walked around to the front of the couch, swung his right leg over her, and stood on his knees above her hips. He was shoving himself into her when Portia looked up over his left shoulder, and her eyes went suddenly calm and happy and expectant and loving. Bucky thought for a second it was for him, for his entering her, but then something made him turn his head and look over his shoulder, and there at the window, outlined against the lightening sky, was a man's face and a gun coming up to it.

Bucky had a chance to throw his left arm up and duck and scream one word before the full-choke load of steel shot caught him in that arm, tearing it off at the elbow.

What he screamed was *"Red!"*

CHAPTER NINE

Bill opened his eyes and came awake into what felt like a world full of dread. "What happened?" he said.

"You fell asleep. I gotta walk around for a minute, get some air," said Dray, who had taken over the driving around one-thirty and had just pulled over onto the shoulder of the road.

"How long have I been asleep?"

"Coupla hours, I guess. We're just above Groveton. I nearly hit a fucking moose a minute ago—on *his* side of the road."

Dray got out of the Jeep and Bill followed him, looking at his watch. It was a little after four o'clock. They walked around on the empty highway in the warm, still air, swinging their arms and breathing deeply for two or three minutes, then got back in the Jeep and drove on northward. Bill was wide awake now and he could tell that Dray was, too. A little while later they were through Pittsburg, and there was nothing after that but road and black woods, and Bill knew that Dray was waiting on him.

"Okay, the way I see it, there are three possibilities up here. One, they aren't here: We just apologize to the man and go. Two, they are here and don't want to be . . ." Bill paused.

"Yeah?" said Dray.

"We either take them back ourselves or go get help."

"And what's the third possibility—that they're up here in the middle of nowhere at some woodchuck's deer camp, Portia and Clair, with the closest Saks four hundred miles away, and *want* to be?"

Bill knew Dray had said that for his sake. "You know what I mean."

"Yeah, I know and you're fulla shit," Dray said. "Now let me tell you what I think. What Clair did when you two were separated is her business, and besides, all we're going on there is the story of some crazy Indian broad. She damn sure wouldn't be fooling around with another man now, any more than Portia would, so you can put that crap right out of your head. Personally, I'd give you three-to-one odds they're spending the night at Bob and Sue Ray's in Hopkinton or up in Hanover—I mean there are a *hundred* possibilities. But if we get up here and find out they're *here*, my friend, and this little paranoid nightmare of yours is *right*? Then we got guns in the car and we know how to use 'em."

Along with the straight-ahead determination that was always there, Bill could hear relish in Dray's voice. "Maybe you were right," he said after a moment. "Maybe we should call the police now."

Dray looked over at him and grinned. "Nope, Billy Boy, *you* were right for a change. We get the cops and the girls aren't up here, we look like idiots, wimps, and pansies, which *I'm* not anyway. And if they are up here, there's no cop in the state of New Hampshire I want doing that job for me."

About fifteen miles the other side of Pittsburg they found the dirt road running due west toward the Canadian border that, according to a red line on the map, led to Red Sizemore's deer camp. And then they were on that road, wallowing at fifteen miles per hour or less through potholes and cave-ins and a dry streambed, with each narrow, hilly, tortuously slow switchback leading them farther into country as wild and harsh as any left in the eastern United States. Bill wanted to talk about something happy and not real, and as far from where they were and what they were doing as possible, so he said, "So, let's say you sell the company tomorrow. Let's go over again what you're going to do. I need to examine it for flaws."

Dray was lighting a Swisher Sweet and he grunted enthusiastically around the cigar, this being a subject he would always warm to.

"Well, first of all, it won't be tomorrow, or next month or next year even. These lawsuits get any worse, it may be never. I maybe won't be able to *give* the fucking thing away."

"Alright, let's say two years from now."

"Two years from now? Two years from now is a maybe. First thing, we sell Portia's business too. And that's not for chicken feed, my friend, the way she's built that thing up, working her *ass* off to do it."

"I know that," said Bill.

"I'm talking eight, nine hours in the shop, then coming home and her and Becky cooking another three hours for a party, then catering the goddamn thing *herself*, and cleaning *up* . . ." Dray paused, smoking and nodding his head. "*That*, Billy Boy, is a woman. They don't make 'em like her anymore. I swear to God, I . . ." his voice thickened suddenly, and he stopped talking and cleared his throat. "You know I kid around and everything, but she's it for me: the *whole* ball of wax." He was silent for a moment. "Hey, what did the leper say to the prostitute?" He cleared his throat again. "Aw, fuck it. Never mind. You know what's heaven to me really? Me and Portia by the water *anywhere* with, like Sarah Vaughan singing 'How High the Moon.' Or even without Sarah Vaughan . . . Even without the water."

"Okay, so now you're both free," Bill said. "You're rolling in dough . . ."

"Yeah. I call the yacht broker and have the sixty-foot Hatteras delivered. And then we're outta there, pal. Put the house on the market and it's sayofuckinara, Boston. Sayonara sirens and shoveling snow and traffic and bustin' butt six days a week. Our *feet* are up then, my friend—just me and my baby and lots of blue water and sunshine."

"Where?"

"Down the Inland Waterway. Base in Marsh Harbour or Walker's Cay all winter and cruise the islands. Anchor up in the lees at night, dive for crawfish. I'll fax you all about it from the boat."

Dray and Portia had had this itinerant, nautical retirement planned out in elaborate detail since long before they knew how they were going to afford it, and Bill had always loved hearing about it. He knew Dray was just warming up, and he settled back into the seat and listened, seeing Dray on the flying bridge at the wheel of the big white Hatteras, and Portia in the fighting chair on the deck below, reading a magazine, a pair of Ray-Bans on her nose. . . .

After they had driven for about half an hour on the dirt road, they passed a turnoff to a marked snowmobile trail. Dray stopped and studied the topo map under the dome light. "That's gotta be this trail here," he said, pointing to a dotted line on the map. "Which means we're nearly halfway there." He looked at his watch. "We should be there by six-twenty, six twenty-five. I want to come in quiet and wait until there's enough light to see before we do anything."

Dray measured with a pencil the distance remaining to the X on the topo map that they believed marked the camp and figured it at 7.7 miles. Seven and a half miles farther up the road, he turned off the Wagoneer's headlights and crawled along, using just his parking lights, for another tenth of a mile. Then he stopped at the bottom of a little rise and turned off the engine. Bill looked out his window and saw that the trees lining the road were beginning to become distinct.

"We'll wait until we can make out the limbs on that big pine up there, then we'll walk over the hill and see what we can see."

"You know, they probably *are* at the Rays' house or somewhere, and I'm going to feel like an idiot for waking this guy up."

"He'll be up pretty soon anyway if he's deer hunting. We'll get him to feed us breakfast. Tell him we drove up because we heard about the dynamite breakfasts he cooks."

In another two or three minutes they could make out the individual limbs on the pine tree thirty yards up the rise, though the narrow strip of sky above the road still had no color. They got out of the Jeep, closing the doors quietly, and walked up the rise on the balls of their feet. At the top Dray slid into the woods and Bill followed him. Below them a hundred yards or so down the road, standing together in a little clearing, were two shacks, a small, domed wigwam-like structure and an outhouse.

A thin thread of smoke rose from the chimney of the smaller shack. Some sort of light was on in the larger one, and they could hear the hum of a generator. They were facing the rear of the shacks, with the smaller one closer to them. Staying in the woods across the road from the buildings, Dray edged downhill for another sixty feet, then stopped and motioned Bill up beside him. They could see now, around the corner of the larger shack, a Dodge truck parked in front. And standing next to it was Clair's Volvo.

Dray turned around quickly and walked back up the rise in the woods, then jogged down the other side to the Jeep with Bill following him.

Dray rolled down the rear window and took out his shotgun and a box of duckloads. "Party time, Billy Boy," he whispered fiercely, breathing hard and filling his pockets with shells. "You were right, goddamnit. *Goddamnit,* you were right, and I'm sitting there at the farm with my feet up watching a fucking *movie* while Portia's up here with . . ."

"Let's take it slow," said Bill. "Let's think about it."

"I'm thinking. Get your gun."

Bill pulled his shotgun out of the case. He slid two shells into it and snapped it shut and put a handful of shells in his pocket. Seeing the gun, Brando stood up in his kennel and started to whine. Dray rolled up the rear window, locked the car, and put the keys on the driver's-side front tire. "Let's go," he said.

In the growing absence of dark, Bill could see that Dray's face was locked into the unquestioning, unanswering resolution that took him through and over anything, and he realized at that exact instant how much he had always depended on Dray to be his opener—going in with his head down, clearing the way—as well as his closer, the guy who put the deal in the bag when all the talking and tap dancing were over. He had been about to suggest again that they think about it, come up with a plan, but instead he just threw his arm around Dray's neck and hugged him hard.

On the top of the rise they squatted in the woods and Dray whispered, "We'll go down in the trees, then crawl across the road to the shacks. You look in the small one and I'll check out the one with the lights. It's six-forty. We'll meet at that little wigwam thing in, say, ten minutes, and see what we got and decide what to do with it."

Bill followed Dray through the woods down the hill. When they were directly across from the smaller shack, he got onto his belly and crawled across the dirt road to the rear of the building and then slowly stood up along its back, tar-paper wall. Looking around the corner, he could see Dray beginning to crawl quickly across the road on his elbows and knees, holding the shotgun out in front of him. Bill looked at his watch. It was six forty-five. Crouching, he crept up to a back door and listened, but could hear nothing inside, so he kept walking in a crouch around the windowless shack. Attached to the end of the building opposite the road was a shed roof, and sitting underneath were two big Honda four-wheeled, all-terrain vehicles with deer racks over the front tires.

Bill had just started coming around the shed when a woman screamed. Turning the corner, he saw Dray getting to his feet at the rear of the other shack, then running in a crouch toward the front. As he started running himself, across the forty yards or so of dirt separating the two buildings, he heard a man's voice shouting something and then Dray's shotgun—booming and reverberating, the sound seeming to hang for seconds in the quiet of the clearing—and then the man shouting again.

When Bill came around the corner of the building the shouting man was standing on the bare dirt a few yards in front of the shack, huddled around himself and splayfooted, holding the bloody stump of his left arm and shouting, "*Rehhhht . . . Rehhht . . .*" He was naked and small and thin and very pale, and he looked to Bill in the half-light like some skinned animal with a missing leg. The arm was spouting blood, and the man held the stump with his other hand and stared at it as though he were waiting for an answer from it, and shouted, "*Rehhhht . . . ,*" like the bleating of a sheep.

Then Dray stepped out of the door of the shack, his face a terrible mask, and aimed the shotgun carefully and shot the little man in the left foot, blowing the foot and ankle into pink and white pulp with splinters of bone showing in it.

"How does that feel, my friend?" said Dray in a conversational tone of voice. He broke the gun and dropped in two more shells and closed it again.

Bill said, "Where are they, Dray?"

"I don't know where Clair is," Dray said, not looking at Bill but at the small, naked, skinned-looking man, who had fallen to his knees and was crawling away from the shack. "Portia's in there and she's not good, Bill." The mask holding his face together slipped for a second and Bill saw an awful, hopeless pain behind it. Dray said again to the little man, "How does that foot feel, bub? Hurt?" He walked off the deck of the shack and followed the man as he crawled on one arm and his knees, his foot, pulped beyond recognizing as a foot, trailing behind him. "How does it *feel*, you little motherfucker? Tell me about it."

"Where is *Clair*, Dray?" said Bill. But Dray didn't turn, didn't even seem to hear as he followed the man, walking slowly behind him, with the shotgun pointed upward and resting on his shoulder, the way he carried it when they were bird-hunting.

Bill ran into the shack. A television was playing. There was blood on the floor, and Portia lay on an old green sofa, her shirt torn open, her jeans and underpants pulled down around her knees. Her big, sweet, joking eyes were open, staring at Bill.

He turned away from the sight of her, feeling how she would hate the lewdness of it, and threw up before he reached the door.

When he walked back out, Dray was aiming the shotgun again and saying, ". . . but we're going to Memphis at the end of this month and she'll finally get some time off then . . ." The shotgun boomed again, the moist reverberation hanging and hanging on the air, and the man's other foot and ankle and part of that lower leg were pulp, too.

"*Rehhhht* . . . ," screamed the man, rolling over on his back then and looking from Dray to Bill, his eyes wide and empty.

"Where is *my wife?*" Bill shouted at him.

". . . we'll go to some catfish fries, listen to a little jazz, take it easy with the family. Portia loves her family . . ." Dray's voice was still conversational but Bill watched the mask breaking up as he talked, and then he was crying, the muscles around his mouth and eyes jerking.

Dray walked abruptly up to the little man and stepped on his throat, stopping the shouting. Then he pointed the shotgun at the man's groin and blew away his genitals. He took his foot off the man's throat and cracked the shotgun to load it again. There was a great, ragged, shining hole between the man's legs. He was motionless and Bill thought that he might be dead, but he sat up, pushing himself up with his good arm, and looked at his gone groin. Then he began to cry, too, sobbing almost silently. Turning on his arm to look toward the other shack, he said, "Red." And for the first time, Bill recognized the word he had been shouting over and over: It was *Red*.

Bill began turning, too, to look toward the other shack when he heard a sound like paper being torn and then a *thhupp*, and when he looked back the little man had an arrow buried in his back almost to the feathers and was slumping forward onto his side.

Bill turned again, crouching instinctively and swinging around the muzzle of his shotgun and saw Dray already on his belly, firing toward the other shack. Then he heard one of the ATVs start up and saw it buck out from under the shed behind the other shack, with Red Sizemore, unmistakably, driving it, and Clair—unmistakably Clair, though she was dressed in camouflage overalls—tied to the deer rack on the front.

"Don't shoot!" he shouted to Dray and took off after the ATV, crossing the forty yards of clearing between the two shacks in a sprint, then running blindly into the woods following the receding noise of the machine for another thirty yards, branches whipping his face, until he tripped over a log and fell, his legs tying up beneath him in a deadfall of spruce.

After he had freed himself, he stood and listened but could no longer hear the ATV. Then, in a moment, he did hear it again, faintly over the rise in the direction of Dray's car, going away and finally losing itself in the stirring noises of the morning.

Bill stood listening to the chatter of a jay and the rustle of branches and felt a wave of cold, hopeless terror rise up and rush over him like nausea; it swamped him for a moment and then it was gone, leaving him weak-kneed and sweating but clear in his head, and feeling gutted and empty, stripped of everything he had ever had that mattered.

He ran back to the smaller shack and entered it through the rear door, hungry for some sign of Clair. Inside there was nothing to see but some black skins spread on the floor in front of a woodstove and a half-empty bottle of whiskey. He found he could neither look long at nor contemplate the bottle and the skins, so he closed the door on the room where his wife had just been and went back to find Dray.

Dray was inside the other shack, sitting on the green sofa. He had re-dressed Portia and was holding her across his lap, with her face tucked into his neck, and was rubbing her back and talking to her in a slow, nonstop whisper. Her left arm hung down between his knees; after a moment he lifted it and curled it into his chest. The television was still playing.

Bill stood in the door, wanting to sit down on the floor and cry for a month but knowing that he had to think and act and that he would not be able to do either if he took even one small step into the paralyzing loss and sorrow and guilt of Portia's death.

He looked quickly through the shack for a radio, then walked back outside past the body of the little, nude man—whose head, he noticed with no feeling, Dray had beaten into an unrecognizable pulp with his shotgun. The gun now lay with its stock and action broken off beside the man's body.

Bill checked the Dodge truck for a cellular phone and did not find one. His mind hollow and thoughtless now of everything but what he would have to do, he found the generator and turned it off, then jogged over the rise to Dray's vehicle. He let Brando out of his kennel and drove back to the shack with the dog running happily behind the car until he came to within a few yards of the dead man. There he froze, the guard hairs rising on his neck, and lay down whining.

Bill parked the Jeep in front of the shack, opened the tailgate, and spread the topo map across it. It was seven-twenty. Clair and Red had been gone for maybe twenty-five minutes and everything in him now was clamoring to follow them. But he made himself study the map carefully and slowly, trying to read in it where Red might go and what he might do, and trying to keep himself dispassionate and clear-thinking.

The trail Red had taken into the woods wasn't shown, which meant there could be an entire network of four-wheeler and snowmobile trails in the area. Due east of the camp was Highway 3, the only real road in that part of the state. Bill doubted Red would go in that direction, or south, toward towns and civilization. To the north and west lay the Quebec border, which looked to be only about ten miles away to the west. With the exception of a small lake called Goose Pond, which was about halfway to the border, the map showed nothing but woods between the camp and Canada.

He remembered Red's wife saying something about going to Canada, and the more he thought about it, the more it seemed that north or west into Canada was where Red would go. The topography of the land to the north looked a little easier, but it was four or five miles closer to the border going west, and to the west was the small lake. He could already tell that it was going to be another hot day, maybe the hottest one yet. There was a good chance Red had not thought to take water with him, and Bill was certain that the two small brooks shown on the map to the west would be dry.

He pulled everything out of the back of the Jeep and did a quick inventory. He had the two emergency fanny packs that Dray had assembled. He had food and water, a compass and a topo map of the immediate area. He had camouflage clothing and a gun. And he had Brando, he remembered, looking over at the dog still flattened and whining.

Just then Dray stepped out of the shack. He stood on the bare dirt staring at Bill but seeming not to see him. There was drying blood on his mouth and cheeks and throat, and Bill thought that he looked painted for war, and threatening in some way he couldn't name.

"I'm going after Clair," Bill said.

"Not without me, you're not," said Dray. "I'm going after *him*."

Bill stared at him, seeing the threat now. He said, "Listen, Drayton, I'd rather be dead myself than have had that happen in there. I want him dead, too, but what I care about now is getting Clair back alive."

"Yeah? Well *fuck* what you care about, my friend. If you'd cared a little more about controlling your wife's hot pants none of this would have happened." Dray walked off fast toward the other shack, shouting now: "The motherfucker didn't even cut the tires on the Jeep—he's trying to make it easy for us to run. Well this is *me* and *him*, Billy Boy. I'm going to find him and cut the mother-fucker's heart out. C'mon if you're coming and bring the gun. Mine got broke."

Bill followed Dray, walking as fast as he could to keep up, with Brando following him. "I'm not going to chase them, Dray. I'm not going to pressure him into doing anything that would get Clair hurt. I think I know where he's going. If we can get there fast enough and if he holes up . . ."

"We're following the tracks of that ATV. That's *exactly* what we're doing, my friend. And to the North fucking Pole if we have to."

Bill didn't say anything else then but followed Dray and waited—as he came around the rear of the other shack and saw the second ATV, as he threw open the door to the shack and tore through it, throwing things onto the floor and breaking the legs off a table until he found a key hanging from a pegboard over one of the bunks, and as he went back out to the ATV, sat on it, put the key in the ignition, started the machine, then turned it off again. Dray said, "Go get the Jeep and bring it down here. We're going to need some things. I'll check the oil and gas in this thing."

And then Bill was finished waiting. He took the key out of the ignition of the four-wheeler, threw it as far as he could into the woods, and said, "This is not your show, Dray. That's Clair he's got and you're doing this my way with me or you're not doing it at all. I'll tie you up and leave you here if I have to. I swear to God I will."

Dray looked at him and then down at the gun Bill was hold-ing and then back at Bill. He grinned. "Uh-huh. So what's your plan, Billy Boy?"

"There's a pond between here and the Canadian border. I'm going to walk to it. I believe he'll go there."

"The ATV went east, man, didn't you *hear* it?"

"Yeah, I heard it. I can't waste any more time, Dray."

"You just never want to get your fucking hands dirty, do you? You want to just go sit by a pond with your camera while your wife runs off with her boyfriend . . ."

Bill brought his right hand up across his body off the stock of the shotgun and backhanded Dray hard in the mouth, realizing the instant he did it that he would never forgive himself for it.

After a moment Dray straightened his glasses and looked at Bill, and his face started to break up. His face broke up and came apart in an agony, and then he was sobbing. Bill dropped the shotgun and took Dray in his arms, holding him for a couple of minutes while Dray sat on the ATV and sobbed against his chest.

When they were walking back to the Jeep with Brando following them, Dray said, "What about the dog?"

"He goes. I can't leave him here."

"Some posse." And Bill believed from his voice that Dray was back.

They each strapped on one of the fanny-pack emergency kits. In a small backpack they put the sandwiches Dray had made for their lunch that day, an extra canteen of water for Brando, a sweater, a flashlight, a pair of binoculars, a coil of rope, and a first-aid kit. Then Bill took the Silva protractor out of the fanny pack, spread the topo map on the ground well away from the metal of the car and got down on his knees.

"You're better at this than I am," he said.

"Go ahead and take the bearing," Dray said. "I'm going in the shack for a few minutes. I'll check it when I come out. Hey listen, I wanted to tell you something." Bill looked up at him. "First of all, I know Clair's not with him because she wants to be, so forget I said that shit. It's not her fault or your fault or anybody's fault but those two cocksuckers'. And here's the thing: Nobody ever had better friends than you and Clair. Nobody. Portia loved both of you more than anyone alive." Bill stared at him, not able to speak. "And so do I, pal. That's it. I'll carry the shotgun, okay? You take the pack?"

"Okay."

"Get the bearing. I just need a minute or two." He lingered, looking at Bill, then he grinned. "Good luck, Billy Boy."

Bill watched Dray walk to the shack, stand the shotgun beside the door, and go inside. Then he carefully laid the straight edge of the compass housing in a line connecting the camp with the pond and turned the bezel until the meridian lines of the compass were parallel to those on the map, and north on the compass corresponded to north on the map. At this point Brando came over and walked across the map to lick him in the face and Bill shoved the dog away, reoriented the compass, and saw that they had to travel 10° north of due west, or 280°, to reach the pond. Then he remembered declination—the difference between true north and magnetic north, which in New Hampshire he thought he remembered as being 16°. In order to have an accurate bearing to the pond, he would have to add—or maybe it was subtract—16° to or from 280°. He stood up then, rolling up the map, knowing Dray would know what to do with the declination.

He put on the backpack and walked to within a few feet of the open door of the shack, with nothing left to do now but go try to find his wife and take her back. Brando looked up at him miserably.

"Dray?" he said. There was no answer from inside. Then Bill noticed that his shotgun was gone. When he looked inside the shack, he saw that Dray was, too.

CHAPTER TEN

A raven sat on one of the top branches of a forty-foot balsam fir looking into the little glade, its head cocked in fierce attentiveness. A red squirrel clung to the trunk of a beech and watched the glade, too. And a red-tailed hawk that had been circling a few hundred yards away swooped in at treetop height and settled noiselessly in a pine, its dagger feet rolling forward to take the branch like plunder. Ten minutes later a six-month-old doe, her rear haunches still mottled with fawn spots, stepped into the glade one foot at a time, and swept it with her dark eyes. Directly underneath the squirrel, she dropped her head for a mouthful of beech mast, then lifted it again, chewing and waiting, along with the raven, the squirrel, the hawk, and Red Sizemore—all of them watching the glade silently, attentively, as though a play were about to begin there among the dying ferns and leaves.

Red, for one, did not believe that anything was going to happen, but his body had told him to wait and watch for an hour, so he was doing that, sitting on his tree stand in a tall, straight, limby fir, on the same level as the squirrel and below the raven and the hawk, but more conscious of them than those two vigilants were of him.

He felt good. It was his favorite time of day in his favorite month of the year—sharp, acrid, virile, red October, when there was still enough time left before the snow flew to gather and kill and take all you needed but not enough time to waste any of it— and he felt as perfectly blended into the moment as the deer, and as perfectly, thoughtlessly capable in it as the hawk.

He sat on the stand without moving, identifying sounds— squirrel chatter and blue jay, a partridge drumming out behind him, a far-off woodpecker. Nowhere among them was the sound of Bucky's ATV, and his mind told him again that this waiting was a waste of time; but his body told him wait. Moving only his eyes, he checked his watch and saw that there were twenty minutes left in the hour.

The deer had browsed now into the center of the glade, and Red thought about shooting it. But there was a chance of losing or breaking an arrow if it passed through the little doe or if she jumped the string, and then he would be down to only five, since he had not thought to grab the other quiver out of the shack. It and water were all he could think of he had not taken from the camp that he might need, which was not bad considering how quickly and unconsciously he had left. Between when the big blond woman screamed, waking him, and the second gunshot, he had thrown on the rest of his clothes, snatched his day pack out of the duffel and the bow and quiver off the bed, gagged C. J. when she came awake at the first shot, and carried her over his shoulder out to the ATVs. He was trucker-hitching her to the deer rack with a rope when he watched the stocky man shoot Bucky a third time, blowing away another part of him, and heard Bucky scream his name again, and that had decided it. Red hated to see anything suffer, so—even though his body was telling him to leave, that there wasn't time for this—he nocked an arrow, and when Bucky sat up, Red had put his little cousin out of his misery.

At close to fifty yards it was a long shot, but Red knew he had gotten heart. He had not shot the man shooting Bucky, though he held a second arrow and badly wanted to do it, because the man had immediately dropped to his stomach and was already firing at him with a shotgun. He probably could have killed the husband, but he had no particular gripe against the husband, and Clair was watching him, her eyes wide with terror, and there was no need to kill him anyway, since Red knew that he and the man's wife were uncatchable.

When the four-wheeler hit the woods, C. J. had raised her head and tried to lift an arm, and Red had turned around to see the husband running after them and his friend lying on the ground but still no one else, which made him believe there was no one else there, though he could not be sure of that. He had turned east when he came to the trail, then south on the other side of the hill, where he cut the road and saw the vehicle they had come in and stopped to check it for a phone and saw it had none. He had thought about pulling the distributor cap but then thought to hell with it, he'd make it easy for them to clear out. Then he bush-whacked south for a quarter of a mile before turning west and then north to pick up the trail again.

Red had been sure the men would not follow, that they would drive out for help; but his body, apparently not so sure of that, had him stop a half hour down the trail toward Canada, hide the ATV in a spruce thicket, get into the tree stand, and wait—to see if anyone would follow and kill them if they did, and to give his mind a chance to catch up and decide what to do from then on out. It had done that before Red had been ten minutes in the tree, figuring in but not regretting the absence of the second quiver of arrows and a bottle or two of water on what was going to be a long, hot day. And now all there was to do was wait, and enjoy being a seeing but unseen and lethal part of the passing October moments.

After awhile he found himself thinking about Bucky. The first thing he thought was that Bucky would have been damned proud of the shot that killed him and would have bragged about it in the sports bars. Red didn't know exactly what it was Bucky had done in the cookshack that got him shot up, and that turned him, Red, into a kidnapper and killer when those two things had never been part of his plans. He didn't know, but he had a pretty good idea that Bucky had lost it with the big blond woman—something that had not occurred to Red might happen. Now that he thought about it, though, it almost seemed predestined that when Bucky lost it for the last time—the time Red had always known had to come, for which they would lock Bucky up in a jail or an institution or someone would kill him—it would be with a woman, the single thing on earth, because of Celia, that Bucky had the highest regard for.

Celia had been a saint—there was no other word for it—who kept getting turds in her punch bowl for men. When Red's parents were killed in their pickup truck by the train between White River Junction and Montreal and Celia took him in to raise, her third husband, a trucker, had just left her and she was living with a laid-off Sheetrocker named Harold. Harold had seemed okay for the first few months that Red (whose name was Allen then) lived in the house, though he got drunk every evening before supper and sometimes passed out at the table.

Then one night in February they were eating pork roast and onions and listening to *The Barber of Seville*, and Bucky, who was three or four, spilled some food on the floor. Harold threw the rest of Bucky's food onto the floor and told him to get down there and eat it like a dog. Bucky had started crying and Celia had started shouting at Harold, and Harold had stood up then, stumbling and yelling to the melody of some aria, "Bow wow *wow*, bow wow *wow*," picked Bucky up out of his chair, and threw him headfirst against the refrigerator. Red and Celia had heard Bucky's skull break. It was the first time Red had ever felt the red heat of his anger or had his body throw him into action. He was a big eleven-year-old. He had knocked Harold down with a chair, jumped onto his chest, and stabbed the Sheetrocker over and over again in the face with a fork, blinding him in the left eye.

They had to put a plate in Bucky's head. He had been a sweet and affectionate boy before Harold broke his head, and he still was, but from then on whenever someone made him feel worthless, Bucky would lose it, just blank out and start putting hair on the wall. Ever since childhood it had been Red who had had to pull him away from most of the incidents when Bucky lost it, including recently a fight at a Fourth of July barbecue when Bucky had a turned-on garden hose pushed into a garage mechanic's mouth and was holding his nose shut.

Red had always known it was just a matter of time before Bucky killed someone, and he guessed it was the big blond woman who had finally paid Harold's bill. Now Red had paid Bucky's, and he hoped Celia, looking down from heaven, was satisfied. But whether she was or not, Bucky was history and so was Red's promise to look after him—which would have been history anyway. Actually, he told himself, it was better this way—this way neither Bucky nor Celia would have to deal with Red leaving Bucky behind when he moved into his new life.

As far as Red could see, nothing that had happened that morning or was likely to happen for the rest of the day had to change any of his plans for that new life, except for his plan for the woman. He had it figured out how to get to Canada by that night, or the following morning at the latest, without leaving a trace, and he knew that once he was in Canada, he was gone. But

things were different with the woman now. She had seen him kill
Bucky and she knew his plans, down to the name of the lake he
was going to. He could no longer let her leave. Either she had to
want to go with him or Red would have to kill her, and she would
have to want it badly—enough so that he could be certain he could
trust her, not just now but weeks and months down the road.

Red believed there was a good chance that she *did* now want
for herself the life he had described for her the night before in the
sweat lodge, even though this morning he realized he had left out
a few important details. She had listened carefully to what he told
her, sitting with her thin, naked, animal-beautiful body still and
open to him, and both then and later in the shack Red had seen
that she was imagining herself cutting the cedar ribs for the canoe
they would build, or running the beaver and muskrat line with
him at dawn in the glistening snow by the river, her face hooded
in coyote fur. He was positive he had seen her imagining herself
living with him that free, clean life without a single piece of junk
in it, and seeing that had made him want her more than ever. Carrying her wrapped in the towel back into the shack, doing her hair,
and then as they lay together on the bearskins, Red had wanted
to own her like his flesh, to carry her inside himself like his blood.
He had wanted to possess her more than he had ever wanted his
own life, and when he put his hand on her breast and she closed
her eyes and sighed as though she were being carried off but it was
fine to go, he had known that she was nearly there, where he
needed her to be—wanting him, too, all of him and his life—and
he had asked her what she wanted then.

"Sleep," she had said, but she had made sleep sound like just
a bridge that would bring her to him overnight. And Red himself
had slept more deeply and longer than he had in years, knowing
she was there beside him traveling that bridge. Then he had waked
to the blond woman's screaming and realized the moment he heard

the first gunshot that C. J. had either safely crossed over and was his or she was dead.

He had almost asked her right then, but his body slapped a towel in her mouth instead and then roped her to the four-wheeler, so he still did not know what she would say, though he would soon.

There were only a few minutes left in the hour and Red now knew for a fact that no one was following him. He knew it would be at least four more hours before a team of men with ATVs could start after him from the camp, and probably two or three hours before they could get the police chopper up from Concord, if it wasn't being used somewhere else. That gave him plenty of time for everything, but he was anxious to get on with it and to find out what would happen. His visions were not as dependable as Joy's, though hers could be way off, too, sometimes, but he had had one this morning in his first five minutes on the tree stand that he believed: He had seen that he would either die that day or the next, or live the life he wanted for thirty years.

And either way was fine by him. One advantage Red knew he had over other people, one thing that made him freer and more dangerous, was that he had always held his life very lightly in his hands, valuing it as he did now, but at the same time knowing it was of no value at all and that he could drop it in the dust in a second and never think about it twice. He hadn't set out to kill Bucky or even to kidnap the woman. He was now playing a game he hadn't asked or wanted to play. It was a game he was so good at, he didn't even need to think about it, but just play—the way those drivers at Indy drove their cars. Red believed there was no way he could not win it, and then take everything he now knew he wanted for the next thirty years, with or without the woman; but if he went into the wall, that was finest kind too.

The hawk had flown, and so had the raven, and Red no longer saw the squirrel. But the deer was still browsing in the glade.

He took his Sony Walkman out of his day pack, slid in a tape of Luciano Pavarotti singing Italian love songs, and put on the headphones. Red always gave away the sense of hearing when he hunted, listening to music on the Walkman as he stalked or sat in the tree stand, because he could afford to give it away. He turned up the volume on "Celeste Aida" from *Aida,* and when the little doe looked up he put an arrow in her. She walked two dainty steps forward as if nothing had happened, and then fell dead. Red came down out of the fir feeling that the woods were his personal arena, his concert hall—that he might as well be the great Pavarotti himself, singing with the Orchestra of Teatro Comunale to all of Bologna.

He walked over to the spruce thicket where he had hidden the four-wheeler and saw C. J. glaring at him from the rack, her eyes fierce as a hawk's. He stood looking at her for a moment before he untied her, letting her eyes claw at him, struck as he had been the night before in the sweat lodge with how her beauty did not seem human somehow, but was lean and smooth and flawless as a mink's.

He untied the rope holding her spread-eagled to the rack and then the towel around her mouth, and she stood up, not taking her furious eyes off his face, and slapped him.

She said, "I don't know or care how you're accustomed to treating your women, but let's get this straight: I don't get gagged, I don't get tied up, and I don't get hit."

Red didn't know what to say to this, so he said, "I didn't hit you."

"I'm talking about from now on. Not *ever.*" Clair walked a few steps off, dropped her overalls and then her shorts, and squatted to piss. "The women you're used to may take that shit, but I don't. And I'm out of this deal if it happens again."

There might have been another moment in Red Sizemore's life when he felt as complete and inevitable as he did just then, but he could not recall it. "I shot you a deer," he told her.

He skinned the little doe while C. J. watched, saying that he would teach her how to tan the skin and make herself a shirt and a pair of moccasins from it. Then he showed her how to take the liver and heart and backstrap. Sitting on a log, her arms wrapped around her knees, she watched all this silently without speaking until he had finished and put the meat into his day pack and wrapped the skin around the axe he carried on the rear rack of the ATV.

Then she said: "It's going to take me awhile and you will have to go slowly. I don't know much about the woods. I've never built anything. I want to learn it all, but can you go slowly?"

"Yes," he said.

She drew a deep breath and let it out. "Thank you for not killing my husband. I know you could have."

"I've got nothing against your husband. And I didn't have to kill him. He didn't follow us."

"What chance would he have?" said Clair simply. "I guess he's gone to get someone to look for us."

Red didn't answer but watched her, wanting badly to have her then but knowing it would be better to save it for the afternoon when everything had been done and they were at the pond and in the clear. Clair lifted her head and stared back at him. Red looked into her face for some sign of lying but couldn't find any. Her eyes looked almost merry.

"But they won't be able to find us, will they? No matter who he gets."

"No."

"How are we going to get to Peribonca Lake? Tell me."

"You'll see."

"No, I want to know. I want you to tell me so I can watch us do it together and know what I'm seeing."

Red walked over to the log, put his hands under her arms, and lifted her to her feet. He bent his head and kissed her, and her lips were there for him, and it was all exactly as he had imagined it.

"We have to go now. I'll tell you on the way."

With C. J. sitting behind him on the four-wheeler, he followed a series of ATV and snowmobile trails east, away from Canada, making it look as though he were trying to hide his tracks.

When he hit the railroad tracks running between Boston and Quebec City, he turned south, following the tracks. By then he had told C. J. about his friends in Saint-Malo, just across the border, who would keep them for a week or so until Red could arrange to have someone fake a murder/suicide for them in Florida or South Carolina; about how and where they would get (he did not say steal) the few tools and supplies they would need up north, and the four-wheel-drive Suburban and snowmobile with trailer; about how they would live that winter in a hole in the ground they would excavate themselves by the lake, and hunt and trap for food; and how in the spring they would build a cabin over the hole and plant a garden—and from then on things would be easier.

No one, he told her, would think to look for them, going into winter, on a wilderness lake three hundred miles north of Quebec City, and she laughed and told him that she believed that. He did not mention the child she was not going to have.

About a mile and a half down the railroad tracks, Red drove the ATV into a thicket and covered it up with brush, then he drained the gas out of the tank, so it would look like they had run out of gas on their way south.

"Are we going to hop a train?" she asked him, looking pleased with the question.

"We want them to think we hopped the freight train that comes by here in about three hours going south. They won't find the four-wheeler until tomorrow, if then. These north-country boys ain't all that sharp. And when they do find it, it will look like we're on our way south."

"What do we do now?"

Red had tied either end of a rope to the axe and swung it over his shoulder with the doeskin wrapped around it. He opened the day pack and handed Clair a bag of nuts, raisins, and hard chocolate, then he closed the pack, put it on his back, and slung the bow and quiver of arrows over his other shoulder. "We hoof it north up these tracks a way to lose our scent in case they bring dogs, then we go back the way we just came. All the way to the border."

"On foot?"

"There's a pond about eight miles from here and five miles from the border. We should be there by four or four-thirty. We'll make a little camp, have something to eat, take it easy for a few hours." He looked at her in the eyes. "Then we'll go across the border and into Saint-Malo at first light tomorrow. It's a pretty good hike to the pond, and we may not find any water on the way. A lot of things won't be as easy as you're used to for a while."

Clair ate a handful of gorp and gave the bag back to him. "That's fine," she said. "I don't need things to be easy anymore."

Red had her follow him while he walked alongside the tracks for thirty or forty yards south. Then they backtracked to where they started from and walked north up the tracks, and he took the can of Scent Away that he used to cover his odor when deer hunting and sprayed away their scent for a hundred yards. He knew he was being more careful than he needed to be, but he had the time to do it and it felt like a little performance for the woman, and she seemed to enjoy it.

In fact, she seemed to enjoy it almost too much and kept stopping and asking him questions about it, and at one point she dropped the yellow scarf he had bought her, and when he went back and got it for her she laughed and said she hadn't even noticed dropping it, that she had taken it off her neck because it was hot and put it in her pocket and it must have fallen out. There was no reason not to believe her, but when they turned off the track and entered the woods, with her following him twenty or thirty feet behind, Red had a funny feeling about her for the first time, and his body, which was in the saddle now, decided to test her. He stopped to let her catch up.

"I won't ever gag you or tie you up or hit you," he told her. "I want you to know that."

She looked at him with no expression and said, "I believe you."

"Then believe this too," he said, leaning into her face and squinting at her. "If you try to run, what I *will* do is fuck you and kill you and bury your body."

She stared at him, not lowering her eyes, looking shocked at first, and then, slowly, angry and angrier, but never frightened. She dropped her head and started to walk on ahead of him up the trail, but he caught her by the shoulder and she swung her face up to him, looking exactly as pissed off and hateful as he wanted her to look. "Not if I fuck you and kill you and bury your body first," she said. "And what do I do if *you* try to run, asshole?"

Red roared at her then—laughing until he thought he'd bust a gut.

* * *

It was a long, hot, dry walk, only part of it on trails, and Red knew the woman got tired and very thirsty, since they had had nothing to drink all day, but she didn't complain and she kept his pace. He tried to make the walk interesting, identifying plants and birds and animal tracks for her. He showed her how to make her watch work as a compass and how she could find out where east was by placing stones at the end of the shadow thrown by a stick stuck in the ground. He pointed out a few edible mushrooms, and told her about the inner tree barks that could be eaten and the various nuts and berries, and how to make teas out of pine needles and pond algae, and soups out of cattails and arrowroot.

The woods were as hot and bright and windless as they were in midsummer, and Red pleasured in being in them as he always did, particularly when they were off the trails and bushwhacking, relying only on the sense he could not remember ever having been without of knowing exactly where he was in relation to where he wanted to go, in any woods, day or night. He had read somewhere that geese and ducks in their annual migrations can return each year to an exact wintering pond, or in the spring to a precise nesting area, and Red figured he must have been given some of the same mysterious navigational equipment those ducks and geese had. He had been to Goose Pond only once, tracking a heavy buck in the snow three years before, but he knew he could return to it blindfolded from anywhere in these woods. To make it more challenging for himself, he decided to come onto the pond at its southeastern end, exactly at a little cove he remembered being there.

Just before one o'clock, backtracking along one of the trails he had followed earlier on the ATV, he heard the far-off buzzing of a helicopter. When it got closer he led the woman off the trail to a big rock maple, and they crawled underneath it and lay on their stomachs with their heads down as the chopper circled over them and then flew on to the northwest. He watched her face as the chopper droned away from them, its sound tapering into silence, and saw nothing there. He put his hand on the back of her head and took the coil of hair he had greased and braided and brought her face to his and kissed her hard, and she kissed him back, running her tongue across and under his. He had turned then under the maple and pulled her body to him.

C. J. drew her head back, breathing quickly, and began to say something, but he slapped his hand over her mouth and held it there, telling her with it and with his body on top of hers to be silent and not to move. He raised his head and listened for two minutes or more as she stared up at him wide-eyed. Then he dropped his head to hers and said into her ear, "Don't move from here or make a sound until I tell you it's alright. You understand?" She nodded once and he rolled quietly off her.

He drew one of the skinning knives out of its sheath and crouched behind the big maple, feeling his senses come up to where he seemed to be able to see around trees, and to hear anything stirring in the woods for a square mile around him. He already knew that it was one man following the ATV tracks, moving quietly and expertly and stopping along the trail as if still-hunting. He also knew which man it was and exactly how far away he was.

Red slowed his breathing and gave C. J. a look to reinforce what he had told her, then he crawled into the woods on the other side of the trail. He moved between trees in a silent, crouching trot until he was directly downwind of the man and had his scent along with the little sound he was making. He wished then for the Walkman, so that he could put on the earphones to make this more interesting. He could tell that the man knew what he was doing in the woods, and he believed that hunting him down and killing him might be made interesting, perhaps even without the Walkman. He waited until the man was across the wind from him and was stopped and listening, then he picked up an old, dry limb from the ground and broke it in half with his foot.

The limb made a loud pop and Red waited, grinning, to see what the man would do. After three minutes he still hadn't heard any movement, and he congratulated the man on his patience. Then in another few seconds he caught scent again from upwind and realized that the man *was* moving and had been for a while, but not away.

With exhilaration Red realized both that the man was stalking *him* and that somehow he had been able to move at least forty or fifty yards without Red hearing him. Still grinning, feeling killing adrenaline rise up and spread through him now like a drink of liquor, he lay down and pinpointed the scent coming to him along the ground. The man was crossing the wind again, headed for a narrow gulley that would lead him in cover downwind of Red. He let the man reach the gulley. Then he crawled on all fours parallel to the gulley until he came to the end, where he reckoned the man would turn uphill to come in behind where Red had broken the branch. He stood up, holding the knife against his leg, and went as motionless as the tree he put his back to.

In two or three minutes he heard the man, and after another minute he saw him. He was holding a shotgun waist-high and moving with skill and lightness, preceding his body with the shotgun muzzle. Red watched him approach, then pass his tree, amused at his dumb *cojones*, admiring his soundless movement, and deciding on the spur of the moment as he passed by not to kill him just then.

The next time the man stopped to listen, Red walked up behind him and laid the blade of the knife with pressure against his cheek and neck and told him, "Let go of the gun." He had had the man's scent for at least ten minutes and now it was very strong—of dried blood, fear, and rage—and as the man stiffened,

Red believed he could smell him thinking of doing something that would get him killed. "You don't have to die," he said. "Just let it go." He could smell the man thinking and knew when he decided. "Go ahead, then," he told him.

As the man started to turn, bringing the gun up, Red stepped back and kicked him hard in the crotch. He screamed and fell to his knees and then onto his side and lay there doubled over, groaning and holding himself.

Red stood above the man watching him, letting him decide what would happen to him, and in a moment or two C. J. ran up panting and said, "Please don't hurt him."

"I've already hurt him," Red said. He picked up the shotgun and threw it into the woods. He had never liked guns. "I told you not to move."

"And I'm telling you not to hurt him," said Clair.

The man looked up at them from the ground. His face was fierce and vengeful and unafraid as a wolverine's in a trap, and Red could see in it that he wanted to die and therefore couldn't be dealt with. C. J. put both hands on Red's arm and the man watched that. "I want you to let him go," she said. "He can't hurt us."

"Portia's dead, Clair, did you know that? They raped her and killed her. You're with him because you want to be? Tell me."

Red felt Clair's fingers tighten on his arm, felt her freeze, and then begin to cry. After a moment, crying, she walked over to the man. She sat down beside him and reached for his head, but he slapped her hands away.

"Tell me," he said again. "Just tell me."

"Yes," she said, crying, but saying it so that neither Red nor the man could doubt it was true. "I'm so sorry, Dray."

"Don't act, Clair," the man said. "For God's sake, don't fucking act for me. Not now." He groaned and tried to sit up. "Listen: Tell your friend to kill me, because if you don't, I'll kill you both, I swear to God. If it takes me the rest of my life."

"No problem," Red told him. "You got it."

Clair stood up. She had stopped crying, and she looked calmly over at Red now as though they had been together for years and she had the weight to tell him whatever she wanted without trying to make him want it, too, and he liked that. "Let him go," she said.

"Truth is, I'd rather kill him, like the man said."

"We'll tie him up when we get to the pond and let him go when we leave in the morning. He can't hurt us, and that's what I want."

Red knew she was right, that the man couldn't hurt them. On the whole, he would just as soon have killed him for what he had done to Bucky, even though it sounded like Bucky had pretty much earned the shooting-up he got. But it was not a big deal to him either way, particularly since he could see that living for the man was going to be more painful than dying. "Okeydoke," he said.

"Where is Bill?" she asked the man.

He looked at her with hatred, and Red thought he wasn't going to answer, but he said, "He drove back to Pittsburg. He had a date, I guess. I just pray to God he's got balls enough to kill you when he finds you."

Red laughed. He put his knife back in its sheath and walked toward the man. He said, "You'll have to get up now, citizen."

And then the little cocksucker *charged him*: One second he was lying on his side holding his nuts, and the next he was rushing at Red with his head down and his arms spread like some fucking football player, and that pissed Red off for the first time. He stepped aside and kicked the man in the throat and then again in the head when he fell.

"Don't say a word, woman, or I *will* hurt him," he told Clair. He slid the axe off his back and took the rope off it.

The man was pulling for breath and coughing. Clair knelt beside him, putting his glasses back on and then stroking his bald head, but looking ready to get on with things. Red turned him over and tied his hands behind his back and gagged him with a strip of doeskin. Then he pulled the man to his feet.

"Now," he said to Clair, finished with this interruption, "I'll see if I can find us some edible roots in the next mile or so. I want you to know what they look like."

They heard the helicopter once more around three o'clock but did not see it, and at four-thirty they walked through a small marsh of alder and cattails, and fifty yards ahead of them was the little cove, exactly as Red remembered it, with the ten-acre pond widening out of it to the northwest.

He skirted the pond for a few hundred yards to the north, looking in the heavy spruces there for a place to tie the man up. When he found it, he pushed him down into a sitting position and tied his ankles and wrists around a tree.

"He needs something to drink and eat," C. J. said.

"I'll bring him something after awhile." Red drew one of his two knives, lifted the man's tied feet, and cut the Achilles tendon of his right leg. The man screamed around the gag.

"No!" shouted C. J., running for the man. "What are you *doing?*"

He caught her and held her and sheathed the knife as the man laid his head against the spruce and screamed again, this time, Red could tell, in rage.

"I'll let him go when we leave, like I told you, but I want him walking slow."

"He'll bleed to death," said Clair.

"No he won't. Let's go."

He led her back through the marsh to the cove, and she wanted to keep walking into the water to drink, but Red took her up a bank and into the woods and told her to sit there while he lay on top of the bank, well back in the trees, and studied the shoreline all the way around the pond and as far into the woods as he could see for five minutes; then he stood up and walked back to the woman.

"I'm thirsty," she said. "I want to get something to drink."

"In a minute," he said, wanting to stretch her now when she was tired and very thirsty, he knew, because he was himself—to work and stretch her for toughness, as he would a skin he was tanning. "We make camp first."

They were in a stand of mature, evenly spaced pines, fifty feet from the water, and the ground was level and carpeted with pine needles. Red hung his bow and quiver in a tree and opened his pack. He unwrapped the doeskin from the axe and cut three straight pine branches about four feet long and built a small shear-pole tent with them, covering the branches with a poncho out of his pack. He lay the doeskin inside the tent, hair side up; then he quickly built a small fire and impaled the deer heart and liver and part of the backstrap on sticks and stuck the sticks in the ground so that the meat hung above the fire to cook.

"Alright," he said when all of that was done. "Now you can go get some water."

The woman ran down the bank and across a few feet of pebbly beach and stopped at the water's edge and undressed. Red sat cross-legged on the edge of the bank watching her drink and then swim. He wanted to stretch out his own thirst a little further and remember the walk in. They had crossed three ridges, one steep, with a scree cliff on its far side, and had gone through a dry bog and alder thickets, matted spruce woods, and still brightly leafed hardwood stands. Red had felt as though he were flowing through and over all that country, as certain and unimpeded as water running downhill. He had felt himself sliding over the ridges and around granite outcroppings, his feet bringing him back on course each time as dependably as gravity, without once thinking about it. And now, sitting cross-legged and straight-backed on the edge of the bank, he felt that he had been carried to this place as unavoidably and effortlessly as if his personal history were a river that had finally reached this pond and emptied here; and that he would flow from the other end the following morning at first light with the woman not only toward and into a new life, but as a new thing—newly composed and charged, with no past other than this pond.

Feeling reborn and unstoppable as rain, Red stood up and jumped off the bank, landing lightly on the pebbled beach eight feet below. He did not like to swim, but he took off his shirt and walked into the pond up to his knees. He bent over and drank from his cupped hands until his thirst was gone, and then he threw water over his head and neck and shoulders, baptizing himself in the water that had just received and swallowed all the junk and sewage of his last forty-five years and three months.

CHAPTER
ELEVEN

The sun was just cracking through the tops of the tall spruces on the rise above him. The air was limpid, warm, and livening with birdsong, but otherwise the little clearing was blessedly silent now and the quiet, clear, brightening warmth had an anticipative feel to it, as if the morning itself in that place was attendant on him.

Bill sat down on the tailgate of Dray's old Wagoneer, closed his eyes, and let his mind go blank for a couple of minutes. When he stood up again he felt rested and certain.

"Let's put it on the road," he said with self-conscious good cheer to Brando, who was sitting on his haunches looking worried.

Then, with Brando on heel, he walked away from the camp without looking back.

His plan was to walk to Goose Pond as if he were traveling over country and still-hunting for deer at the same time, taking a few dozen steps, then pausing for a few seconds to look and listen. From having still-hunted like this with Dray, he knew he could cover a mile of woods in about forty-five minutes. According to the exact measurements he had made on the map with the scale end of his compass, it was a little over five miles from the camp to the pond. It was eight-thirty when he walked away from the camp. Adding another fifteen minutes per mile for navigation, he figured he should be at the pond around one-thirty.

He knew the chances that Red would go to the pond at all were only fair. He also knew that if Red *was* going to stop at the pond on his way to Canada, the chances were much better than fair that he would have already done so and left by the time Bill got there. But something told him that if Red was not feeling pushed, he would rest up for part of the day, and the pond was a good place to do that. He also doubted that Red would leave a followable trail, which meant that he would have to ditch the four-wheeler at some point—probably in the opposite direction of where he was headed—and having Clair with him would slow him up if he was walking.

All in all, Bill knew that logically his chances of finding Red and Clair, on foot, in thousands of acres of woods before Red made it to Canada, were remote. But he believed he was doing the only thing he could do and that it would lead him to Clair no matter what the odds were against it, so he did not worry about the logic, or about what he would do if he did find Clair and Red with no weapon other than a knife, or even about Dray finding them first. Like Portia's death, those were all things he knew he couldn't both think about and function through, so he left them behind at the deer camp and walked into the woods behind the smaller shack until he cut the four-wheeler trail that Red had used.

The trail ran east to west and Red had turned east on it, but Bill thought he would have done the same thing if he wanted to go west and believed he might be followed. He had hoped the trail would follow his bearing, and it did follow it closely enough so that he was able to stay on it for about a quarter of a mile. Then the trail turned off to the north and he was in the woods.

Thinking they were hunting now, Brando tore off into the big pines and hemlocks ahead of them, snuffling for birds. After three or four times calling him back to heel, Bill gave up and decided to let him run, having no attention to spare on the dog. After a few minutes of stumbling around and running into trees with his eyes glued to the compass, he remembered about picking a landmark as far away as possible along the bearing, then walking to it without looking at the compass and picking another landmark from there. In the relatively open woods he started out in, this method, once he remembered it, made for easy going. He would pick out a tree at 280° as far away as he could see and walk to it. Then he would stop there, whistle for Brando to sit, and look and listen for thirty seconds before picking out another tree at 280° and walking to that one.

But after about a mile of this the land dropped through a spruce thicket into a dry streambed where the ground was stony and covered with green moss. The trees there were whippy, clinging poplar and birches, and he couldn't see far enough ahead in them to find landmarks, so he had to walk straight ahead, following the compass's directional arrow over whatever was in his way.

The streambed led him finally to a bog of hummocky marsh grass that was a couple of hundred feet across and about the same distance wide. His bearing lay directly across the bog, so he stepped into it to walk across and immediately sank to his knees in sucking black mud.

He backed up and sat down on the edge of the bog and watched Brando flush a pair of grouse. He took the pack off and drank some water out of one his canteens. Brando came over and lay with his happy yellow face in his lap, and he split a sandwich with the dog. There was one turkey sandwich among the six he had brought—an aberration for Dray. Bill decided to save it for Clair.

When he had finished the sandwich he was calm again and he believed he remembered how to get around an obstacle like this bog and then get back on the original bearing, and the method made sense to him whether he was remembering it properly or not.

Counting off thirty steps, he walked due south, 100° off his bearing, until the bog ended, then back west until he was on the far side of the bog. Then he walked thirty steps 100° north of 280°, which brought him back to his original heading. Starting out again along good old 280°, with Brando now at heel on his own, Bill was certain he had gotten it right and felt a surge of confidence.

After the bog he crossed a valley of dense pine and tamaracks and another dry streambed, then a ridgeline of oak and beech and maple trees where the hot midmorning sun ignited the red and yellow leaves on the ground and made them glow like embers. He stopped at the top of a second ridge and gave Brando some water and drank some himself. Then he pulled out the map and looked at it. The ridgeline he was on and the one he had already crossed were shown there on the way to the pond, along with a third, steeper one farther along, but all three ridges ran from north to south for miles, and it was impossible to tell from the map if he was on course. In the spruce thickets he had gone through he had not always been able to follow his heading exactly, but he felt like he had compensated for the times he had come off it and he believed he could not be far off the heading.

At about ten of one, as he was climbing the third ridge, he heard a helicopter. His first instinct was to run to the ridge top and wave to it when it came over him. Then he realized that if he attracted the helicopter, it would announce to Red that he was being followed. So instead of waving, he got down on his stomach under a tree and hid, and the chopper—with its promise of authority and manpower and safety—banked above him, fell away down the other side of the ridge, and faded out of hearing.

He had counted on being able to see Goose Pond from the top of the third ridge, which showed on the map as being less than a mile from the pond if he was on course. But when he and Brando got to the top he could see nothing to the west but more trees, stretching on and on, matted and spiky and silent, toward Canada. From the ridge top it looked like the entire world was either a paradise or a hell of trees, depending on who you were and what you were there for, and nowhere among them was there any sign of a pond.

Bill directed himself to stay calm as he walked north and then south along the ridge top, a few hundred yards in both directions, and still had no sight of water; his mind seemed to pay attention for a while, but his body did not. His breathing quickened and so did his step, and when he returned from ranging the ridgeline to where he had left his pack, he realized that he was humming "The Yellow Rose of Texas" over and over out loud.

He put the pack back on and started trotting down the west slope of the ridge, his eyes on the compass held out from his waist, humming to himself and feeling panic starting to seep now into his mind, and thinking: Maybe the compass was broken; maybe some metal had thrown it off when he took the bearing off the map, or was throwing it off now. . . . Then he heard Brando bark, and looked up from the compass just in time to see the ground disappear from under his feet.

The cliff was a shallow slope of scree and Bill slid and rolled, feeling oddly peaceful, over the loose rock for sixty or seventy feet to the bottom, where he lay for a minute or two not knowing whether he was injured and afraid to move and find out.

Brando, who had barked for a while from the top of the slope, had now gotten down it and was lying beside him, trying to lick his face. His left wrist hurt, and when he looked at it he saw that he had broken his watch and that there was a bruise forming on his forearm just above the wrist. Otherwise, he seemed to be okay when he finally did stand up. Then he looked up the slope and saw his compass lying smashed into four or five pieces on the rocks above him.

Bill stared at the broken compass for a full minute, struggling with another urge to panic. When it was gone, he sat down on a rock and stared at the scree between his legs, knowing that he was beaten. Below him was a swale of tall, tan grass and dying golden-rod. He looked up across the swale at the endless woods in which he was lost and no longer had any chance of finding Clair—and hated them.

He remembered his recent sentimentalizing of the woods as a safe haven—his fatuous sense as he followed Dray into the wood-cock cover that he could just slide invincibly into them now any-time he wanted as if into a warm bath—and his smug renunciation of the kill-or-be-killed mentality that Dray had always brought to the outdoors. And remembering all that, he hated himself along with the woods. "Meat," he could hear his father saying, "you're meat, pal," turning over his cards.

When Bill and his brothers were kids, his father had played a game with them on long car trips. He called the game "Life or Death."

"Okay . . . Sean," he would say. "You're out in Cape Cod Bay by yourself and your sailboat sinks, what do you do?" And Sean would say, "Do I have a lifeboat?" "You're towing a dinghy, yeah. But there are no oars in it." "Do I have a bottle of water?" "Nope, no water." And they would go on like that, with Sean trying to figure out what to do to survive until Jack Joyce said either, "Okay, congratulations, you made it, you get Life," or, "Tough luck, buddyro, you just bought the farm." Then the next kid would get a turn.

"Okay, Billy," Bill said aloud to himself now. "You can't find the pond. You have no compass and no idea how to get out of the woods, let alone how to find Clair. What are you going to do?"

He didn't know. But when he thought about what his father would do, or Dray, he immediately knew that both of them would stand up and start putting one foot in front of the next.

His father had been a tough man, and Dray was, too—not in the vainglorious sense of that word, though they could both be that as well, but in the sense of always doing what their characters demanded they do and never quitting on themselves. His father had always hated mortgages and had never had one, and it occurred to Bill now that his father's toughness, like Dray's, had had to do with owning his life, like his property, free and clear. Realizing that made him see for the first time how he had taken out far too big a mortgage on his own life when Clair came back to him. The terror of losing her again, to Red Sizemore or anything else, owned so much of his life now that he was no longer certain from moment to moment if it was himself or his lien-holder the gremlin making the decisions. In the past year he had reclaimed much of himself along with Clair, but a crucially important part of that self, he saw, was still missing—the unmortgaged, uncompromisable part that could go implacable when it had to and simply put one foot in front of the next. And at that moment Bill knew that he could no more give up now on finding that missing part than give up on finding Clair.

He and Brando watched a great blue heron fly over, and then a flock of ravens flapping like black rags out of a fir to chase the heron. He would keep walking west—in the general direction of where the sun would set—and hope to stumble onto the pond. And he would do the same thing the next day, and the day after that too if necessary. The weather looked like it would continue to hold. He had food and water. He had everything he needed.

He slipped out of the backpack and split one more of the sandwiches and the last of one of the canteens of water with Brando. Then he stood up, put the pack back on and walked across the swale of grass back into the woods. They no longer looked to him like the home of evil trolls, as they had from the scree slope, but neither did they seem a safe haven—only something neutrally and unknowably other than himself.

Walking out of a thicket, he saw the flock of ravens settling fussily back onto their fir tree, and that caused him to think of the heron and to wonder what it had been doing out here, since herons, he knew, were never far from . . . water.

Thanking God for that small curiosity, he headed out in the direction the heron had been flying from, putting one foot ahead of the next as fast as he comfortably could, and in less than ten minutes of walking to the northeast he was at the pond. Coming into it at what he could tell from the map was its western end, he realized he had originally overshot it to the south, probably because of the 16° of declination he hadn't known what to do with.

Goose Pond was a little glacial tarn at the bottom of a shallow bowl, which explained why he had been unable to see it from the ridge. The western end of the bowl was the higher end, and Bill got on his knees as soon as he spotted the water through the trees and crawled up to where the land began to fall away, and then lay there on his stomach, with Brando sitting well behind him, and studied the pond and the woods around it. It was a friendly-looking body of water: a deep, cool blue color under the high sun, maybe eight or ten acres large, he guessed, with a shallow cove at the far end. After he had watched the pond for a few minutes and seen nothing but a beaver swimming, he backed up on his belly until he could no longer see the water, then stood up and walked in a crouch to the north, following the edge of the bowl, where the land continued to rise gradually, looking for a good place to hide and keep watch from.

Within fifty yards he came to an ATV trail that ran up to the lip of the bowl from the west. Just off the trail he found an old Labatt's Canadian beer can with the print on it in French as well as English and realized that this had to be the trail into Quebec. He walked down the trail away from the pond for a minute or two, looking for fresh ATV tracks or footprints, but saw none.

Only forty or fifty feet farther to the north of the trail, close to the highest point of land around the pond, he found a deer bed in a cavelike V formed by three short but densely branched spruce trees. The little evergreen cave was around ten feet deep and three feet wide at the opening and commanded a clear view of the trail, the pond, and most of the bowl.

He took off the backpack and the fanny pack and shoved them under some branches near the mouth of the cave. With a piece of nylon rope he cut from the coil in the pack, he tied Brando to the center spruce so that the dog was confined to the deep end of the cave and could not follow or be seen if Bill wanted to leave quickly.

He lay down then on his stomach to wait and watch the pond. He figured it must be around two-thirty, but it didn't really matter what time it was: this cave of needles and branches was home until either Clair came or he knew she was not going to come, and that would not be until the following day.

As he lay watching the pond and waiting, Bill felt calm and knitted together inside himself and ready for whatever might happen. He wondered where Dray was and what he was doing. He didn't believe Dray would be able to find Red by tracking him and he prayed that he was right about that. Waiting for him here might not work, either, but Bill felt comfortable at the mouth of the little evergreen cave and content and right to be there. He had spent nearly every one of the past twenty-four hours trying to get somewhere other than where he was, and it felt to him now as if he had traveled a million hectic miles in that time. He had always been his best and happiest watching from a good place; that was always when things happened for him that he wanted to happen. Playing no one but himself, watching, and waiting for the game to come to him had won Clair back once before and he believed now that it might again.

He woke sometime later to the sound of a helicopter. It was the same one he had seen earlier, and it flew over the pond, hovering every couple of minutes, as it had before, but this time Bill did not wish he was on it or regret its leaving.

He slept again, and the next time he woke it was to Brando whining, and when he looked down the pond he saw smoke curling up out of the big pines at the far end. He pulled the binoculars out of his pack and focused in the far end of the pond. There was a small, rocky beach and a high bank and, behind the bank, the tall pines with a ribbon of smoke rising from them. He trained the binoculars on the top of the bank and waited.

In a couple of minutes he saw Clair run out of the woods down the bank and across the beach to the water. Then he saw Red Sizemore walk to the edge of the bank and sit there cross-legged, looking down at her, his face in the binoculars relaxed and possessive. Bill watched his wife undress on the beach and then walk naked into the water, the dropping sun flashing off her skin. He watched her drink for a long time from her hands and then swim, breaststroking out into deep water and back again into the shallows of the cove, as comfortable-looking as if she were in their swimming pool back at the farm. After awhile he watched her walk out of the water and use a pair of camouflage overalls to dry herself—starting with her left foot first, as he had watched her do a thousand times after swimming or taking a shower. While she was drying off, Red Sizemore jumped down off the bank, took off his shirt, and went into the water up to his knees to drink and wet his head and upper body.

Then he walked out and Clair was there on the beach waiting for him. Bill watched her stand up on her tiptoes, her beautiful calf muscles knotting, to kiss the man. He watched Red Sizemore cup her buttocks in his big pale hands and pull them into his hips, and he saw Clair hold herself there and bring her nails down along his back in a way that Bill knew. He steadied the binoculars and watched Sizemore lift his hands and pull Clair's face away from his with both hands in her hair and say something to her, and then he watched Clair smile and kiss the man again quickly but with a ready heat that Bill also knew well and could see all over her through the glasses.

He watched Clair dress, putting on cutoff shorts and one of his old shirts and then the overalls and her shoes and socks, while Sizemore put on his shirt without buttoning it and stood watching her dress. Then Clair took the man's hand and they walked across the beach and up the bank and disappeared into the pine woods.

He watched for another two or three minutes and saw nothing more happening in the cove. Then he put the binoculars back in the pack and saw that his hand was shaking, and he thought fleetingly about how much of his life had come to him through lenses. Bracing himself, he took his head in his hands and closed his eyes, still seeing Clair up on her tiptoes, her face turned upward—but the sickening terror he was waiting for didn't come. Instead, Bill felt himself go suddenly and completely calm and available in a way that seemed instantly familiar. It was the way he had always felt just before soccer games: when there was nothing left to do but play, and he was actually trotting onto the field and his consciousness seemed to have drained out of his head into his body. And after all the frustration and fear and horror of the past sixteen or seventeen hours, Bill felt nothing now other than an exuberance of readiness riding up over his exhaustion and filling and energizing him like pure oxygen.

Holding Brando's muzzle, he told him in a whisper to be a good dog and a quiet dog, and that it was important for him not to bark, and Brando looked back at him sleepily and fondly with his amber eyes, lay down, and tucked his nose under his tail.

Then Bill strapped the Buck sheath knife onto his belt and crawled out from beneath the spruces.

CHAPTER
TWELVE

She had never been so glad in all her life to see water as when they walked through the marsh of cattails and spotted the pond for the second time a little way ahead of them. She had wanted to please and impress him with not getting tired or thirsty, but in fact she was very tired, and thirstier than she had ever been, though she had not complained or even let him know that, and when she saw the water she wanted to run to it and throw herself into it and drink until she burst. But he caught her arm when she started for the pond and led her uphill into some tall pine trees and had her sit out of sight of the water while he lay on the ground a few yards ahead of her, looking down at the pond for what seemed like an hour, lying as still as if he were dead.

She had never seen anyone who could be as still as he was when he was still, or as quick and fluid when he moved. He moved and was still like an animal, she thought—some large but quick, graceful animal like a lion whose life depended on movement and stillness. That was one of the reasons she was with him, she told herself, and she would learn to move and be still in the same way.

When he stood up and walked back to her, she watched him come and looked up into his face when he stopped in front of her, and told him simply, without whining, "I'm thirsty. I want to get something to drink."

But he said they would make camp first. He wanted, she could tell, to make her wait for the water, and she knew she could wait all night if he wanted her to. She watched him build a tent and make a bed for them inside it with the skin of the deer laid over a mattress of pine needles he heaped together. She watched him build a neat, quick little fire and, when it was going well, put some of the deer meat cooking above it on sticks, and watching it cook, she realized she was almost as hungry as she was thirsty and felt she could happily eat a piece of the meat raw.

"Alright," he said finally. "Now you can go get some water."

She ran down the bank and over a stony beach and took her clothes off quickly at the edge of the water, knowing he was watching her. She walked into the water up to her waist, drinking from her cupped hands as she walked until she couldn't drink any more. And then she swam out into the pond with the lowering sun still strong and hot on her head and shoulders, taking strength from the cold grip of the water on her body. When she felt thoroughly cleaned and renewed, she swam back in. While she was drying herself he jumped off the bank, landing on the beach below silently, with a cat's poise, and walked out into the pond shirtless to drink and splash himself, and she stood on the beach in the last of the sun watching him, feeling possessed and controlled by his size and strength and will as completely as if he were an ocean current that she was caught in and would ride in until she died, and outside of which she had no way of moving.

When he walked out of the pond she went to him and kissed him with all the heat that was on her then, and he put his fingers in her hair and pulled her face away and asked if she was ready to tell him what she wanted, and she said yes, more than ready, but she was hungry too, and he grinned and told her he would feed her. After she had dressed she took his hand, feeling the coarse hardness that every part of his body had, and it led her back up the bank and back into the pine trees.

They sat on the ground beside the fire and ate part of the deer heart and liver and all of the tenderloin. He cut pieces of the meat off the sticks with one of the two knives he wore on his belt and put them into her mouth. She chewed each piece slowly before swallowing it and felt like she had never really tasted meat before. He ate silently, watching her, and she could tell from his face now that it was finally almost time.

When they finished eating he walked back down to the pond and filled a metal cup with water. He boiled the water in the cup and poured tea into it, and after the leaves had settled to the bottom of the cup they drank the bitter black tea with a little sugar that he carried in a small leather bag. During all of this he didn't say anything but watched her in a way that made it clear what he was thinking, and it pleased her that she knew exactly how to act and move to keep his eyes on her.

"You're not much of a conversationalist, are you?" she said to him once, teasing him as she passed him back the cup of tea.

"My ex-wives talked all the time," he said. "I'm tired of it. I'll talk enough to you when we get to where we're going and I have something to say. You might be surprised how much I talk to you then and what I have to say."

"I want you to talk to me when you're ready," she said, "so I can know about you. How many ex-wives do you have?"

Red tossed the last of his tea and the leaves on the fire and watched the smoke they made.

"Answer me. I want to know. Tell me about them."

"One was German, one was Canuck, one had one eye. The last one was an Indian. There's nothing to tell—all of them were garbage. Don't worry," he said, looking at her. "You'll know about me all right. And what do you want now?"

"Now?"

He didn't answer her.

"I want to take some water and meat to my friend. And then I want you up inside of me," she said, holding his eyes. "All afternoon and all night. That's what I want. Can you do that?"

He didn't answer her for a while and his eyes didn't say what he was thinking. "Your friend can wait."

"All right. But first I want to rub your back. Then I want you to rub mine."

"I don't rub backs," he said.

"You can learn," she said. "That's what I want."

He grinned at her faintly and said, "Alright."

"Take off your shirt and lie down," she told him.

"Where?"

"Here. By the fire."

He slipped off his shirt and lay down on the pine needles by the fire with his face turned away from it. She kneeled over his narrow hips and put her hands with the fingers spread down onto the strange, hard terrain of his back, resting them there until it felt familiar and her hands were warmed. She began where his back came out of the buckskin pants in two rounded ridges of muscle along his spine, pushing down and upward along those ridges to his shoulder blades, then drawing the heels of her palms back down them slowly. His muscles were tense at first and it felt like massaging stones, but then he began to relax, and when she could work the muscles with her fingers she moved up to his shoulders and the humps of muscle rising from his shoulders to his neck.

As she was rubbing his neck, pushing with her thumbs held together from the base of it up to his skull, he grunted and the eye that she could see closed. Her hands were hot now and she could feel his waist between her thighs rising and falling slowly against her in his relaxation, and she leaned down and drew her tongue along his neck where she was rubbing and then up around his ear. She put the tip of her tongue lightly into his ear and lay down along his back, massaging his head with her hands now, and whispered into his ear, "Don't move. I'm not finished, but I want to do the rest with my clothes off."

He didn't move or say anything or open his eye as she stood up over him.

She backed up a few steps and then reached behind her, without taking her eyes off him, to exactly where she knew the axe was, standing at the base of the tree where he had hung his bow and pack, and picked it up with her right hand and brought it around her legs and took it in both hands, and the feel of it made her think of herself chopping firewood on canoe camping trips with Bill in Maine, and she held that image in her mind.

She stepped astride him, her feet just as they had been when she stood up from him, and raised the axe quickly overhead and swung it down as hard as she could.

She didn't even see him open his eye, but in the second while the axe was falling he must have felt or heard or sensed something, and just before it hit him squarely in the back of the head where she was aiming, he started to rear upward and the blade caught him behind the left ear and she felt it glance off his skull rather than crack through, but it had still hit him hard and it carried away his ear and what looked to her like part of his jaw along with a patch of scalp, and his upper body—which had been humped up and rising—collapsed again, and his hands pushing him upward opened and closed, opened and closed, opened and closed, digging holes through the pine needles into the ground, and then stopped moving and he was motionless, with Clair standing over him still holding the axe, certain he was dead.

When she saw no movement from him for a full minute, she turned and threw the filthy axe away from her into the woods, but as the momentum of her throw carried her body around she saw him lurch up off the ground as if he were being pulled upward by strings, with what looked like half his face hanging away from his head and a knife in his right hand. He looked at her, his face pale, his eyes blinking rapidly, blood coursing down his chest, and lifted his left hand tentatively and pressed the hanging part of his face back in place, standing in a crouch and wobbling on his feet, holding the knife out in front of him, pointed at her. Clair watched him and waited for him to fall, believing he could not live long with his head that way and with all the blood, and wanting to see him die. But he held his face in place with his hand and took an unsteady step toward her. Then in the next second he seemed to be flying at her out of the crouch, the knife flashing ahead of him, and Clair turned and ran into the pines, hearing him shout something and then a muffled thudding sound, as if he had fallen or run into something. But she did not turn to look back.

She ran, feeling winged, dodging the trees and cursing herself in her mind for having thrown away the axe, until she was out of breath. Then, still running, she looked behind her over her shoulder and did not see him. She ran for another fifty feet and threw herself to the ground behind a big fallen pine, crawling up into the branches and pressing herself flat against the trunk, and lay there listening to the blood pounding in her head and the ragged heaving of her lungs.

She did not move for five minutes by her watch. Then she looked up over the trunk and scanned the woods carefully in the direction she had run from without seeing or hearing anything.

She was certain he was dead. He had to be dead with that wound and loss of blood, and he had probably fallen and died right after rushing her. But he had surprised her once, and Clair did not intend to let him do it again. She would wait here, she decided, for another fifteen or twenty minutes before letting herself be positive. Then she would go back the way she had run and find Dray and set him free, and both of them would go and see the man dead.

She pressed herself against the trunk of the fallen tree, listening to her breathing slow, feeling potent as some wild animal. All of her life she had hated violence, thinking of it as belonging to a world she didn't even inhabit, let alone understand. Not once in that life before ten minutes ago had she ever struck another human being, and now she had hit a man as hard as she could in the head with an axe, and Clair felt no guilt or horror or pity over that violence, but only a thrilling freedom and strength in knowing that she had surely killed him, with help from the woman C. J.

She had first begun to get C. J. in the sweat lodge the night before—seeing that version of herself living the cold, pure, severed life he had described to her, hearing what the woman would say while taking a dead muskrat out of a trap, while canoeing with him the fourteen miles into town once a month for supplies . . .

She had gotten more of C. J. seeing his deerskin clothes and having her hair greased by him. And when he lay down with her on the bearskins and kissed her throat and chest and breathed against her, and she felt the drowsiness starting to take her and carry her away, she had rested her hands on his wide, strong back covering her and realized as she drifted off that she was feeling that back with hands that wanted to massage and explore it, and then she had known that she had a role now, all of it—the logic, the voice, the movements, even the thoughts—if she should need it.

And after the horror at the camp that morning, she had lain tied and gagged on the four-wheeler while he sat in a tree waiting to kill her husband if he followed, realizing a little at a time how much she did need the role and then looking at it, examining it, feeling herself in it, before she put it on and zipped it up. Seeing herself in the role, Clair had believed that she could make it win both his confidence and as much of his attention as she would need if she played it perfectly, and she was so certain she could do that that she decided to risk everything from the very beginning on her sense of what he wanted the woman C. J. to be.

As soon as he untied her and removed the gag from her mouth, C. J. slapped him and told him that she would not be gagged or tied up or hit, and Clair could tell by the way he looked at her that she had it right and would not have to think about it again, but just drop into the woman's head and body. And so C. J. walked a few steps away and took a piss, something Clair badly needed to do, too.

She had not once, all day, come out of the role: not when they were backtracking up the railroad tracks with him spraying away their scent and her nearly panicked with the realization that there was no way now that Bill could find her, that she was on her own; nor when the helicopter passed over them the first time and then flew on, its disappearing sound seeming to mince her last hopes of rescue; nor right after that when the man caught Dray and she believed he would kill him and from then on had to act for Dray as well as herself; not even when she learned that Portia was dead—the worst and hardest moment of the day— and had to tell Dray she was with the man because she wanted to be (having to *believe* that and *feel* it—seeing the awful hatred on his face and having to meet it with indifference on her own);

not even when she found out that Bill had not come after her, as she needed more than anything to believe, but had gone back to town for help. Though it had taken everything she had, she had acted through those terrible minutes with Dray—and later through watching Red tie him to a tree and cut him—by telling herself over and over that now she had to kill the man for Portia and Dray as well as for herself, and that the more believing and trusting she could make him, no matter what it took, the more insulting his death would be.

And then they were at the pond and C. J. had brought Clair up to the exact place to which she had to bring her: With her hands rubbing the man's back, with her tongue in his ear, C. J. had gotten Clair the relaxation, the closed eyes, the moment of trust she needed, and when that moment came, Clair had not hesitated but thrown off the role as she stood up, picked up the axe, and struck— not even needing, as she had been afraid she might, to think of Portia murdered, or of Dray tied to a tree and screaming around his gag, or of the baby the man would have had her kill.

She had simply taken the axe in her hands and swung it without hesitation; then she had felt all through her body that she was free. She had run through the woods with the wild strength of that freedom, feeling reborn into some new winged form. And now lying pressed into the fallen tree, she realized that whether the man was dead or not, the old Clair was.

When fifteen minutes had gone by she stood up and stretched, looking around at the woods now as if she knew them. She would go back and get Dray and they would go see the man dead. Then they would walk around the pond until they found the trail Red had told her about that led to Canada. They would walk until it got too dark to walk anymore, then sleep in the woods, and walk again the next day until they came out somewhere or until Bill found them. She wasn't worried about getting out of the woods. She wasn't worried about anything now, not even the moment when she could no longer put off dealing with Portia's death.

She walked toward the pond, then turned up the bank above the shoreline. A raven flapped and cawed out of the woods behind her and Clair watched it fly out over the pond, cawing irritably. She was watching the raven's shiny blackness against the steely, dimming blue of the sky above the pond when she thought she heard something move behind her, then did hear a hoarse whisper.

She started to turn, her mouth opening involuntarily to scream, when she was grabbed by an arm around her waist and a hard hand against her mouth and hauled backward off her feet into the woods.

CHAPTER THIRTEEN

Bill crawled on his stomach through the woods behind the cave of spruces until he was well away from the rim of the bowl. Then he got to his feet and started walking, stopping beside a tree after every half-dozen steps to look and listen. Staying a few hundred feet back in the woods from the western edge of the bowl, he walked south, watching and listening as much as he walked. He knew Red could not hear him this far away even if he were sloppy with his walking. But he also knew that everything depended on his being able to come up onto the place where Red and Clair were without being seen or heard, and that he would need all the practice he could get in moving quietly and slowly before he got to that place. Because of the fire Red had built, Bill believed that he was convinced he was not being followed, and that he was probably planning to camp where he was until the next morning. He figured there was less than an hour of daylight left, and he wanted to time his stalk on Red's camp so that he arrived within sight of it with just enough light to see where he was walking. Then he would wait there until dark—until the right chance came to kill Red Sizemore.

As he stalked down the woods, Bill thought about how best to use the knife—whether to stab with it underhand or overhand and where exactly to plunge it to find the heart—and those uncommon thoughts felt familiar, even comfortable to him. A number of times he put his hand on the knife's handle at his hip, pushing his thumb up against the metal tang, and felt a strong, sure, thoughtless hunger for using it, and behind the hunger a hatred he didn't need to look at but knew would be there giving him whatever killing strength and appetite he needed, until either he or Red Sizemore was dead. Thinking how he would kill the man whose friend had killed Portia and who himself had stolen Clair, Bill felt that all the things he was in the real, normal world had become only one thing now, and that thing more real and with more purpose than any of the others.

After fifteen minutes of stalking, he believed he was a little over halfway to the southeastern end of the pond. Brando had not made a sound and he knew there was no way his travel could have been seen or heard from Red's camp, so he got onto his hands and knees and crawled to the edge of the bowl to find out how far he had left to walk.

Lying on his stomach, he could still see the smoke rising from Red's fire, though there was less of it now, and he figured the camp was about a quarter of a mile away. He decided he would wait where he was, well hidden in a clump of yellowing tamaracks, for ten or fifteen minutes and stalk the last quarter mile as close to dark as possible. The oval of sky above the pond had gone a dim, silvery blue. Long, feathery mare's-tail clouds were pushing into it from the west, announcing a front that Bill guessed would finally end the long stretch of hot weather with rain that night, almost certainly followed by cold.

He had just lifted his head to look down the pond again when he heard a sound behind him in the woods. It was the sound of something walking, and it was coming his way. He rolled farther into the clump of tamaracks, drew the knife out of its sheath, and got to his hands and knees. The walking passed him, very nearby, and then stopped as a raven came cawing out of the woods and flew over the pond. Bill looked up through a screen of yellow needles and saw Clair, standing six feet away at the edge of the bowl staring out over the pond. He waited for a moment without hearing any other movement. Then he put the knife back in its sheath and stood up very slowly.

"Clair!" he whispered. The instant she started to turn he could tell she was going to scream and so he leaped at her, grabbing her up from behind with his right arm around her waist and covering her mouth with his left hand, and pulled her backward into the tamaracks and then onto the ground.

He lay on top of his wife, holding her face to the ground with his hand over her mouth until she quit struggling. After a moment he still didn't hear anything outside the trees and Clair was struggling again, so he let her turn over, with no means other than faith of knowing who would come up looking at him—the woman he had watched kiss and hold Red Sizemore on the beach as if she belonged to him, or his own Clair. Her head came up and around, her eyes searching for his, and when they found them seeming to Bill to fly out of her and into his own eyes and to come home there and slam the door and lock themselves in. Then he let his hands and his heart really touch her for the first time, feeling relief and joy and love and gratitude going off inside himself like little bombs, feeling exploded with relief and happiness, and whispered, "Hello, Dill," his name for her. "Where's your friend?" Clair looked up at him, her face as torn with joy and relief as he felt his own was, and Bill knew without needing another word from her that he had his wife back. He knew too that whatever it was she had done with Red Sizemore that had brought them to this place meant no more to him now than the dead tamarack needles he was lying on.

"I killed him," she said, her face fierce and exultant and loving. She pulled his head down to her and kissed him, her hands in his hair. She pulled away finally and said, "Back at the place where he made a camp: I hit him with an axe. I knew you'd come. Oh God, Billy, sweetheart, I knew you'd come. How did you get here?"

"I walked and waited for you. Are you sure he's dead?"

"He got up after I hit him and tried to follow me. But he has to be by now. There was so much blood. Half his face . . . I ran and hid and waited and he didn't follow. I was going back to get Dray and then go see him dead and to kill him again if he wasn't."

"*Dray?*"

"He followed us, and Red caught him. He told me you had gone to town to get help . . . And he told me about Portia."

"Where is he?"

"On the other side of this pond. Red cut his Achilles tendon and tied him to a tree. But what am I going to do about Portia, Billy?" she asked in a lost whisper, looking up at him. "How am I ever going to be able to live with that?" Bill didn't answer her, nor did he know how to. She stared at him for a moment, then looked away and said, "I want to go and see him dead."

"So do I, but not now, Dill. If he's still alive, we need to get to Dray before he does."

She reached up and closed the eyelid of his right eye and stroked it with her forefinger as she did at night when they were twined together before they went to sleep because it made her feel safe. "I can't tell you how sorry I am. Or how hard I prayed for you," she whispered.

Bill bent and kissed her lightly on her nose, on each eye and then her mouth, with so much feeling and with so much to say that he could say nothing, but took her hand and stood up and pulled her to her feet. "Can you find where Dray is?"

"I think so. Yes."

"We'll go around the north end. Follow close behind me until we get to the other side and walk quietly, Dill," he told her.

They walked carefully going around the pond, pausing frequently to listen and watch and not speaking. When they were well down the east side, Clair motioned to a thick stand of spruces and they both got down on their bellies and crawled into the trees. In a minute or two they came to a little opening and Bill could see Dray sitting on the far side, his hands and feet tied together around a spruce, his head hanging back motionless and directly away from the tree, as if he had stretched it back to scream. Bill watched him for almost a minute without seeing any movement. Signaling to Clair to stay where she was, he took the Buck knife out of its sheath and crawled across the mossy opening, certain his friend was dead.

But when he touched Dray's back he felt the unmistakable warmth of life, and when Dray lifted his head and grunted, Bill felt like shouting with relief.

"It's me. Be quiet," he whispered. On his knees, he cut the gag off Dray's head and then the ropes from around his wrists and ankles, seeing the dried blood on Dray's pant leg and boot top and hearing him grunt again, with pain this time, when the cutting knife drew the rope tight around his ankles.

When Dray was free he rolled over onto his side, holding his right leg, his face gray with suffering. "Up to spec, Billy Boy," he said.

"Can you crawl?"

"You bet."

"Let's go."

Back in the spruces Bill watched Dray and Clair look at each other and knew instantly from Dray's eyes what he had seen and what he believed.

"Dray . . . ," Clair began.

Bill interrupted her, whispering. "Clair hit him with an axe. He may or may not be dead. I want to assume he's not until we can find out for sure tomorrow in the daylight. I have a hide at the north end of the pond. We can spend the night there. Can you walk?"

They found that he could, supported by Bill on his right and Clair on his left, as long as he put no weight on his right foot. The three of them walked that way, silently except for Dray's occasional grunts, back up the pond through the darkening woods.

When they were fifteen or twenty feet from the little cave of evergreens, Bill heard Brando start to growl in the low monotone that always preceded his barking. "Quiet," he whispered. "Hush."

"Brando?" said Clair, grinning at him around Dray. "You brought that idiot?"

"We sort of brought each other."

They lowered Dray to the ground at the entrance to the cave and Clair dove into the spruces, pulling Brando's ears and kissing his muzzle as the dog rolled round delightedly under her, licking her face.

"He's been tied up here for three or four hours," Bill said, watching them. "I'm going to fix Dray up and then we should walk Brando around before it gets too dark."

"I'm all right," Dray growled. "Just give me the Percodan from the first-aid kit, then you and Shirl go walk the fucking dog."

Bill took off his fanny pack. He looked at Dray's eyes and saw that they were exhausted with misery and bleak beyond saying, but that the cold hatred and lifelessness was out of them. Shirl was an old, fond name of his for Clair, one all tied up with Portia.

"Watch who you're calling Shirl," she told him lightly from the back of the evergreen cave. Dray chuckled, and that, Bill knew, was that.

He took Dray's boot off, sterilized his ankle, wrapped it loosely with an Ace bandage from the first-aid kit and gave him the bottle of Percodan and his canteen. Then he took the space blanket out of the fanny pack and spread it next to Brando in the back of the evergreen cave and helped Dray onto it.

"We'll be back in a few minutes," he said, pulling half of the blanket over Dray.

Dray grabbed Bill's hand and squeezed it. "Hey, Clair," he said.

"Drayton?" said Clair.

"Thanks for chopping up the motherfucker." He made a noise that might have been a laugh and laid back, staring up at the knitted branches. "I couldn't have lived with him alive. I mean that."

They took Brando out into the hardwoods north of the pond and then cut back in the last of the light to the ATV trail, coming out on it farther west than Bill had walked before. The trail was wide and well cleared and ran due west.

"Do you think this is the trail he told me about that goes to Quebec?" said Clair. Bill told her he believed it was, and she stared up the trail toward Canada.

"It would be nice to just walk out, wouldn't it?" he said.

"It will be nicer tomorrow," Clair said. "After we've seen him dead."

Dray was asleep and snoring in the rear of the evergreen cave. Bill tied Brando beside him and spread the other space blanket just outside the mouth of the cave. He and Clair lay on it side by side looking out at the pond, whose outline they could still just distinguish. A wind was rising out of the southeast, and they listened to it begin to hiss in the tops of the trees along the rim of the bowl.

After awhile Clair said, "You don't believe he is dead, do you?"

"I don't know. But I know we have to think he's not until tomorrow. We have to keep each other awake and stay ready until midmorning, or even noon. If he hasn't shown by then, we'll go look for him."

"He's dead, all right," said Clair. "I killed him. I want to tell you about it now, okay? All of it."

She started talking then and talked for half an hour, in a whisper so as not to wake Dray, telling him for the first time how miserable she had been during their separation, and how hopeless and frantic it had made her to see at his father's funeral that he was his old self again and doing fine without her.

She told him about the day with Harry in Los Angeles, and then about the sheepshearing weekend at the farm and about taking the man in the barn and how it had felt like shoplifting something you didn't need or want but had to take anyway, and about how she had felt all kinds of things afterward—a little shame but also a little proud of herself, a little replenished, a little fear, a little exhilarated from having played with fire; and then the next day, nothing but a sure, absolute determination to go back to Bill and beg if she had to to stay.

She told him what Red had said to her in the phone calls all summer, and how frightened she had been that Bill would find out, and how relieved she was when the calls stopped. And then she told him what had happened the previous day and night. She told him about the life Red Sizemore had planned for her and how and where he had described it to her, and when she had realized that she could play the woman he wanted her to be and the moment that morning when she had known that she *had* to play that woman to have any chance of saving first herself and then Dray. And she told him how she had become the woman C. J. and played her perfectly, even through the awful moments with Dray, and then how she had stepped out of the role when she had to take up the axe and do the only thing she could do, and how doing that had freed her of ever having to act for a man again. She said she wanted him to know this: that whether the man was dead or not, the old Clair was definitely dead—the old, submissive, needy Clair who had danced and acted for her father all her life; who had allowed Bill to wreck their marriage by not standing up and telling him what she wanted, what he would have to do, instead of acting first the Happy Wife, for years when she was not, and then, for years also, the Patient Sufferer. That Clair, she said, was dead and gone and she wanted to tell him about the exact moment when she died. And as she described raising and bringing down the axe and the joy and liberation she had felt when she ran, Bill could hardly believe it was Clair he was listening to or, rather, knew he was hearing the exact truth from some exact truth-telling part of her he had not known well, or maybe at all, before.

When she had finished talking they lay silently for a few minutes with their arms around each other, her head on his chest.

"Is that everything?" he asked her finally.

"Everything but one thing." Clair lifted her head and looked at him, and Bill thought that he could die very happily looking up at that face, even in the dark. "I'm pregnant," she said.

He stared at the outline of her face, wishing he could see her eyes. After a moment he said, "Is that true, Dill?"

She laughed and he knew that it was.

"And here's the thing. You know it just *happened*, and when I first found out I was petrified, Billy. I've been afraid the whole time. I thought, oh no, what if . . . Well, the wonderful thing is, I'm not afraid anymore. I feel like I've been let out of jail. We'll just have it and love it and love each other, and it will grow up fine."

"It?"

"Do you want to find out? Do you care?"

"No and no."

"I don't care, either, but I hope it's a girl."

He put his hands on her cheeks and held them there, believing that even if he lived another hundred years, his life would never again have in it moments that felt as completed and achieved as these dark, silent moments felt.

He said, "Let's make a deal."

"Okay."

"Two deals. We get rid of the sheep and we stay out of the woods."

"Deal and deal," said Clair.

A few minutes later he said, "Do you smell smoke?"

After a moment she said, "I don't think so . . . Maybe, though."

Bill crawled to the edge of the bowl, and from there he could see the flicker of a small fire back in the pines at the far end of the pond. He was crawling backward to the spruces to tell Clair that they no longer had to wonder if Red Sizemore was alive or not when the music started, and it stopped both his crawling and his breath and brought the hair up on the back of his neck.

Carried across the water on the rising wind, each word distinct, a marauding female voice was singing in German, and the warlike voice and tumultuous music behind it seemed to him to be the night itself singing of coming storm. Bill crawled on back to the spruces and took his wife in his arms, and though he could not make out the features on her face and she did not speak for a moment, he could feel that she was different. He could feel with his arms that something had gone out of her and she was different.

"I thought he was dead," she said quietly, feeling light and tentative now in Bill's arms as the music rose up off the pond and whirled around them. "I wanted to kill him for Portia and Dray, and for me. But he's still *alive*, Billy, and he's playing that music on his Walkman with these little speakers that he bought to play opera for us when we got to Canada," she continued, her voice speeding up and starting to fray. "He's down there with his goddamn music *telling* me he's not dead . . ."

"Alright, alright," Bill said, pulling her head into his chest.

"Oh shit, Billy," she whispered, starting to cry noiselessly against him. "What about Portia? What are we going to do without her? Oh God, Porsh, I'm so sorry . . ."

"Baby," he said, pulling her closer to him, feeling in her crying voice and in her small body the surgings of a pain big enough to swamp them both right then. "Don't. Don't talk or think about that now. We've got to say, fuck him and his opera. Can we do that, Dill? Answer me."

After a moment, she nodded against his chest and her dry, silent crying stopped, and she said, "Yes."

"Let's say fuck him and his opera good, okay?"

"Okay," she said.

Bill looked up and saw the waning moon with a hazy ring around it just topping the pines at the lower end of the pond. "'I see the moon and the moon sees me,'" he said to Clair, the first words of a song they had sung to each other for years. Her head was resting on his chest in the place where it had rested so many times before, it seemed to Bill there ought to be a groove there for it.

After a moment she said back, "'Down through the leaves of the old oak tree,'" her voice stronger now and with more of herself in it.

Bill found her lips and kissed her, and told her with the kiss exactly how he wanted to tell Red Sizemore and his opera to go fuck themselves, and felt through her mouth and then her tongue how she thought that idea was perfect.

"We may wake up Dray," she whispered against his cheek.

Kissing her again without answering, he started to undress her and then himself and she began to help him. Without taking their mouths apart they removed their clothes slowly and quietly together, except for his shirt on her, which he unbuttoned and left under her when he rolled over on top of her and finally broke off the kiss and lifted his head to look at her in the new moonlight, the opera surging with the warm wind through their spruces.

"'That same moon that shines on me,'" he whispered to her.

Clair closed her eyes and he watched her come back completely into her face, and she smiled and reached for his head and brought it down to her chest and whispered back to him, "'Shines on the one I love.'"

Afterward, they lay still, listening to the opera and the wind rising in the trees, and the singing then was nothing more than entertainment. After awhile Bill could tell from Dray's breathing that he was awake and listening, too, and Bill wondered how long he had been awake. There were three or four angry-sounding females all singing together, and the music behind them sounded like horses and battle and people dying. And then the performance stopped suddenly, and there was just the urgent hissing of the wind in the treetops to listen to for a moment before Red Sizemore's voice boomed down the pond:

"The Valkyries, C. J. Wotan's handmaidens . . ." Bill crawled out to the edge of the bowl again, and from there he could see Red in the dim moonlight, standing at the far edge of the pond, shouting through his cupped hands: "The Valkyries carry off the *dead,* C. J. . . ." Bill backed up under the spruces and wrapped Clair in his arms and held her, but she felt full of herself now and un-afraid. "They ride down the *night* and find you *wherever you are,*" Red shouted. "And that's what *I'm* going to do, C. J. Find you wherever you are . . . Then the Valkyries can have you . . . And they'll need a *box,* C. J., to put the pieces in . . . You and your friend *sleep tight.*"

"Nice touch, the box," said Dray after a moment or two of quiet. "You guys really know how to pick your handymen."

"How do you feel?" Bill asked him.

"No pain. The Percs fixed me up."

"Good, because we're going to carry you out of here in a little while."

"To where?"

"Quebec."

"Look," said Dray, "I don't want to get into it with you again about plans, particularly since you were right the last time. But that's about five miles through the woods as I remember it from the map. At night."

"There's an ATV trail. It's shown on the map. It goes right to a little river called Halls Stream. That's the border. According to the map there are some big fields on the other side, and then a town only a couple of miles from the border."

"How do you know the trail you saw is the one on the map? How do you know it's not part of a *maze* of trails back here?"

"I don't," said Bill.

Dray sighed. "The thing is, I can't do it anyway. There's not enough Percodan in the world . . . We'd be too slow, too noisy. There's a million reasons."

"Then we all stay."

"And do what? Listen, we stay here and he hunts us down tomorrow at first light in fifteen minutes. He doesn't know you're here, right?"

"I don't think so."

"You and Clair walk out to Quebec tonight, or try to. I stay here."

"Why doesn't he hunt *you* down at first light?"

"Okay, listen to this because I'm too tired and too fucked up on these pills to talk much longer, or probably to see it straight more than once. If he comes up the east side of the pond, our tracks would lead him here for sure, unless it rains, which it's gonna do. But he won't—he'll go up the west side because he figures Clair and I will head for Canada. Cut some crutches. Drag your right foot for a mile or so. He'll think you're me with Clair and follow your tracks, and he'll take his time because he knows we'll be moving slowly. If you make it out by daylight, you can have a chopper in here before he figures out he's not going to catch you. And he wouldn't come back here then anyway. He's after Clair."

Bill didn't even have to think about it to realize that Dray had it all right. It was the only thing to do. "He won't get caught this way. You know that. The son of a bitch won't get caught."

"Yes, he will," said Clair.

Bill looked at Dray but Dray didn't say anything. "There's another way. I could go to him. Tonight. Go down there and find him and kill him."

"Dumb, Billy Boy. That would be something *I'd* try to do, except maybe not anymore."

Bill smiled. "You wouldn't charge?"

"A man learns. Either one of us or anyone else we know would wind up nothing but dead. You've already got all the flags, my friend. All you have to do is walk out."

Bill looked at Clair. "It won't be easy. It'll be a long night on that trail, and cold and probably wet." She grinned at him and didn't have to say anything. "We could leave Brando with you if you want," he told Dray. "For company."

"And protection," said Clair.

"Uh-huh," said Dray. "Well thanks, but see I might be forced to eat him. I'd take him with you if you don't want him maybe eaten. Speaking of eating, you have any of those gourmet sandwiches left?"

They split the turkey sandwich and another one four ways with Brando and finished off the last of the water. Then Bill took the flashlight out of the pack and he and Dray looked at the map, figuring bearings and distances with Dray's compass.

"Basically, any kind of west will get you to the border," Dray said. "That southeast wind is probably going to stay up all night, so if you lose the trail and the flashlight goes out on you, just keep the wind on your left shoulder."

Bill stuffed his space blanket into the pack and took out the sweater for Clair. He left Dray with one of the remaining two sandwiches and the first-aid kit, and he set up one of the canteens for him outside the spruces to catch rain when it came. When he and Clair were ready to go they crawled to the back of the cave and knelt by Dray.

"We have about nine hours until daylight," Bill said. "We should be able to make it to a telephone somewhere by then. I'll get back here as soon as I can."

Dray said, "Maybe the motherfucker will die overnight. I haven't been to church in awhile, but I'm going to lie here and pray he dies overnight. Listen, do me a favor."

"Name it."

"If he doesn't die, don't get close to him, Billy. Just get Clair out as fast as you can and leave him in the woods for the cops. Promise me."

Clair leaned over and kissed Dray on the cheek. Bill watched her rub Dray's bald head with her hand and stare into his face for a moment, and then kiss his other cheek.

"Anytime he's not performing, Babe," Dray said. "Like maybe he wasn't completely on his game a little while ago? Irishmen are famous for having this problem. See this girl comes into the cop station and says, 'An Irishman grabbed me by the tush.' 'How do you know he was Irish?' says the sergeant. 'Cause I had to show him where it was,' she says."

Bill laughed. "You were awake."

"I mean it, Billy Boy. Don't take any chances with her. Or with you."

"No," said Bill. Dray squeezed his shoulder with his right hand, and when he let him go, Bill caught a glimpse in his palm of a wallet picture of Portia. "Good luck, doofus," he said.

"You too," said Dray.

Bill untied Brando and put on the pack. Then he crawled out of the cave, followed by Clair and Brando, and stood up, holding Dray's compass and the flashlight, and stepped off into the night. "Stay close," he told Clair over his shoulder. "And keep Brando on heel."

The moon was slipping in and out of clouds now and the rising wind was bending trees against the sky. Using the flash-light occasionally, he followed the route he and Clair had taken Brando on earlier until they ran into the ATV trail. When he stopped to cut a cane, Clair said, "Shouldn't we maybe not use the flashlight?"

"I don't think he'd be looking for you now. He can't see to track until daylight. But yeah. We shouldn't need it on the trail anyway as long as we have a little moon."

He cut a forked maple branch and walked with it, drag-ging his right foot occasionally, to create a track like Dray would make. He had Clair walk ahead of him and he kept Brando in the woods, paralleling them, so the dog's tracks wouldn't show on the trail.

For a while—as he limped behind Clair's thin, light-stepping form—the chilling darkness and wind, the swaying trees and scud-ding sky produced in him an anxiety that felt like suffocation and gave him an almost irresistible urge to drop the cane and grab Clair's hand and run. But he made himself think, and walk as he imagined Dray would have to walk, and after a half hour or so his mind seemed to adjust to the night as his eyes had and he felt that he was simply walking up a trail with his wife and could do so for as long as he had to, and that the theatrics of the night could go ahead and do whatever they had to do.

The moon continued to appear through the clouds, and even without the flashlight they made pretty good time, covering what Bill figured was about a mile of the trail in well under an hour. The map had shown mostly flat terrain between the pond and the border, and he began to let himself believe that they would make it out before daybreak.

They were taking their first break, sitting off the trail beside a granite boulder, when the music started up again. Bill felt Clair freeze next to him. Brando whined and lay down. The wind was blowing the sound around but he was fairly sure it was coming from up the trail, in the direction they were headed: it was the howling German women, the warring music, and it was not far away.

"Oh God, no," whispered Clair.

"Lie down and be quiet," Bill told her. He put his arms around her and held her against the boulder while the music got weaker and then stronger. Then it stopped. In a minute or two it started again, just north of them now.

"He knows where we are," Clair whispered frantically. "He's circling us, Bill."

"He couldn't know," he told her, though he was fighting the panic of that same thought. "Be quiet."

The singing stopped, and this time it was five minutes before it started again—from behind them on the trail and very close.

"Come on," he whispered. "Take hold of my belt and don't let go. Keep Brando on heel."

Walking as quietly as he could through trees with no light other than a glance or two of moon, and struggling to keep himself from breaking into a run, Bill led them north away from the trail for a hundred yards or so and then turned west, feeling the wind come onto his left shoulder and cheek as the rampaging singing started up again, upwind of them now to the east and louder, though he believed it was no closer.

Clair started sobbing then and pulled him around and buried her head in his chest.

He let her cry and held her, staring into the windy blackness. It was growing colder. He knew that he couldn't go back to the trail. Ahead of them were at least four miles of lightless, path-less woods. Bill stared into the night with desperation so heavy on him, it felt like paralysis, and thought: We could lie down here and just go to sleep. Why not?

After awhile Clair quit crying and said, "It hasn't started back," and in the dark he thought how he loved the sound of her voice.

"I don't believe it will."

"He *doesn't* know where we are, does he?"

"No. He was trying to find out, I think."

"Billy?" She put both hands on the back of his head and he knew she was looking up at him. Her voice was calm. "What are we going to do?"

He didn't know. Red Sizemore either knew where they were and was playing with them, or he was trying to find them. If he was trying to find them, the more they moved the easier they made it for him. But Bill didn't believe that even Sizemore could track at night with a disappearing moon, and he knew he had to make it to the border by daybreak if he was going to get Clair and Dray and himself out of the woods safely. Staying put felt impossible. But so did going ahead: as he looked west into the dark, all he could see there was terror and exhaustion and Red Sizemore waiting for them behind every tree.

"Billy?"

He found her mouth and kissed her. "We're going to put one foot ahead of the next."

At one point, leading Clair and Brando through the black woods in what felt like a blind lifetime of struggle and fear and frustration—feeling for almost every step with a foot before he took it, and for trees with his hands, using the weakening flashlight briefly only at an impasse and every fifteen minutes or so to check the compass—Bill suddenly remembered his father frying squirrels and singing "That's Amore" on a fall morning in the kitchen at the farm, and the memory brought him a moment of peace and comfort. Then he saw Jack Joyce splitting wood with one hand. He smelled his father's good, boozy smell and felt the warm, utter softness of his English cashmere jackets. And then he heard his father say, as if he were there walking next to Bill, "Uh-oh, Billy, I seem to have twisted this damn trick knee." "Hop aboard, then," Bill told him, as his father used to tell him, swinging his youngest son up on his shoulders to keep him up with his brothers.

"What did you say?" Clair asked behind him.

"Nothing," he said, but smiled. And for the next couple of hours he had the odd sensation that he was carrying his father with him through the woods—and it was a good, welcome, strengthening weight.

Sometime around midnight the rain began as cold, gusty showers that became a downpour. They walked through it for another two and a half hours, falling occasionally on the slick, invisible ground, feeling their way through drenched spruce thickets—just breathing, it seemed to Bill, and walking through fear as relentless as the rain, and keeping the wind on their left shoulders. And then Clair tugged at his belt and stopped and said that was it. She gave a short, self-conscious laugh and said, "I'm sorry, Billy. I can't go any farther."

The land had been sloping downhill for ten or fifteen minutes and the trees were thinner. Bill said, "Let's just get to the bottom of this slope. The last contours on the map before the border go downhill to about twelve hundred feet and then flatten out right before the border. Ten minutes," he said, and took her hand.

In ten minutes more they stopped and Clair lay down on the ground. Just ahead of them Bill could hear moving water. "I think we're here," he said, not really believing it. "I think that's Halls Stream. The border."

"Can we just rest for a few minutes, though, even if it is?" said Clair. "And try to get warm?"

"For as long as you want. Until daylight. If this is not Halls Stream, we're lost. And if it is, we have to be able to see to cross it."

With the last of the flashlight's power, Bill looked around until he found a pine blown down at the base of a little cliff out of the wind. He cut away branches from the fallen tree with his knife until he had made a space underneath it large enough for the three of them to crawl into, then he laced the branches back together over the top.

"Do you know what this reminds me of?" said Clair when they were wrapped together in the space blanket under the tree with Brando between them and with only a little of the rain making it through the branches. "The berth on that train we took that time from Montreal to the Gaspé. Do you remember that wonderful little thing?"

Bill said that he did, and also remembered having his salmon rod stolen off the train in Matane. Feeling giddy and wide awake, they talked about anything they could think of in order to stay awake—anything that didn't have Portia in it. They talked more about travel, and food and books and dumb parties they had been to. As the hours passed and the rain stopped, the subjects all began to run together and the talk got silly, and Clair said it felt like sleepover parties she had gone to at Laura Clark's house when she was in grammar school. More than once, it seemed to Bill that he was talking or listening to Clair and dreaming at the same time.

Around four o'clock, they split their last soggy sandwich three ways with Brando, and afterward Clair said she wished she had a cigarette, even though she hadn't smoked in ten years. Bill said he was glad she didn't.

"It would kill the smell of wet Brando, anyway. Don't you think he smells like a root vegetable when he's wet?"

"A rutabaga, maybe. Or is a rutabaga a root vegetable?"

"The question is, what is a rutabaga, period?"

"I have no idea," Bill thought he said. "Unless it's a root vegetable that smells like Brando."

He thought too that sometime after Clair went to sleep he observed the exact moment when the black dark cracked and began its slow dissolve. It was the third morning in a row that he had witnessed night's sleight of hand into day and felt with a lightness in his lungs and throat that moment's prerevelatory hush—its brief, stirring, unattached poise between dark and light. This morning the knowledge came to him with a small shock that one way or another this would be the last such moment he would witness for a long time if ever again, so he paid attention to it, and when it was over and the woods around him began to emerge as if being created just for him, he thanked God for the life he had had and the mate it had been his good fortune to find and have.

The next thing he knew, it was daylight and he was looking out through evergreen branches at a view he knew he would remember every detail of with inexpressible joy for as long as he lived. What he saw in that view was that Dray had been right—Bill had all the flags; all he had to do now to put Clair and Dray and himself out of danger was to stand up and walk off the field—and seeing that made it almost easy to acknowledge consciously to himself what he now realized he had known all night: Winning the game would not end it. The game would never be over for any of them until Bill found Red Sizemore in these woods and faced him.

CHAPTER
FOURTEEN

"Help me!" Red had shouted out to her when she ran and he knew he couldn't follow. And he hated that now almost as much as he hated how his body had lied to him. When he lunged at her with the knife he had known it was C. J., but when she turned and ran and he tried to follow, holding his face and scalp together, the blood had run into his eyes, blinding him, and he had somehow believed it was *Joy* he was chasing and knew he couldn't catch, blinded, and he had shouted to *Joy* to stop and help him.

Then he had run into a pine tree, and gone out again—as he must have gone out when she first hit him, because he couldn't remember anything between hearing the axe in the air and then pushing to his feet as she was throwing it away into the woods, comprehending in that instant the double treachery, hers and his own fooled body's.

When he could think again after running into the tree, his first thought had been that he didn't want to bleed to death before he could find and kill her. He crawled back to the dying fire and wrapped his buckskin shirt around his head and lay on his side away from the bleeding, slowing his heart rate to forty-five or fifty beats a minute, until he could no longer feel fresh blood welling into the wound. He knew he had to attend to his head quickly or infection would shut him down before morning, so as soon as he had felt strong enough he tied the shirt as tightly as he could around his head, leaving his right eye clear, and walked carefully down to the little marsh that he and C. J. had crossed coming to the pond, and gathered there and in the woods around it what he didn't already have in his pack. On the way back he checked on the man in the spruces, figuring he'd be gone and he was, and not even looking for any tracks because he knew where the man and C. J. would go eventually.

He had gotten back to his camp just after dark and rekindled the fire. Then he had set up the Walkman with the speakers and put on the opening of act 3 of *Die Walküre* and pointed the little speakers up the pond to begin what he hoped was a long, slow night of terror for her.

Then, with that done, he sat down beside the fire in the closing dark, hating how he had shouted to her to help him, and began working on himself. The compact he had bought her had fallen out of her pocket on the beach when she had taken her clothes off to swim and he had found it there when he went down to drink and put it in his own pocket, and now he untied the shirt and used the compact's mirror to look at his head. The lower half of his ear was gone, and the entire left side of his face from the scalp above where his ear had been to just above his chin was cut away from the white bone of his skull and jaw. Looking underneath the flap of his face and scalp at the angle of the cut, Red saw that a quarter-inch less deflection would have killed him, and he was grateful to that quarter-inch and the sharpness of his hearing that had won it for him only because there were deaths and deaths, the only significant difference in them being—as the

Indians had known—the amount of humor that could be drawn from them at your expense. And he knew precisely how much humor would be drawn in sports bars all over New Hampshire and Vermont from his being killed by a flatlander woman with an axe.

Red ate some partridgeberry leaves for his pain. He shoved a shredded mixture of beech bark and leaves under the flap of his scalp and into his jaw to act as an antiseptic until he could prepare a poultice. He covered what was left of his ear and the length of the axe cut with oak leaves, which were astringent and would stop any further bleeding, and bound his head up again in the shirt.

All the Valkyries were singing together when he stood up and turned off the Walkman, his head hurting too much for their overwrought, bitchy German voices. He walked down the bank to the pond and shouted into the night to C. J. exactly why he had chosen that particular musical selection for her listening enjoyment. Then he drank, and washed some of the blood off his face and chest and filled his cup with water.

Back at the fire he boiled white pine inner bark and a root of wild sarsparilla together with yarrow, bearberry, alder leaves, and juniper needles until the mixture was black and thick as molasses. When the poultice had cooled, he took the beech mulch out of his wounds and poured the thick liquid into them. Then, lying on his side with a stick of alder between his teeth to bite on, he used the compact mirror, a needle he had fashioned out of a long, supple sliver of pine, and thin strips of buckskin cut from his shirt to sew his scalp and his face back together.

When he was finished with the sewing he was tired of the company of brother pain, but he burned the end of a pine stick into a glowing point and cauterized the flesh where most of his ear had been cut off, nearly passing out twice before he finished that job. Finally, he poured the last of the poultice onto a square cut from his shirt and folded it into a bandage, and tied it tightly to the ear and along the cut with buckskin strips.

Then Red pulled his pack over to him and took from it the pint bottle of rye he had thought about for the last hour and a half and saved for now. He lay on his back and drank off half the whiskey slowly while he studied the storm-announcing moon and felt his face and head already beginning to burn from the poultice.

In a little while he was hungry and he took what was left of the deer heart and liver off the sticks and ate them, feeling that he could eat fifteen deer hearts and livers if he had them, and the size and passion of his body's appetite amazed and gratified him as it often did.

All of his life Red had been hungry for everything there was, and never full, so that now hunger and living seemed to be the same thing to him and death nothing but a permanent loss of appetites. All of his wives had been hungry, too, or at least had started out that way, and he had believed he recognized a bigger hunger than any of theirs in the Joyce woman, though it was more hidden and subtle, and at first had been hard to see at all under her flatlander, rich-woman prissiness.

Red had believed that her hunger was a monster, like his own, that she kept locked in a cage. When he saw it roar out of her in the barn, he had seen that it was not only like his own but equal to it, for once, and had seen on the barn ceiling in living color that she was the right one to share the big meat course of his life. His body had seen that. His mind had thought from the beginning that she was twenty-five miles of bad road, but his body had won out as usual. And after a rocky start the woman *had* seemed, even to his mind, to have come overnight to exactly where he wanted her to be. All day she had seemed perfect, or even better than perfect. And now that he let himself think about it for the first time, Red had no idea what had gone wrong, only that his body had let itself be deceived, and that had nearly gotten him killed in a laughable way. It was because of what she knew about him that the woman had to die, but it was because of that deception that she would die a little at a time.

After a few minutes he felt strange in the head from the beginning of the fever that he knew he would have to go through, and his pain was bad. The wind that had come up was rising, so he crawled into his tent and pulled the little doeskin over him and ate some more partridgeberry leaves and finished the bottle of rye. In a sort of waking dream then he saw Joy, as she had been when he first met her five years ago, when she served him breakfast at Bradford Junction—thin, but even then with big tits—and thought maybe if she could get thin again he would take her north with him: get thin and drop the hokey Indian shit, and learn finally how to dream big, which she had never figured out how to do, hard as Red had tried to teach her. But then, he thought, no woman seemed to be able to learn how to dream big, or to remain big-hungry. Sooner or later they all settled, like Joy.

He had met her in the middle of his Indian obsession—when he was learning herb, root, and plant medicine, learning tanning and canoe- and bow-making—and Joy was full-blood Abenaki, even though she had been adopted and raised by a white couple in Nashua. She had gone to some college in New York on a minority scholarship and had been out of it for only three years and was teaching at Kearsarge Junior High and waitressing on weekends when Red met her and gave her a life.

She had been a thin, smart, pretty Indian girl with a big appetite for sex and beer and for fitting into white society and being a success there. She had had no real knowledge of her roots, no real pride in being Native American, and no anger. Red gave her those things. He had gotten her reading the right books, gotten her proud, and finally plenty pissed-off at whites. And he had gotten her dreaming a little. He had made her see that the entire country had a guilty hard-on for Native American crafts, and that there was serious money to be made there. "Support your heritage, and your heritage will support you," he advised her, quoting a bumper sticker he had seen on the Toyota 4×4 of an Indian bowmaker.

Joy had learned to make baskets, jewelry, skin clothing, fetishes. Within a year he had talked her into quitting her teaching job and changing her name to Swift Otter, and for a couple of years the two of them had traveled around to fairs and powwows together, and Joy would sell her crafts while Red gave archery and knife-throwing demonstrations, both of them dressed in buckskins and beaded things that she made.

Then Red had gotten sick of the whole Indian gig. He quit going to the fairs and started up again with other women and staying out all night. He told Joy that she wasn't getting rich because she wasn't hungry enough and was too dumb to learn to dream big.

She went from beer to vodka. She got fat. She got jealous. She got angrier and angrier. And then she had a kid on him, something he had warned her not to do.

Right after Red had moved Joy into the old, ruined house in Bradford that had belonged to his parents, he had married her in it, using himself as the minister this time in a sort of half-invented woodland Indian ceremony in which they had cut their palms with a knife and mixed blood and sworn that with the mixing they would carry each other's hearts with them wherever they went.

Then a week later they had burned the house down in what Red told her was a purging of their old lives, and had built a tee-pee to live in, and then a hole in the ground for the winter that he told her would be the foundation of their new house and life. But he had never gotten around to putting up the house with the insurance money he collected, and after Joy had the kid on him he had no further intentions to.

He was just waiting then for his life to change again. And to calm her down on the few occasions when he was home, when she got drunk and started throwing things and blaming him for how fucked-up her life was—with nothing in that life anymore but liv-ing in a hole and dragging her crafts around to pissant little fairs while he tried to screw every white-trash bimbo in New Hamp-shire—he had made up a story about taking her and the kid to Quebec to live on a lake away from everything, and he would tell her about that life and she would shut up.

Now, going into the fever of poultice healing, with that clean, remote life perfectly planned and only days away from him but with no one else to live in it, he thought again that if Joy could lose weight . . . if she could drop all the Indian shit that she had settled for along with the kid, and lose weight and learn to dream . . .

After awhile when he felt good enough to walk, he got up. The southeast wind was high now. It was colder and he could feel the coming rain. He put on what was left of his shirt and cut a hole in the middle of the doeskin to put his head through so that it hung down over his chest and back. Then he took the little tent down and put on the poncho over his day pack and shouldered his bow and quiver.

His plan was to make the rest of the night as terrifying and sleepless as possible for the woman and her friend, and then at daybreak to station himself along the old ATV trail to Quebec and wait for them to come to him. He knew that if they didn't try to walk out on the trail, he would find them anyway and probably quickly, even if it rained hard. From daylight on he figured he had no more than two hours of work to do—an hour to find C. J. and the man and to kill him, and another hour to kill her. Then he would scatter pieces of her body all the way to Saint-Malo for the coyotes and stay with his friends there until he was well enough to put his black ship in the water and sail it north, with a pirate's face now as well as soul. Between now and daylight all he had to do was keep moving through the fever and keep himself entertained.

He walked northwest, closing his eyes for a couple of minutes at a time to accustom himself to moving through the total darkness he knew he would have when the moon was lost altogether, feeling his body come up to that challenge sense by sense through the fever and pain, as if a bunch of little emergency switches were being thrown, until by the time he cut the ATV trail a mile and a half or so from the pond, he felt as capable in the dark as a lynx.

He stopped there and played a little music, just in case they were hiding near the trail. Then he moved around, making circles off a west-to-east axis, turning the Walkman on and off and holding the speakers out from his waist. The bitchy shrieking bothered the pain in his head, but he figured it bothered C. J. more. His plan was to go all the way around the pond this way, making certain she heard him no matter where she and the man were hiding. But when he crossed the ATV trail again nearer the pond, his head happened to be down when the moon cleared for a second and he thought he saw boot prints on the hardpacked dirt of the trail. He waited for the moon again and this time he could see plainly her track heading west, followed by a man limping with a cane.

"I'm a sonofabitch," said Red, and he would have laughed out loud if it hadn't been for his head. C. J. and a guy with a sev- ered Achilles were trying to walk out into a rain- and windstorm in the dark on a trail that led to Quebec, alright, as he had told her it did, but through jogs and intersections with other trails that would be impossible to follow at night. Ballsy as it was, he figured it was C. J.'s decision, and he applauded her for it, though the net effect was that it would get her killed sooner rather than later.

Red stowed the Walkman in his pack and set off up the trail, wanting to catch them while he still had enough moon to watch her face when he killed her. Though he was walking quickly and knew the first trail intersection was a couple of miles away, he kept his eyes, out of habit, on the track—a strange track, a track he didn't like much—and when it stopped he noticed it.

He walked another hundred yards up the trail and saw that it didn't resume; then he came back to where it ended and looked around the large granite boulder just off the trail, waiting on the moon, and saw there what it was he hadn't liked about the track: Going north from the boulder it was now the track of a woman, a dog, and a man with no limp or crutch. Too neat. Too regular, too quick for a man in the kind of pain C. J.'s friend would be in. He wrote it off to the fever that he hadn't realized all of that ear- lier. She was probably with her husband and the dog he had seen in the Jeep back at the deer camp—which made no difference to Red beyond the facts that they could move a little faster and that he had less appetite for killing the husband than the stocky little bald man who had shot up Bucky and who he now knew was cached up somewhere nearer the pond.

He figured C. J. and her husband were looking for a lie off the trail, a place to spend the night, and that they might have found one close by, so he walked carefully, having to wait once almost ten minutes for moon enough to follow their trail north; but then when he saw, with the very last of the moon, that the track turned west again, Red changed his mind.

Reeling a little from the fever and the wind, he stood facing west and closed his eyes in the total dark and let his body take over. It told him what they were trying to do and how they were doing it, and Red knew that he could follow them with just his body's intuition as he had followed deer when he couldn't track for some reason, and that he would find them if he could stay well enough. He even thought he could see with his closed eyes the place where they would meet at dawn, and he directed his body to take him there.

The fever peaked in him about an hour after the rain started, and the visions it brought, along with the pounding pain in his face and head, nearly drove him crazy. With the wind keening in the trees and the rain thundering against his poncho and clawing at the bandage on his face, Red believed for a while that he saw Joy running ahead of him in the woods and he needed her to help him, but there was blood in his mouth and he couldn't make her hear. Later he saw Joy again, who became C. J. this time, who was on a horse and galloping out in front of him, and when he tried to run after her he fell into a hole in the ground, the cellar hole of some old, dead life.

Over the next hours, while his body traveled the black ground on autopilot, C. J. and Joy and his German wife, Katrina—who had dreamed big enough to sell her house and her mother's jewelry to start up the first of the karaoke taverns that Red had told her would go into franchise and make them rich, but not big enough to borrow money and try again when that one went tits up and so had settled for managing a little bar in Concord after Red had thrown her out—and his French-Canadian wife, Annette, and his first wife, the vivacious, one-eyed biker slut, Jill, all ran from Red, sometimes taunting him, and his mouth or eyes were always filled with blood and he couldn't make the women hear him or stop. Shifting into and out of one another, they ran and rode down the stormy night ahead of him, weapons flashing, their laughter like thunder, calling out to each other "Ho-Yo-To-Ho"— as uncatchable and proud and overwrought as the Valkyries themselves.

At one point, in pursuit of Jill, he fell—something he had never done before in the woods, not even as a child. He lay where he had fallen on his back and let the rain pour over him like accusations and he demanded of the fever that it break and fall away. But when he stood up fifteen minutes later the fever was still raging and he knew then that he was not going to be well until he could get to some real antibiotics and maybe not even then, and he told all natural medicines that they could go and fuck themselves.

In less than another hour he was where he wanted to be and he felt a little better, though light-headed and with a ringing in his ears. He knew that C. J. and her husband could not possibly have reached the border yet, and he figured that even if they did reach it before daybreak, they would not cross the river in the dark.

Red climbed the tallest tree he could find, one just inside the woods where they met the meadow running down to Halls Stream. From the tree in daylight he knew he would have a view of nearly a mile up and down the stream, with the Paquette Boy Scout campground and fields on the other side. He expected that C. J. and her husband would appear in that view sometime after daybreak and he would walk up to them and kill her so that she could see him when he did it, and also watch herself die. The husband he would kill first and quickly with an arrow, and he would be sorry to do it.

If for some reason they did not appear by seven or eight o'clock, Red knew he would have to go on into Saint-Malo and get himself well. Finding her and killing her after that would be more work and would put off his new life for a while—but not much work, and not for long.

He sat in the crotch of the tree in a cold, rain-clearing wind. The moon was back out, low in the western sky, and Red watched a flock of birds fly across it from north to south, a flock so large, it took over thirty seconds for its length to pass across the face of the moon. The birds were too small to be ducks and he thought maybe it was a huge migrating flight of woodcock or wisps of snipe headed south—probably flying with their eyes closed. He settled himself against the tree to wait for dawn. He could hear his mind telling him not to wait, but to get down out of the tree, walk into Paquette, rouse a doctor, and get a shot of something quick; telling him he might be killing himself just to kill the woman. But his body knew that a man had to stand for something—even if it was not letting a deceiving flatlander woman get away with hitting you in the head with an axe after making a complete fool and potential joke-butt out of you. His body was happy where it was in the testing, honest October cold and it told the cowardly mind to shut the fuck up and go to sleep for an hour or two.

What Bill was looking at when he came awake seemed at first to be some dream vision of a new world. The wind had died. There were big, voluptuous autumn clouds in the western sky, fluffed and white as fresh laundry and shot through with pink and orange from the sun rising behind him. And between the clouds, widening as he watched, was the tenderest, freshest blue sky he had ever seen, a sky so guileless and new that it might have been the first blue sky of the first morning on earth. It was a sky to give anyone courage and hope, and beneath it and the clouds were miles of fenced and cultivated fields—a treeless paradise, it seemed to him. In the foreground was a meadow at the edge of the trees, dropping to a small, lively river, and on the other side, only seventy or eighty yards from where and he and Clair and Brando lay, were a dozen gray tents in a field. Best and most miraculous of all, moving around the tents were human beings—men and boys in uniforms, building fires, boiling water, brushing their teeth . . .

He woke Clair and watched her see this idyll of salvation across the river, watched her eyes widen as she realized it was not a dream, and saw the happiness and relief flood into her face. Then they crawled out from beneath the fallen pine and walked out of the woods, letting Brando run ahead of them and across the little meadow.

Before they reached the river, the people in the camp spotted them and stood gaping, and Bill grinned, imagining what he and Clair must look like. As he stepped into the water, holding her hand, the sun breached the trees behind them, illuminating the water and the field and warming his back. He took a deep breath of the cool, misty air above the river and thought that breathing had never felt so good, and he swore to himself that he would never again take anything for granted.

As they waded through the knee-deep water, a heavy man with a florid face and a black handlebar mustache walked down to the river to greet them, followed by three or four boys. The man and the boys were dressed in tan uniforms with red waist-to-shoulder sashes and navy neckerchiefs and berets. In midstream Brando spotted the boys for the first time and started barking delightedly. When they stepped out of the water into Canada the man nodded to Clair, extended his hand formally to Bill, and loudly said, *"Bonjour."*

"He says they are two Boy Scout troops from Sherbrooke and they come here every year in the fall for a wilderness adventure retreat. He says they have never seen anyone come out of the woods before and he wants us to have breakfast with them," said Clair, translating for Bill as they walked across the field to the Scout campground. "I haven't gone into us yet. I did ask him if they had a cell phone and they do, so we . . ."

Bill had stopped and turned around just a second before to look back at the woods from which they had finally been delivered and to which he knew he had to return, so that he was facing those woods—a dark line of mostly pines and hemlocks, with the sun not yet fully emerged from behind them—when the music began there.

It sounded like Italian opera this time, a man singing, and Bill and Clair, the Scoutmaster, and the Scouts all stood in the field staring at the woods and listening.

Bill looked at Clair and saw that she was fighting back tears. He took her arm and led her on into the campground to a picnic table and sat her down there. He tied Brando to one of the pine posts holding up the fly on the Scouts' cook tent, then he knelt beside Clair.

The opera was still playing. They were surrounded now by Scouts and Scoutmasters asking questions in French. Bill looked only at Clair and said, "Listen to me because this is important. Call the police in Pittsburg and tell them to get a helicopter in to Dray at Goose Pond." He slipped out of his backpack. "The map's in here. You can give them the coordinates. Tell them about Portia and the man at the deer camp, which is marked on the map, too. And tell them about Red. Tell them he's here."

"You're going back in there," said Clair, not looking at him.

"I have to. For Portia. And for Dray, who won't have anything as long as this guy's alive and free. And mostly for us. We can't let him have our life, Clair."

"Dray told you to leave him for the police. You promised him you would."

"He said that for me. He knows there are no police here or anywhere else who would catch Red in the woods."

"I thought he was dead. All night I kept praying he would die, and then this morning when we saw that river and the fields and the sky, I knew he was dead and out of our life . . ."

"He will be. Call the police." Bill stood up.

"What are you going to do?"

It took him a few seconds to answer. "I don't know."

Clair began to cry then and held her face. "He'll shoot you with that fucking bow before you get across the river."

"I don't think so. He probably could have already shot both of us. I think he wants to talk—I think that's what the music's about this time—that and telling us he's there in the woods waiting, and always will be waiting for us."

"Go ahead, then," said Clair, sobbing through her hands. "Go ahead, big man, and get yourself killed."

Bill knelt beside her again and took her hands off her face and kissed them. "I'm not going to get killed, Dill. You and I are going to die together of old age on a dock in Florida watching manatees. Go call the police."

When he stood up again, he said to the heavy man with the mustache, speaking slowly, "Please let my wife use your telephone."

He held an imaginary phone to his ear. "Please keep her here and take care of her," he said, hoping some of this was understood.

"Of course," said the man in perfect English. "And you please be careful of the man with the bow and the Verdi."

Then Bill made himself turn and walk away from the campground, back toward the dark woods where the music was still playing.

Red's body had let him sleep longer than he wanted for two mornings in a row now and he wondered if that meant he was getting old. But the sleep had done him good and he had come awake to the dog's barking still feeling light-headed and weak from the infection but with his mind clear and strong again after the bad night it had had. He had looked out from his tree and seen a beautiful morning and C. J. and her husband walking out of Halls Stream and greeting a Scoutmaster and some Boy Scouts, elements he had not planned on. They were within range and he thought about dropping them both, but it was not the way he wanted to kill her, and then his clear mind told him, "Relax. You have plenty of time—months, years, as long as it takes. But let them know that."

He pulled the Walkman out of his day pack and popped in Pavarotti because he was sick to death of Wotan's handmaidens. The man seemed to be looking directly at him when Red turned the Walkman on and the pure, hero's voice poured out across the field. C. J. and the others turned toward him, too, then, though he knew he was invisible, and all of them and the other people in the camp stood stone-still and staring toward his woods as if watching him perform there.

He had intended to play the music only for a few seconds, then drop out of his tree and trot the woods to Saint-Malo, to his friends and medicine; but he was enjoying the singing and the stares of his audience so much that he left it on for a while, singing along with some of the phrases he had memorized, and the next thing he knew the Joyce man was crossing the river again and headed his way. Red was not surprised by much anymore, but he was surprised by this.

He took his bow off his shoulder and nocked an arrow. He left the music on to guide the man in.

Bill walked across the meadow toward the singing. He kept his right hand on the slick handle of the Buck knife, pushing his thumb against the hilt, and tried to keep the fear out of his mind, but a dreamy fatigue overtook him before he reached the stream and he found himself remembering picnics that his mother had organized at the farm every Sunday during the summer when he was a child. There would be eight to a dozen adults and as many children: they would carry hampers of food and a Sunday *Globe* and a cooler of soft drinks and beer up into the meadow above the house and lie in the tall grass that was almost the color of the grass he was walking through now and eat cold salmon and fried chicken and deviled eggs and play horseshoes or fly kites when the wind was out of the south as it was now, and whenever a child got too close to the woods, Bill's mother, with the eyes in the back of her head, would stand up and call out in her high, fun-loving voice, "Yoohoo! Don't go too close to the trees, lamby—that's where the bears eat *their* picnics." After the meadow was fenced, their first goat, Stew, just disappeared one day, and months later Bill had found his bleached bones and long, toothy skull at the top of the pasture near the edge of the woods and believed he saw finally what his mother had been driving at.

Wading the stream seemed to take a lifetime, and when he stepped out on the other side the music was louder and almost inviting somehow, and with only thirty yards or so to walk before he entered the woods Bill found that his right hand had begun to shake uncontrollably. He decided he had better sit down until his mind cleared and his hand calmed down, but it now seemed to him very important not to let the music end, so he continued to take one dreamlike step after another, feeling on the precipice of an irresistible exhaustion, and thought of the first time he had gone rock climbing with Dray at the old railroad cut in Newbury. The little granite cliff was neither steep nor tall and Dray had had him on a top-rope belay solid enough to hold a falling train car, but less than twenty feet off the ground Bill's left leg had started to jerk and he couldn't make it quit. "Sewing-machine leg," Dray had called it (the result, he explained later, of the body knowing it had no business being where it was, doing what it was doing, regardless of what the mind believed), then had yanked the rope, causing Bill to lose his footing and swing away from the cliff and learn with his flesh that he would be held by the rope; and when he swung back his legs were too busy climbing to jerk. Now, a few feet away from the woods, Bill could still tell himself, as he had Clair, that he was not walking to a sure death—that he would somehow find a way to survive this face-off with Red if only because he had to survive it for Clair and Dray. He could tell himself that and mean it, and had done so over and over on the walk from the campground. But his body was no longer listening.

"*Fuck* you and that sissy music," he shouted as he stepped into the trees. The music stopped then and so did the shaking of his hand. It was shadowy in the trees in a way that felt like running water on his skin and that brought his head suddenly sharp and wide awake again. Bill closed his eyes and breathed deeply for a moment. Then he started walking forward.

He had taken no more than five steps when an arrow dove into the ground inches from his right foot. He stared at it, and then up into the trees ahead of him without finding the man.

Concentrating on the words, he sang to himself, "'Her eyes are bright as diamonds, they sparkle like the dew.'"

He took another step, and a second arrow slapped into the ground beside his left foot. Bill looked into the trees again and said, "If you're going to shoot me, why don't you just go ahead and do it?"

"You're looking too high. Deer and people aren't imprinted to look up, which is why this works."

Bill dropped his gaze and after a moment he saw Red Sizemore sitting in the crotch of a tree fifteen or twenty feet off the ground. He was holding his bow with an arrow on the string and his face was so terrible that Bill had to force himself to look at it, but he did that.

"That's what the books say, anyway. Did you know your old man beat the shit out of me when I was eleven or twelve years old?" Red asked him.

"I heard that from my brother. I never knew if it was true or not."

"I caught trout out of that pond of his right at daylight two or three mornings a week all of June and July. One or two fish. I'd string them on my bicycle handlebars and ride through Newbury with them on my way home. Then one morning that old one-armed fart stepped out behind the barn there while I was pulling in a fish and laid into me with a willow branch." Red gave a short laugh. "I was trying to fight him. He put me down on the ground and put his knee on my back and tore my butt up with that willow. After awhile I said, 'Look here, if you don't hit me anymore, I won't take any more of your fish,' and he let me go then. He told me to call him if I wanted to fish in the pond and he'd teach me how to fly-fish, but don't ever steal from him again." He laughed. "Hell, it wasn't his trout I wanted anyway."

"What was it?" asked Bill.

"Why son, I wanted his whole fucking *life*. I'd of settled for that Garwood boat, though. The one I used to see you and your brothers in."

"And what would you settle for now?" Bill asked him. He was no longer curious about Red Sizemore or frightened of him, only angry. "You can't have my wife. You can't have a damned thing of mine."

"Uh-huh. Well now let me ask you something. What did you walk out here to get, other than dead?"

"You," said Bill.

Red laughed again, loudly. "Me. Who do you think you are, Wyatt fucking Earp? Are you *shitting* me?"

"Either you have to go to jail or one of us has to die. I'm not Wyatt Earp but that's how it is," Bill said.

Red dropped lightly out of the tree and put his bow and quiver on the ground. He stood up and looked at Bill and it seemed he was glowing—the ruined skin of his face and neck were bright red.

"You want some kind of a gentlemen's duel, right? Am I right? Okeydoke, citizen, tell you what I'm gonna do—I'm gonna kill you right quick and then walk over there and take your wife up north with me and kill her wicked slow. Maybe for a week." He pulled one of the two knives on his belt out of its sheath and tossed it handle-first to Bill. Then he drew the other knife and held it loosely with the blade down by his knee. Grinning crookedly at Bill, he reached up with his other hand and pulled away what was left of a bandage on his head and Bill saw that the left side of his face was a dangling, bloody flap, attached to his head only at the nose and down somewhere around his chin, and that his ear was gone. "See what your missus did? I'd stay on her good side if I were you." He started walking toward Bill then, raising the knife.

He was fifteen feet away and coming. Bill held the big knife out in front of him. He was crouched, on the point of charging Red and hoping for some advantage for momentum, when he heard Clair's voice behind him. What she said was: "You're nothing but a pathetic, low-rent old redneck with a little dick."

Red Sizemore stopped and looked at her.

Bill looked at her, too. She was standing just to his right and behind him, her legs spread wide, holding the folding knife out of his backpack with an overhand grip. Seeing her brought no fear up in him, but only an exuberant joy and love that made him want to laugh. "I hope to hell it's him you're talking to," he said, feeling wonderful with her there, holding the knife like a ferocious little girl.

Red laughed. He said to Bill, "Here's your duel, asshole. This is *real* life."

Then Bill watched his hand—all in one blurred, unbroken motion—flick the knife up in the air, catch it by the tip, and throw it. He felt the stinging thud against his chest and then a quick, dizzy weakening, and he looked down and saw the knife, buried to the tang high up in his chest under the collarbone, and felt his legs starting to go.

From his knees Bill watched Clair run at Red, stabbing at him overhand with the little folding knife, and watched him catch her wrist and break it with a jerk in the air and heard her scream.

And then she was on her back and Red was straddling her, talking to her conversationally, and Bill pulled the Buck knife from the sheath on his belt and believed that he could crawl to them, though he could feel himself being sucked down and out of his body like water out of a drain.

"I want you to watch this thumb, C. J. People don't know how easy you can take an eye out with your thumb . . . ," he heard Red saying as he crawled. And then he heard a crashing in the brush off the trail and there, somehow, was Brando coming toward them at a full sprint through the woods, towing the fly-post Bill had tied him to, and he felt like laughing again, but kept crawling as Brando bounded out of the woods and onto Red Sizemore, hitting him squarely in the chest and knocking him off Clair.

And then Bill could see Brando with his forepaws braced on the trail, pulling at something, the way he played tug-of-war with a sock, and Red Sizemore was lying on his stomach screaming and clutching his head with his right hand, and Bill rose up on his knees and saw that Brando had the flap of face in his teeth and was pulling, backing up, his feet braced, and Red was clutching at the separating skin with his hand. Then Bill saw him find his knife with his left hand and flail out at Brando, and the dog howled and jerked his head and Bill saw him carrying off the flap of Red's face in his teeth, and the knife in the rolls of fat around his shoulders.

Then he was there and didn't see anything but Red, or feel anything but strength surging through him as he threw himself astride Red's back and pulled his head up out of the dirt by the ponytail and cut his throat. Bill cut the big man's throat just below the Adam's apple. Then he raised the knife and cut it again under the chin. He pulled back on the ponytail and cut up to the hilt all the way across, and then yanked the ponytail higher while the man jerked under him and cut his throat a third time when the jerking stopped, digging, feeling and cutting bone this time, until the head swung freely on the spine.

Then he dropped the head and felt Clair's hands on him and nothing after that but the last of himself disappearing into the drain.

The Bell Jet Ranger helicopter, piloted by Sergeant Elmore Hines of the New Hampshire State Police and carrying Paul Keeler, sheriff of Coos County, and Mrs. Joy "Swift Otter" Sizemore with her child and dog, took off from Pittsburg, New Hampshire, at 7:15 A.M. on Monday, the tenth of October, the last day of the long Columbus Day Weekend and peak day of foliage season for the 1464 slow-driving tourists admiring the beautiful woods of New Hampshire from their car windows.

Sheriff Keeler had radioed in to Concord for the helicopter the day before from the scene of a double-slaying at a deer camp some twenty-five miles northwest of Pittsburg. He had been led to the camp by Mrs. Sizemore, who told him that she believed her husband, who owned the camp, had some involvement in the slayings and was presently fleeing and holding hostage a man and wife named Joyce and another man. Mrs. Sizemore, a Native American, had further told him at the crime scene that her husband was headed for Canada, and that she knew this from a vision, the same vision that had informed her about the slayings at the camp.

Sheriff Keeler frankly did not know whether he believed in visions or not. Moreover, the woman did not look all that credible. In fact, she looked like someone out of the circus that came to Pittsburg every June. She was very large, dressed in skins and beads with a knife on her hip, and carrying on her back both a child and a small dog in twin, buckskin-covered cradle boards. She was calm at the crime scene, but she appeared to want to find her husband very badly, and for some reason Sheriff Keeler believed that she actually did know where Mr. Sizemore was going and was telling him the truth about it.

So despite the fact that his men had found ATV tracks that morning leading east from the camp and then south, and late that afternoon had found the ATV itself hidden in a thicket of spruce near the railroad track, Sheriff Keeler had concentrated his helicopter search north and west near the Quebec border. And even though they had seen no sign of anyone all afternoon, when the woman told him on this Monday morning that she had had another vision overnight and now knew exactly where and how her husband would be found, the sheriff told Sergeant Hines to fly directly to the Boy Scout campground just east of Paquette, Quebec. And no sooner were they in the air than his dispatcher was on the radio telling him the Joyce woman had just called from that very same place saying her husband had just gone into the woods after Red Sizemore.

Vision or no vision, Sheriff Keeler was glad Mrs. Sizemore was right. He had promised to take his oldest son partridge hunting that afternoon, and if they did find her husband quickly and dead, as she assured him they would, he might be able to keep that promise.

By the time the helicopter landed in the meadow by the river where the Scoutmaster with the mustache and two other Scoutmasters and about twenty Scouts had carried Bill, Clair and the Scoutmasters had done everything they could do medically for him, and Clair had whispered three Lord's Prayers and was in the middle of reciting what she could remember of the Twenty-third Psalm.

She didn't know whether Bill was dying or not. His heart-beat was strong enough and his breathing was regular, but he was very pale. He had not come to since she rolled him off Red Sizemore's nearly decapitated body and then ran to the edge of the meadow screaming for help; and one of the Scoutmasters had told her that he was in shock. All she could do was wait and pray that he would live—that he wouldn't die now when he would leave her more alone than she could ever have been before.

She had prayed for Brando too as he limped behind her, howling pitifully as she followed the men carrying Bill out of the woods. In the meadow a solemn-looking Scout who seemed to be the troop nurse had told her that Brando's fat had saved him from being badly hurt, then he splinted and wrapped Clair's broken wrist, and when the helicopter came in, she was lying on the grass between Brando and Bill, praying, with her left hand on Bill's cheek so that she could stroke his eyelid with her forefinger and hope that he could feel it and know that she was there.

A man in a brown uniform was the first one out. He called her Mrs. Joyce and introduced himself with a nice, comforting smile. Clair told him that her husband was badly hurt and uncon-scious, that a friend of theirs was wounded and waiting to be evacu-ated from a pond about five miles east of where they were, and that the man who had kidnapped her was dead in the woods be-hind them. "This woman's husband," she said, nodding behind the sheriff at the Indian woman from the fair who had climbed out of the helicopter right after the sheriff and now stood beside it with a dog and a child on her back, looking gravely at Clair through her thick glasses, her arms crossed above her belly.

The sheriff said, "That would be Mr. Sizemore."

"Sheriff, my husband . . . ," Clair began.

"I know. We'll have him down to Dartmouth-Hitchcock ER inside an hour."

The sheriff and the helicopter pilot lifted Bill carefully and put him into the helicopter. Clair was watching them load Brando when she realized that the woman was holding her hand and saying something to her. She looked at her.

"I said I was wrong about you. I'm sorry. I'm sorry about your pretty friend too." Clair stared at the woman, who stared back at her thoughtfully. She squeezed Clair's hand, then let it go and said, "There's not enough room in the helicopter for all of us, so I'll stay here with my husband. They can come back for us. But I want you to know something about me before you leave." She smiled, and her smiling face was sweet. "I went to Vassar College. I graduated with honors in 1987."

Bill came to as two men were putting him into the backseat of the helicopter. When they had finished, he was lying on his back, with his knees up and, after a minute or two, his head in Clair's lap, and he could smell Brando somewhere nearby. He felt dizzy and cold and thirsty and nauseated, but he also felt very happy knowing where he was and who he was there with and where he was going, and feeling that maybe he was not going to die.

"Hello, Dill," he said, and felt Clair jump under his head. She leaned over and looked into his face, grinning, and kissed him quickly and started telling him things.

As the helicopter blades came up to speed and the cabin began to vibrate, and then as the helicopter pulled at the ground, tipping from side to side, then came unstuck and floated off in a bank, she talked to him and he held both of her hands, going in and out of focus on what she was saying as if his mind were a camera lens being turned.

She told him he was going to be alright and that Brando was going to be alright, too. And that the helicopter was going to drop them off at the hospital in Hanover and then go and pick up Dray. She leaned farther into his face so that their noses were touching and told him that they would name the baby Portia, and that the Scoutmaster with the mustache had kissed her hand and called her *"une femme très courageuse"* . . .

The day was clearing from the east. The helicopter lifted in circles and Bill looked down through the window he was facing whenever it tilted toward the ground and watched the woods below getting smaller and farther away, and realized he didn't owe them anything and vice versa. From here, they no longer resembled the woods he had struggled in and spread his fear across, but looked ordered and calm and reassuring and bright with random splashes of color, like the right and safe woods in a child's coloring book.

At the top of its rising spiral the helicopter paused, hung for an instant on the air, and Bill felt that he was exactly on time for once, unattached in front or behind for the first time in his life: poised perfectly and breathlessly himself, like the moment before first light.

Then the helicopter tipped and fell off toward the clear, sunny sky to the east, and, listening to the beloved sound of Clair's voice, he closed his eyes.

Swift Otter walked into the woods where she was directed by the Scoutmaster and sat on the ground beside the body of her husband, stroking the bald top of his head and watching the helicopter circle upward until it was no bigger than a hawk. Black Feather was crying and would need to be fed, but she wanted to get across the river and as far into Canada as she could before she took the time to do that.

She rolled onto her knees groaning and took the skinning knife out of its sheath. It didn't take her long, and when she had finished she stood up slowly and tied the heart to her belt with a rawhide thong. She did not look at her husband again, but, keeping the marriage vow she had always intended to keep, she started walking north and west toward the lake in Quebec.